ETERNAL
CAPTIVE

ELLE MAE

Cover design by Seventhstarart
Edits by My brothers Editor
Proofreader Leticias Edits

www.ellemaebooks.com

NOTE

This is a work of fiction. Names, characters, business, events and incidents are the products of the author's imagination. Any resemblance to actual persons, living or dead, or actual events is purely coincidental.

Before moving forward, please note that the themes in this book can be dark and trigger some people. The themes can include but are not limited to: mentions of past torture, depictions of torture, attempted murder, parental death, self harm to frame somebody, blood play, gore/violence , family violence & abuse, voyeurism, murder, stabbing, sexual violence, biting, physical altercations, depictions of corpses being treated poorly, beheading, verbal, mental and physical abuse by a parent, ableist language, bullying, public sex, public execution, implied abuse of an animal, depression.

If you need help, please reach out to the resources below.

National Suicide Prevention Lifeline
1-800-273-8255
https://suicidepreventionlifeline.org/

National Domestic Violence Hotline
1-800-799-7233
https://www.thehotline.org/

ELLE MAE

ELLE MAE

Blood Bound Series:

Contract Bound: A Lesbian Vampire Romance

Lost Clause

Blood Royale:

Eternal Captive: A Dark Enemies-to-Lovers Sapphic Vampire Romance

Winterfell Academy Series:

The Price of Silence: Winterfell Academy Book 1

The Price of Silence: Winterfell Academy Book 2

The Price of Silence: Winterfell Academy Book 3

The Price of Silence: Winterfell Academy Book 4

The Price Of Silence: Winterfell Academy Book 5

Winterfell Series Box Set

Short and Smutty:

The Sweetest Sacrifice: An Erotic Demon Romance

Nevermore: A Deal with a Demon

EDEN EMORY

The Ties That Bind Us

Don't Stop me

Don't Leave Me

Don't Forget Me

Don't Hate Me

Two of a Kind

Hide n' Seek

Queer Meet Cute Anthology

Patreon Only

Wicked corruption: An FF Mafia Romance

Watch Me

Tales of the Stolen Demon Brides

For those who couldn't get enough of enemies-to-lovers lesbian vampires, enjoy your new grumpy masc and flirty femme~

ETERNAL
CAPTIVE

ELLE MAE

CREATURES

Humans

At the bottom of the food chain, humans have long since been seen as weak compared to vampires. Humans like to keep out of supernatural business for the most part, but it isn't uncommon to see some of the wealthy and more powerful in business with royal vampire families.

Long in the past there was rumored to be hunters. A group of humans that ruthlessly killed vampires for a corrupt corporation but records of the group has been lost to history.

Tiers

None

Weaknesses

Vampires
Witches
Disease
Old Age

Vampires

No one knows when vampires crawled out of the shadows, but the most recent history has had them in positions of power.
In the past vampires stayed in "clans" recruiting those close to them and sometimes engaging in war with the humans.
Nowadays, the vampires have split into rogues, clans, and families.
Some have climbed to fame and have enough power to turn a clan into a family through blood bonds, but the vampires who can do this successfully are few and far between.
Vampires tend to stay away from witches as their magic can do great harm, but they have no problem recruiting humans as feeders for use whenever they see fit.

Tiers

Families

Must be created through blood bonds. Typically see as those with more power as once bonded, can never be broken, if they decide to leave.

Clans

Not joined through blood, but shared loyalty.

Rogues

No connection to others. Typically seen as dangerous

WEAKNESSES

Witches
Magic
Going without blood for long
periods of time

STRENGTHS

Humans
Long life
Wealth (families)

BELIEFS

While vampires are not known to have a religion, there
have been a few royals that have been praying to a goddess
named "Krae".
This goddess is rumored to be the first of all vampires in
existence and some say her blood is still alive in a select few
families to this day..

Witches

Vampires like to think of themselves as the top of the food chains, but it's truly the witches.

Witches keep to themselves, often found in covens of their own or even taking over full towns. Humans are mistrusted and usually, when stumbling upon a secret witch hideout, find themselves turned around with no clue where they are.

Not much is made public about witches. Some powers are rumored to be: seeing the future, healing, blood magic, manipulation of objects and matter, and much more.

Vampires often describe a witch's smell as burning foliage or wood.

Tiers

Unknown

Weaknesses

Unknown

Strengths

Humans

Vampires

WITCHES

BELIEFS

Witches are known to believe in many gods, but the names have never been shared with humans or vampires. They take their beliefs very seriously and it is not wise to scoff or laugh them off or else risk their wrath.

When a witch says that they will pray for you, it is the highest of honors.

PROLOGUE

For some reason, I never thought that my mother would die before me.

In our world, my mother was akin to the goddess Krae. The mother of all vampires. A powerful warrior of a woman whose lust for blood was as strong as her maternal love for her people.

Vampires fled their covens, cut ties with their families, came from all over the country just for a chance to kneel at her feet and pledge their allegiance. If she had been like any other vampire queen, she would have turned more than half of them away.

All those who attempted to appeal to her risked the same. Be rejected by her and forever become an outcast rogue, whose only hope being a small coven who took pity on them.

But she never turned them away.

They loved her for it. Worshipped her because of it.

And I had been born into that love. Blinded by it like the people.

I got firsthand experience with just how much the vampire world was enamored with my mother, and it only made me love her that much more. Without her, no one would join Father. She brought light to his darkness. She brought empathy to his coldness.

Before her, Father simply had a coven. Because of her, it turned into a family. We were royalty because of her.

But this...

This wasn't love.

My hands caressed her cheeks. I desperately tried to wipe away the black vine-like markings on her face, but it was no use. The magic had already worked its way through her entire system. Her eyes were red, her mouth open as her teeth desperately searched for flesh.

She had been gasping for air by the time that I showed up, but it quickly turned into shallow breathing and small whimpers.

This is poison. Witch posion.

But why? I couldn't understand why a world that seemed to love my mother so much would hurt her.

The cathedral was empty, with only the stone-carved goddess Krae to witness the crime.

Normally, the sacred place was reserved for prayer to the goddess and additions to the family. Up on the stage, there was an empty crystal bowl, which vampires used to fill with their own blood as an offering to their king.

Krae was supposed to watch over it all. Give her blessing for our new additions and strike down whichever ones she didn't approve.

But she never interfered. Even when my mother was dying.

She had been sprawled across the steps, her hand outstretched as if trying to crawl toward the goddess. The image of her perfectly manicured hand reaching for help that would never come would forever be burned into my memories.

It's as if she *truly* believed the immobile statue could save her. As if the legend of Krae wasn't just a tool used to control the masses of vampires at her feet.

For the first time in my existence...I felt hopeless.

The woman I owed my life to—the one I loved more than anyone else—was dying, and there was nothing I could do to save her.

"Father!" I screamed, my voice breaking. *How many times had I called out to him?*

Yet he still didn't come to her rescue. He wasn't far. But even so, with our hearing, *someone* should've heard me.

My gaze traveled to the all-powerful goddess, her eyes burrowing into mine. The same expression that seemed so gentle turned malicious. Like she was *laughing* at my struggle.

Mother let out another whimper, this time managing enough strength to bring her hand to my cheek. It was as cold as the stone beneath her.

She tried to speak, but no words came out. The only sound filling the space was the wind being forced from her closing throat.

"*Don't.* Don't push yourself too hard," I pleaded.

Why is no one coming?!

Tears started blurring my vision, and it wasn't long before they started running down my cheeks. I felt bad for the way they fell onto my mother's face and quickly tried to wipe them away so as not to sully her.

"Father will be here soon," I said, looking back to the entrance, but no one had shown up. The doors were wide open and empty even after screaming so hard my voice became hoarse. "Someone, please help! The queen has been attacked!"

There's no other explanation for it. Of course there was an attack. Someone had snuck in—someone who hated the queen and decided to punish her.

Why? Why her? Why us?

What did Mother need to be punished for?

"Aurelia." The voice that left her throat didn't sound like hers at all. It was hoarse, crackly, unrecognizable.

I turned my attention back to her.

"Please," I begged her. "Please don't leave me, not yet."

Anything but this. I knew nothing besides her. I didn't know how to stand in for her. I couldn't nurture the love of the vampires in our family like she could.

I was nothing and more like my father than I ever was her. She used to say it like it was a good thing. Like it meant that I had potential and wasn't the slap to the face it truly was.

"Stay...fierce."

I forced out a smile for her. It'd been her favorite saying for me. Father didn't like when I talked back and often tried to punish me for it. Mother said it was because I reminded him too much of himself in those moments. But she was always there, by my side, reminding me that this fierceness was a strength.

It was the last word she would ever say to me. Not that she loved me. But to remind me that I am just like the man who refused to come save her. I watched helplessly as the last bit of breath was squeezed from her lungs.

Seeing the light die in her eyes was even worse. She was trying to fight it. She was trying to stay for me. She realized that she was on the brink of the inevitable and *still* tried to rip her own soul from death's grip.

But she lost her battle.

I couldn't move. I couldn't speak. Grief, sorrow, anger—all of it crashed over me, filling my little body to the brink until I was about to explode with it. I didn't know how to separate it all. *I didn't know what to do.*

I wanted to explode, even if for just a mere chance that it would inconvenience Father. I wanted it to take me with her while at the same time ripping the foundation from under the building and causing everyone who couldn't help to crumble with it.

How could this happen to her? Someone so loved and adored?

I didn't want to believe it. Not even when her eyes glazed over. Not when my vampire hearing could hear the sound of her body giving up on her.

I leaned against her, selfishly taking one last sniff of her scent. Even after her body became cold, she still managed to smell like sunshine and honey.

The sound of my father's boots squeaking against the floor as he entered the cathedral interrupted my moment with her. There were people behind him, three from the sounds of their footsteps.

I took a deep breath and sat up, but I was unable to turn my eyes away from Mother. I knew I should have stood in his presence, I just couldn't find the strength to. I didn't want to be taken from my mother so soon.

A foolish part of me thought that she might come back to life in the minutes that passed, but of course that wish never came true.

"Pity," he said, though there was no grief in his voice. No hoarseness. No strain. Like commenting on the weather. "I never thought the witches would've found a way in here. I guess it's time to update our security. Take the body, search for the witches."

That's it?

I sat there, numb, as two of his servants lifted my mother's body. I squashed my urge to reach for her as her lifeless form dangled in front of me. They were gentle with her, gentler than my father ever was.

I turned to him, rage simmering inside me. He was dressed in his usual extravagant king's clothing. Covered in furs and jewels and looking as calm as he did that morning when he held court.

His dark hair was too much like my own. The shape of his eyes. The shape of his lips.

Is this what Mother saw when she looked at me? Did she just see a replica of the person who abandoned her?

I didn't know what to expect when Father found Mother dead. Maybe panic. Maybe fear. *Something* that would prove to me that he wasn't the cold vampire he'd shown me my entire life and that maybe it was just a front to keep his power.

But he couldn't even manage to *pretend* he cared about my mother.

Because he never had. All he cared about was that somehow a witch had been able to sneak into his palace, showing a weakness in his carefully curated image.

He didn't care that his queen was dead. He didn't care that the mother of his only child was dead. And because there was no one here to watch this unfold, he had no use for the facade of loving her.

And Krae watched it all, saying nothing.

The two servants were teary-eyed, their love for my mother obvious. But neither of them spoke out as they took her body away from me. Their allegiance was to my father. No matter how much they loved my mother, the blood oath they swore was to the family.

Which he held the power to.

"No one will know about this," he said, his eyes following the servants as they took her body. His lips turned downward at the side. *Disgust.*

There was one more by his side, and the man kept his eyes to the ground.

"We need to let the people know," I said, my voice hollow and dejected. I didn't understand the intricacies of running a vampire family, but surely not telling them anything would make things worse. "They deserve to know. They deserve to grieve. How are you gonna explain the queen's disappearance?"

A small smirk spread across Father's lips.

"We report that the queen died of health reasons, no more information, no less," he answered, placing his hands on his hips. His eyes wandered up to the goddess. "No one needs to know about the witches. Imagine if everyone knew how easy it was to get into the palace."

Then his eyes met mine. There was a silent demand for me to agree with him. As if this notion wasn't an insult to the mother I loved so dearly.

I had no words. All I had was a burning fury inside me. I let it consume me as I launched myself off the ground and at my father. I screamed at him, pounding my fist against his chest.

"My mother died! She's dead, and you could've saved her!"

Pain exploded from my head as my back and neck were slammed onto the cold marble steps. I was dazed in those moments, unable to fully comprehend what had happened to me. I was standing upright one moment, then writhing in pain on the cold floor right where my mother had died the next, my father's hand around my throat.

My eyes widened as I met his glare. I had seen that look before, but never had it gotten to that point. I flailed, tried desperately to push him off, but he was far stronger than me.

"Enough of that," he growled. "Don't you dare say anything of the sort. Not in front of me, and definitely not in front of the rest of the kingdom."

He squeezed my throat painfully, not allowing any air to escape in or out. I was gasping for breath, much too similarly to my mother just moments before.

Was this how she felt when she was facing her death? Was this how it felt to be watched by the goddess as you tried helplessly to save yourself?

"Pl-Please—"

"What's that?" he asked. "I won't accept anything other than an apology from a spoiled brat like you. Do you realize how much I've done for this kingdom? Do you realize what I'm going to have to do in order to make sure that the kingdom still loves us after this?"

I pounded his shoulder. Black covered the edges of my vision. *No more, please, no more.*

"I-I'm...sor-sorry—"

"Some people have already gotten word. I hear them approaching," his servant said behind him. I could barely make out the words. Even my slow heartbeat sounded like it was underwater.

Finally, Father let go of my throat. I turned to the side, coughing and heaving. Sweet, delicious air filled my lungs, providing me with much-needed oxygen while burning at the same time.

I couldn't look at him as he left. His servant lingered and then dropped a small handkerchief in front of me before turning and following him.

I grabbed the perfectly white cloth and wiped up the spit and mucus on my face, secretly glad that I could sully it.

My mother hid this from me, but I had noticed it. I noticed when they fought. When Father wanted to punish me, Mother would take him into the other room instead. What I hadn't realized was that she was taking the punishment for me.

She let me keep my rose-colored glasses on as long as she could, but now that she was gone, those glasses shattered, the sharp pieces embedding into my skin, burrowing so deep that they would be there as a painful reminder for the rest of my life.

It was beautiful with Mother, the walls were glass...but with Father, I was quickly pushed inside a wrought iron cage with only him holding the keys to my release.

There was only one way to survive, and my mother gave me the best hint of all.

VESPER

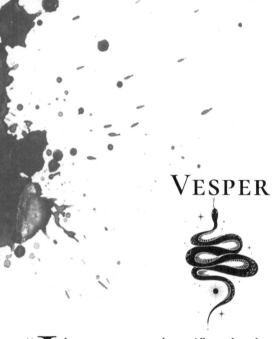

"I'm a seer, you know?" a drunk male witch said to the obviously very uninterested female witch at the bar.

She gave him a polite smile and took a sip of her pink swirling liquid before trying to turn back to her friend.

"And you know what I saw?" he asked, desperately trying to steal her attention. "Us. Meeting. It's destiny, don't you thin—"

"Richard, don't you dare make me kick you out again," an older witch said from behind the bar. "*Destiny*." She let out a huff. "Don't start with that shit again."

I couldn't help the smirk that spread across my lips.

I hated the seers' obsession with destiny as much as the next person. They believed it to be an undeniable truth and bound to happen no matter what a person did to try to change it.

But they didn't realize how binding their words could be.

My *destiny* was solidified in a coastal town in Northern California.

It was a quiet place. The people were nice, the forest that surrounded the town was densely populated and perfect for any creatures that like to stalk their prey in the darkness of the shadows.

It was where I stayed for the majority of my life. Where I worked tirelessly to prepare for something far greater than myself.

A day will come when the singular Castle bloodline comes to maturity, and a child born with poison for blood will usher forth an end to their rule.

I was that child, and that day was coming. Faster than I ever imagined.

But it didn't scare me—at least not anymore. Father had beat it into me for years, making sure the prophecy and the importance of it were branded onto my skin. Sometime between the "training" and taking countless vampire lives, the fear turned to anger.

It festered inside me. Rotting and turning my insides black with every job I took.

How many lives did I take in preparation for this? A hundred? Two hundred?

I had lost count as I tried to erase their faces from my memories.

It only made the anger that much stronger. Instead of jading me, it only made me resent my family and the secretive organization they worked for.

The anger was what had brought me to the city. The main line of the prophecy never said that I was going to die, but the seer had mentioned the bloodbath that would ensue, something a mere human like myself would probably not survive.

And my parents just accepted that as my fate and trained me as such. It was I who decided to go against what destiny proclaimed of me. Going against my father's wishes.

But I needed to do it. I had let my life be controlled by destiny for so long that I had become complacent. For years, I had been ready to give all of myself to the suicide mission. I was too much of a coward to shake it off completely, but that didn't mean that I couldn't at least try to prepare myself a bit better.

The bar I was told to meet at was one I had visited many times over, but it was no place for a human. Even if they let me in, the cautious stares and the potent smell of magic in the air were a reminder of how out of place I was.

It was old, probably more than a hundred years old, and placed in the basement of a laundromat they used as a front. The walls were cracked, and the speakers they played the music out of were fuzzy, but they kept it up well, and I have never seen a fight break out in this place. They respected it. Respected the history and magic weaved into the walls.

Something the humans could never do.

The part of the city where the bar was located belonged to the witches, though the many humans who stumbled upon it wouldn't know it. The storefronts and various businesses all looked normal, but somehow every time a human came through the area without a purpose, they would suddenly find themselves turned around and spat back out on the other side.

So, from the moment I stepped into this bar, they knew not only that I knew what this place was but also that I had probably been invited.

"Don't mind them, darling," an older witch said as she placed a pint of beer in front of me.

Martha, my mind supplied. She was always here when I was and had never given me even so much as a dirty look.

"I understand it," I said, taking the glass with a grateful smile. "Most know what I do, and it's enough for them to want to stay away."

Her smile wavered at this.

"No talk of that here," she said in a hushed tone, her eyes darting around to the other patrons. I couldn't tell if it was for my benefit or theirs.

I gave her a forced smile.

"You mean kill—"

"I charge double if you get us kicked out," a voice said behind me. I couldn't stop the smile from spreading across my face.

A woman with pink hair maneuvered around the table and placed her hands on the elder witch's arms. *Levana.* The only witch I chose to spend my time with. Met at the very same bar and haven't been able to get rid of her since.

But at least she would come in handy.

"You know she can be prickly," she said in a faux-annoyed tone. The light in her eyes and the smirk gave her away. "I'll get us out of here soon."

The older witch nodded before sending me one last lingering look.

"Take care of yourself, youngling," she advised. "There's something sticky in your aura. If you're not careful, it just might overtake you."

I bit the inside of my cheek to stop myself from responding.

The old woman didn't deserve my anger. The witches who could see auras couldn't help their gift. And from her point of view, she was probably truly trying to help me.

That didn't stop it from feeling like a jab to my carefully curated mental walls.

"Still don't like people reading you, huh?"

When I didn't respond, she let out a sigh and pushed a hand through her bright hair.

"So...you changed your mind," she said and pulled out the chair. The sound of the wooden feet scraping against the hard floor caused silence to ripple through the bar. *As if we needed even more attention on us.*

But Levana had even more of a reputation in these parts than I did.

It was the type of reputation that made me respect her, no matter how annoying I might have found her at first.

I leaned forward, getting as close to her as possible and away from prying ears.

"You better fucking be sure about it," I growled.

Her eyes widened for a split second before she threw her head back and let out a boisterous laugh, not at all bothering to hide the two small fangs. It was enough for the onlookers to relax and turn their attention elsewhere.

Thank god.

"You doubt my abilities, human?" she asked and forced the beer from my grip. "They won't smell it. It's my fucking *specialty*."

Specialty. A funny way to say that because she was a hybrid, her magic was less potent than the others. There weren't many of her kind out there, or if there were, they liked to remain as below the radar as possible.

Human and vampire blood could mix easily, but the same wasn't so true about witches and vampires, so her existence was just short of a miracle.

"It's not just any clan I'm assigned to. It's a family, *royalty*, Levana," I whispered. "I *need* this to work, or it risks my life."

For the first time in years, a seriousness fell over her. She gave me a stiff nod before she reached into her pockets and pulled out tiny jars of what looked like various herbs and wildflowers.

"Put these in your bath before you go," she instructed and pushed the pile toward me. I examined a few before pulling my bag from the ground and dumping them in. "Soak for at least fifteen minutes. If you can, wash your hair in them. Hair and cloth are the hardest to get the scent out of. I truly don't think it's necessary, but just in case."

I nodded and pulled my collarbone-length hair to the side. Her eyes lingered on the pitch-black tattoo that traveled up my neck.

"Straight to the point, then?" she asked. "I'd thought you would want to stick around for a bit. Reminisce. This may be the last—"

"I leave in five hours," I said, cutting her off. "Getting home is forty minutes alone."

She swallowed thickly before reaching her hand out and placing it on my neck.

A burning sort of magic washed through me. My first instinct was to jerk back, memories of the same magic being used against me in training attacking my mind, but I stayed as still as possible, pushing all those terrible thoughts to the recesses of my mind.

Focus. It wasn't painful for long. Just a few minutes before the magic cascaded down my shoulder and chest, completely hiding any evidence of the family I came from. The scars would be a different story, but hopefully they wouldn't give me away as easily as my family's symbol would.

When she pulled her hand away, I had a moment to collect myself before I jerkily grabbed my bag and opened it to grab her payment. Panic was ebbing at the edges of my mind, but I concentrated on what I could control.

My heart and my movements.

It allowed everything else to wash away into the ether, leaving me and my task at hand.

The payment was an orb wrapped tightly in cloth, its glow seeping through the thin fabric. It warmed my hand, the magic inside it seeping into everything, even with the extra protection.

Gently, I placed it on her still-outstretched hand.

"This is too much—it's pure magic. Your father will—"

"Be too proud of my sacrifice to notice," I said, letting the smirk fall across my lips with ease. *It was stolen anyway, and from my father's personal collection, no less.* "Thank you."

I barely heard her as I turned away, but somehow her words still made it to me through the chatter of the bar.

"I'll be praying for you, Vesper."

If I allowed myself to feel any of the emotions swirling inside me, I would have to admit that her words affected me enough to cause all the air to escape from my lungs.

Witches don't pray to their gods for just anyone.

But I wasn't feeling them. I had closed them off as best as I could and instead forced myself up the stairs and to where my bike waited for me.

Less than five hours to go.

I ran the towel over my still-damp hair as I exited the bathroom.

My skin was pruny, and the smell of herbs and flowers was so potent I was sure I'd be smelling it for days, but it would work. I had faith. The witches didn't get involved in anything to do with humans, but they were people of their words.

I was down to three hours.

The clothes I wore to the bar had been burned in the fireplace, and I spent extra time making sure the tattoo on my neck was successfully covered before scrubbing my skin violently with the herbs.

I paused as I walked down the hallway that overlooked the living room. Light shone up and illuminated the dark hallway, voices from below traveling up as Mother and Father discussed something with some stranger.

Having visitors in the house was common, but what shocked me was the young teen crouching against the railing, his hands gripping the wooden beams so tightly that his knuckles turned white.

His gaze snapped to mine, dark golden eyes so much like my own.

Instead of asking him to move, I crouched beside him to see what he was seeing. When I caught sight of it, my heart skipped a beat in my chest.

A human police officer stood in our kitchen discussing something serious with our parents. It wasn't often that one of those visited our family. We had chosen this specific town and community because it was safe, and it wasn't common for human law enforcement to come snooping around.

"A nomad," Tate said, his voice a whisper. "It's making the human police look bad, so they're asking us to clean up."

Ah, makes sense.

"They'll take all the credit as usual," I murmured. "Must be bad if they're making house calls."

"Twenty humans drained in the course of two weeks," he whispered. "The humans haven't panicked yet because they're reporting the deaths as natural causes. Apparently they think it's just an insatiable rogue."

My eyes traveled to the teen, taking in his face, devoid of

emotion. He was too smart for his own good. Father would surely notice, if he hadn't already, and I didn't know what was worse— Father's attention or his punishments.

"But you don't." It was a statement.

Tate didn't say anything, just stared at the people below. He had something to say to them. I knew the look.

"Come on," I said, placing a hand on his shoulder. "You have school tomorrow, and if you go to bed now, you can catch a few hours of sleep before then."

"I'm not sleeping," he replied, his lips turning into a scowl. "I'm seeing you off."

I had to look away from him as a wave of sorrow rocked my body. It was such a foreign feeling that it sent me off balance.

"If you wish."

"I do," he said quickly. "I want to remember everything." He couldn't look at me. That made it hurt even more.

I didn't have the words to tell him how much it upset me to see him like this. To know that, once I walked off these grounds, he would likely never see me again and that he would use that memory to fuel the fires of his hatred for our parents.

"In two years, Mother and Father will give you a choice," I whispered. "You can go to a boarding school for people like us or stay with Gabriel—"

"I don't know him," he grumbled.

I leaned into him and rested my head against his.

"He's nice," I said, trying to pull his image from my blurry memories. The firstborn son, the one we all strive to be like. He had left right as Tate was born to build his own business. I might not remember much, but I did remember his hatred for my parents. I remembered how he raised his voice at them when he found me in the basement, starving and full of bruises.

Tate will be safe with him.

They hadn't forced Tate to go through the training I had. He still had time to change his life.

"Forget about me, Tate," I pleaded. "It's easier this way."

He pushed me away, causing me to tumble to the ground.

"Don't say something so selfish!" He turned his back and ran to his room before I could stop him.

My eyes darted to the kitchen, where all eyes were on me. Father's gaze was already narrowed in my direction.

AURELIA

The hard sound of the slap reverberated throughout the meeting hall, followed by a stunned silence.

Pain exploded in my head and traveled far down my neck. I was forced to grip the edge of the table. The polished slickness of the surface almost caused me to lose my balance and crumple to the floor.

All eyes were on me, the heaviness of their weight intensifying the pain. All of them waiting to see if the beloved yet *spoiled* princess would burst into tears at her daddy's firm hand.

I never did, but that didn't stop them from creaming their pants at the possibility.

What was it with men loving to see a woman in tears and knocked down a peg?

Blood filled my mouth for a split second before the wound disappeared.

He didn't hold back. My mind was swirling with bitter, violent thoughts as I forced my gaze to his.

He was standing, his sudden movement pushing his obnoxiously decorative chair back. His eyes were bright red, his fangs bared. Both my stepmother and sister were in their places behind him, standing and looking at me with wicked grins they tried so desperately to hide behind their hands.

"What you *meant* to say was that you will be honored to receive Prince Icas *today* to accept his engagement," my father said, his voice low but not at all hiding his anger. "If I hear one more disgraceful utterance like that again, I will have you flogged, and your blood privileges revoked for a week."

There was a small, feminine gasp from my side. My hand-maiden, Melia, rested her palm against my back. A small, comforting gesture that brought me nothing but more contempt.

Too snarky even for him, huh?

He wants me to go mad. That was the meaning of his punishment. He wanted to show that even his own daughter, the princess, would not be able to escape his control.

And disgrace the Castle bloodline with his disease? The single sentence that I uttered. I tried to keep it inside. Tried to lock it in the small cage in the recesses of my mind.

But then, when they started talking about the money they could make from me once the prince had *claimed* my body and forced a blood bond...I couldn't keep it in. I was angry.

I had done nothing but be the perfect daughter to Father. I was his replica in almost every sense. I was as cold as he was. As cruel. I was there by his side for every moment.

And he was willing to sell me like a broodmare.

"Just a joke, Father," I said, bowing my head to him. "Of course I will be honored to receive Prince Icas."

I forced my hands to grab my dress, trying desperately to hide how they shook with anger.

"Receive, marry, bed, and produce an heir worthy of uniting our families," he added, taking a step toward me. His grubby finger found my chin and forced me to look up at him. He was calmer then, but the bloodlust was still raging in his eyes. "It is what you were born to do, don't forget that."

I was born to rule, just like my mother, until her untimely death.

"How could I possibly forget?" I made my voice as sweet as I could muster. I was asking for a repeat of the slap, we both knew it. *Krae, help me.* And maybe for the first time, the goddess actually heard me.

His eyes searched my face, then slowly the normal blue hues started to appear.

He nodded and righted himself again before sitting on his throne. And just like that, it was over. The meeting with the various court members was back in action, all of them laughing as if it never happened.

I turned to face the group with my hands folded together in front of me. The ache in my cheek was slowly fading along with the pounding in my head. Melia was by my side, her hand holding the back of my dress.

Her actions annoyed me only because of how useful they were at grounding me while the men of the court's eyes roamed over my swollen face.

I wish she would just fucking disappear. Just because my stepmother had assigned her to me for half my life didn't mean I had to like her. And right then, all I wanted to do was finally give them all a piece of my mind.

I wanted to scream. I wanted to rage. To flip the table in front of me. To tear my fangs into the necks of the people who dared laugh at me.

It had been building up for years, and each time, I chose to lock it behind the golden cage in the back of my mind. The same cage that was starting to rust and bend in places as the emotions violently crashed against the bars that held them in.

But for one more meeting, at least, I had been able to keep them back. Been able to stand there next to my father as the hours passed and the sun set. I passed the time by imagining the sun being able to burn me alive like it was rumored to do to our ancestors.

None of my wishes came true that day. I sat through it. Smiled when I needed to. And left when I was dismissed.

Melia tried to follow me as I left behind my father and stepmother, but I gave her a glare, warning her that if she even dared, she would be paying the price.

I couldn't kill her, but that didn't mean I wouldn't make her life miserable.

"The previous queen would have loved to see this day," my stepmother said from beside my father, her charcoal-lined eyes meeting mine as she shot a smirk in my direction.

She didn't even try to hide her slight. Her spawn, who was trailing a bit behind me down the hall, let out a chuckle.

I hastened my steps, trying to close the space between us.

"She would, but I have you standing in her place, don't I?" I asked in a sickly-sweet tone and quickly stepped on the hem of her dress that had been trailing behind her.

She hadn't caught onto my plan fast enough to stop herself from jerking forward and almost losing her balance.

Father didn't even attempt to catch her. Merely turned his head to the side, watching as she struggled to right herself.

"Aw, so shocked by my declaration it caused you to misstep?" I asked and pushed past her as she stayed frozen in the hall. "Never thought I'd see the day."

"Aurelia," Father warned, but didn't pause to help his wife. Her spawn was by her side in seconds, running to grab onto her elbow and help her stand up straight.

Can't even stand without help. Surprising Father kept you around so long.

"Excuse me, Father," I said, bending my head and sending him a smile. "Merely just excited to bond with your wife—"

"Your mother," he corrected without so much as a blink.

"Right," I said through gritted teeth and kept pace with him until we got to the hallway that led to the east wing of the house and my room. "I'll retire for the night. Looking forward to the engagement talks."

He let out a grunt but gave me no other indication of his approval. When his back was turned to me, I waved to the evil duo as they walked past.

"Watch your fucking mouth next time," I muttered under my breath.

Her spawn looked at me with shock while her mother just smirked.

"You really don't know what you're in for, do you?" she asked, her eyes trailing my body as if assessing me. "You're just a tool for breeding, and somehow you've convinced yourself you're still important?"

All the anger from before slammed into my body like a tidal wave. I clenched my fists, willing them to stay by my sides regardless of how red my vision turned.

She let out a light laugh and continued on her way after Father. Her spawn whispered something under her breath. Something that had me losing my entire rational thought.

"*Broodmare.*"

Crystal shattered against the shimmery decorated wallpaper in my bedroom, the sharp pieces scattering across the room, light reflecting off them and shining against the ceiling.

A guttural scream ripped from my throat. I grabbed everything and anything I could throw. Carts. Perfume. Makeup. Chairs. Throws. Paintings.

All of it met the wall with a hard thud, and whatever didn't shatter satisfyingly enough, I made sure to tear it apart myself.

"Fuck you," I growled, tearing a painting of the rows of roses in front of the palace. "Want to sacrifice me? And for what?"

Selling me off would only hurt Father, wouldn't it?

What was it that Prince Icas had that Father wanted so badly that he would sell me?

I had done everything I could since Mother died to get on his good side. I hadn't said anything when he married that *bitch* mere months after Mother died. Nor did I say anything about her baggage.

I sat there and took all their abuse and attempts to steal the power for themselves.

I was a good little princess. One who was fierce enough to remind my father that I was more similar to him than I ever was to Mother.

Even if I were disposable enough to sell off, *why him*?

Prince Icas's father was the head of a family, but it was nowhere near our size. Had nowhere near our power.

The only thing that they had going for them was their wealth.

I let out another snarl. The room was a mess. I had destroyed almost everything in my path. *Almost.*

My pristine four-poster bed with a mountain of fluffy blankets on top caught my eye. I headed straight for it, imagining the entire time that the fabric belonged to the dress of my vile stepmother.

I ripped into the silk sheets with my fangs and claws, imagining that the feathers spilling out were the same color as her insides. I hated her. *Hated them.* Father was the person who allowed all this to happen, but *they* were the ones who inflicted the years of pain. Father's slaps here and there held nothing to what they had done.

There was a pitcher of bright red blood next to the bed, and one sniff told me it was alcohol-infused. I poured it out over the bedding, reveling in the way the color stained the white sheets, forever ruining them.

"Do you bleed like this?" I mused, still imagining my stepmother lying on the bed instead.

I let out a growl. The anger still fresh and threatening to tear apart my insides. I grabbed the pitcher and turned, ready to slam it into the reinforced window, when my eyes met two black, needy ones.

In a golden cage, much like the one I imagined myself in, sat the only true friend I had in this palace. I dropped the pitcher onto the bed, forcing myself away from the mess.

Something else tugged at my chest. Something more painful.

Something that felt similar to the time I found my mother dying on the stone-cold ground, gasping for breath, and holding her hand out for me to save her.

The gray and orange bird inside chirped as I jostled its cage, but it didn't attempt to bat its wings at me. It had seen one too many of these tantrums, but it was not out of its care for me that it stayed regardless.

There was no doubt in my mind that, if given the chance, it would fly as far from here as possible and not once look back. That's why I had its wings clipped long ago. An awful and torturous procedure, but I did what I had to to keep her with me.

We were so similar, the caged bird and me. It had learned how to remain calm in the face of a much more powerful, threatening source. Its non-reaction only served to save it.

But it was okay. *I understood.*

"I'll have the cleaning staff fix it later," I promised her, as if the creature in its once tidy cage gave two shits about what the room looked like.

I took a deep breath, centering myself and looking at the anger deep inside me. It would remain there until I needed it the most. No matter what Father or that bitch tried, they wouldn't take it from me. Because no matter how much they tried, no matter how hard they beat me, the rage would still be there. And as long as I had that rage, I had *me*.

VESPER

Vampires. Once, a millennia ago, thought to be cursed, they had somehow changed society in a way that left them at the top and all those *weaker* than them beneath them.

They looked down on humans like me. Saw us as blood bags with no use other than food and fucking. The time I spent preparing for this mission at Prince Icas's house only made me resent them more.

I had seen too many of them. Especially the spoiled and rich ones. Seen them as they tore apart their victim's neck as others watched for sport and then laughed when their limp body fell to the ground. Seen them as they forced themselves onto humans while they were in that lustful haze the venom left on them.

That's why people employed families like mine. Hate ran deep throughout this world. Humans hated vampires. Vampires took them down a peg whenever they thought they'd gotten too cocky. Humans fought back through people like me.

It was a cycle, repeated over and over again. Job after job. There was never an end.

The prince was merely a stepping stone for my bigger plans, but a necessary one that would open a door for me. But once the door was open, I would be on my own.

"I heard the princess gets her pick of us," one of the guards seated next to me whispered to his companion. He had been relatively quiet the entire ride until that moment. I remember him vaguely from the time at the prince's palace. In one of the training groups.

Before they even allowed us to apply for jobs as the prince's guards, they had us go through rigorous training. Over half the people who applied didn't make it through the three required rounds.

And even if you did, a person was not guaranteed a good position. Though it wouldn't do me any good to gain too much attention. I had to strike the right balance—high enough in the ranks to save me a spot near the princess without making them suspicious.

The travel van they had packed us into had looked large from the outside, but when all of the princess's new hand-picked guards had been forced into it, there wasn't even enough room to breathe without brushing against someone.

The covered tattoo on my neck itched, but the magic was surprisingly quite strong. Not a vampire or human had noticed its presence...*yet.*

"Do you think she'll feed on us?" another asked, his voice sounding a bit too excited. "I heard she's pretty feisty, and you know how those feedings get."

There were a few jeers and laughter throughout, none of the words appropriate for a lady of her status.

"Settle!" came the head guard's voice as he opened the metal window that separated us from those in the driver's cabin. "Keep it up, and I'll personally deliver your tongues to her feet."

His threat shut them up really quick, and the rest of the ride was relatively silent.

It was a gift I didn't take for granted. I leaned back against the cold metal, my hands gripping the vest of my all-black uniform.

Calm down. They can hear your heart. Most of the humans were nervous. Sweat dripping down their forehead, their hands shaking. That's all the jokes were. An attempt to put them back on equal footing with those who awaited us inside the walls of the Castle family palace.

We were being used as fodder disguised as a well-meaning gift from one rich family to another. Even if any of us got close to the princess, chances were they would end up drained before my mission was completed.

I closed my eyes and walked through the layout of the palace for the hundredth time since becoming a guard for the Solei family. My whole life had been spent prepping. Months of grueling training to fit into these ranks for the chance of being handed off to the Castle family.

All of it leading up to the very moment where he would hand us over to her.

You will carry this family's legacy, Vesper. My father's words played through my head during the times when hatred started to seep into the cracks. When my body started to feel like it was on fire and my jaw clenched so hard, my teeth threatened to crack. When only thoughts of murder and pain brought me comfort.

They centered me. Reminded me of what my job was. My *last* job.

One that would forever change the fabric of this society, or so the seer had foretold. It was what I was born to do. What I existed for. My family had given up so much to ensure that *I* was the one who would be able to bring honor to the family's contracting business.

Not my brother. Not my father. *Me.* The seer had chosen *me.*

The truck stopped abruptly, causing many of the men to jostle into each other. Their grumbled complaints were muted underneath the sound of footsteps exiting from other vans around us. The double doors were pulled open, and we were forced out with shouts from our superior.

I was the first due to being near the exit. It was strategic. It forced me to the front of the line as they positioned us behind the prince and his personal staff.

The gravel crushed underneath our booted feet, the guards

choosing not to let us on the brick patch before the prince. He looked at the palace without even trying to conceal his glee. His stance oozed a cocky confidence that I'm sure vampires of his status loved.

My eyes wandered over the trunks of gold and jewels as they were carried out of his car. There wasn't much stacks of cash could do for a family like the Castles. They were rich, old, and powerful. The prince would need something more concrete to make him look good in their eyes.

After all, what else could they even think to ask for?

Though I'm sure in their world, this would cause any vampire princess to swoon. To be lavished and handed more money than she could ever need.

And blood.

His personal staff showed the wealth, and the guards?

They showed the blood. We were here to be of use to the princess. Protect her as an extension of the Solei family. But those men had been right. The princess's family could protect her, we were here for her bloodlust. As a show that the Solei family was willing to give fresh humans. But not any humans. Strong and *healthy* humans that would drop in a moment's notice and offer her their neck.

And I would be just that.

It was why I was first. Why I had freshly washed and styled my hair. Why I had soaked my uniform in a lavender wash two days before. It was why I had a witch enchant the tattoo of my family's crest on my neck.

So maybe I would entice the monster just enough that she would be willing to have me on her staff.

I let my gaze wander to the palace beyond. A power show. Something that looked to come straight out of a dark fairytale rather than vampire royalty. It spanned stories with shimmering windows, but the blackness of the bricks and the shadows the forest around us cast showed its true nature, no matter how many shiny embellishments the family made to it.

"Follow the prince," one of our leaders said as they motioned us forward. "Step out of line, and your first job is as a blood bag."

The already silent guards had nothing to say about this threat. Their nerves were palpable, filling the air and causing a tenseness to run through the crowd.

The prince led us up the long brick entrance and between the hundreds of rows of red roses. Their overpowering smell tickled my nose. The pounding footsteps of the guards walking in sync echoed throughout the courtyard but softened when we reached the expensive marble steps.

The doors were open for us. There were people already waiting with their heads bowed and lined up to lead us down the long outdoor hallway to the throne room.

A welcoming show that none of us would have gotten to experience if we had not given our bodies to these families.

I tried not to be amazed by the inside. Tried not to let the awe rise in my chest as I took in the carefully crafted space. The inner courtyard was filled with black roses, trimmed bushes, and marble pathways. Columns carved with images of the vampire goddess Krae were everywhere, all in different renditions but beautiful nonetheless.

The walls surrounding the inner court were tall enough to cast wide shadows over the palace.

Making it an easy place to hide.

I caught a few glowing red eyes in the dark corners, watching me exactly like I had been watching them. They were in all-black uniforms, much like we were, but there was something about them that made me believe they probably weren't the normal guards the family employed.

The prince was the first to walk into the throne room. We followed him shortly, filing into the room that barely had enough space to fit us all.

Just like the Solei family, the throne room was for show more than anything else. Stairs led up to the single throne. Stained glass with more depictions of Krae stood behind them. And right in the very middle, there they were. Poised, well-groomed, and ready for political matchmaking.

The vampire obsession with royalty was nothing I ever understood.

In modern day, they held the wealthy, and even some countries, in a chokehold. But the crowns? The thrones? The extravagant ball gowns?

It was all too much.

The prince dropped into a low bow, placing one arm behind his back and another at his stomach. We followed his show of submission. Instead of copying his stance, though, we picked something much more fitting for our stature.

We knelt to the ground and placed our foreheads against the cool marble. No simple bow would do. Some struggled to contort their bodies as fast as the others, their mistakes already determining their fate even before we were offered to the princess.

"I, Icas Solei, come to propose marriage to Princess Aurelia Castle," he said, his voice ringing out loud and clear. "I have brought jewels and gifts, as well as fifty guards, at your disposal if you accept. On our wedding day, I plan to triple anything you receive from me today."

Seconds ticked by. Five, ten, twenty. *What were they waiting for?* The silence pulled my gaze up, even if my mind told me not to look.

There was a single throne where the king sat while his daughter, and who I assumed were his wife and child, stood by his side.

Even the princess didn't get a throne.

Another show of who actually held the power in the family.

She was beautiful. Long, soft brown locks flowed down her back, her head topped with a simple yet elegant diamond and ruby tiara. She wore a deep bloodred dress that was accentuated with real gold throughout and hugged her shape before flowing out behind her. To top it off, she had a huge ruby placed in the hollow of her throat, the contrast between the jewel and her skin striking. It twinkled with each breath she took.

But her beauty wasn't what shocked me.

It was her striking blue eyes...that were staring right at me.

My breath caught in my throat, and my heart began to pound in my chest. I had come here with a simple goal, but never did I imagine that I would garner her attention so fast.

I almost couldn't believe it. Suspicion rose in my belly.

Had I done it?

What would happen because of it, I did not know. But what I did know is that it was the first step in enacting the carefully laid-out path that had been determined for me at my birth.

I was going to kill Princess Aurelia.

AURELIA

is offer of engagement was not the first time I had set my eyes on the *wonder* that was Prince Icas.

I was a young vampire when I first met him at a mandatory ball all royal vampires forced their offspring to attend. It was my first time debuting as an eligible vampire. Also the first time I had ever seen so many male vampires looking at me like I was a piece of meat.

Even back then, he took a liking to me straight away. After all, there weren't many other vampire families out there that could match his family's *esteemed reputation* and wealth.

It didn't matter to him that there were already rumors of his engagement to another princess. Or that he was over a hundred years my senior. Or that he had more than his fair share of *fun* with the other princesses in attendance while his bride-to-be was watching it all.

Well...princesses, maids, guards. Icas didn't discriminate who he decided to sink his fangs into. But that's not what made me loathe him. I could appreciate a bit of fun now and then. Hell, sometimes it was the only thing that made this dull life worth living.

What truly made me loathe him was his disgusting disregard for the humans who signed up to be his feeders.

It wasn't uncommon for feeder abuse to occur, and it was especially rampant in rich families. For vampires, feeders were at the bottom of the food chain. These were the humans who signed up to be used by the family. Who gave their blood—and body—in exchange for room, board, and a hefty compensation they accumulated for their service.

They were there for whatever the vampire wanted. At their beck and call, no matter the situation. And often, their deaths were overlooked if the family just quietly paid them off.

I had been witness to more than one atrocity he committed against the poor humans in his service. Watched as his hazel eyes lit up at the begging of his humans as he bared his pearly white fangs in a twisted grin.

I was no saint and had the blood of many on my hands, but even I had a limit with the poor feeders. I would never force them into anything sexual. I wouldn't tear their skin or cause them harm just for fun.

But he did. And he did it because he enjoyed watching the pain of others.

He had that same look on his face as he stormed Father's throne room. He held himself like he belonged here. Like he was the one who was next in line for Father's throne. Like just because he breathed the same air as us, he was entitled to the wealth and status my family worked for all those years ago, when Mother was still alive.

The human guards behind him refused to look at us. All of them had their eyes on the ground as they marched behind him. Each of their heartbeats pounded in their chest, the sound echoing throughout the room.

Did they know that they were already dead? That all of them stood for one thing and one thing only, and that was their blood, promised to me by their very own prince?

I hated it. I hated Icas. I hated my father. But what could I do other than smile down at the monster that would soon have his grimy fingers around my throat like a collar?

I would make him pay for this. Maybe not then, but I vowed I would make his life a living hell for thinking he could use me like this.

"I, Icas Solei, come to propose marriage to Princess Aurelia Castle," Icas said, his loud voice causing my head to pound uncomfortably. "I have brought jewels and gifts, as well as fifty guards, at your disposal if you accept. On our wedding day, I plan to triple anything you receive from me today."

Oh great. Just what I need. How generous.

I didn't respond. It wasn't my place. Per royal vampire law, it was my father who had the power to accept or reject his proposal.

Instead, I let my eyes wander over the guards. *Maybe they could provide some entertainment.* It would at least be better than whatever I could do with Prince Icas. Their bodies were healthy, their blood warm, and most of them probably signed up for this knowing that they had the possibility of warming my bed if I requested it.

But most of them looked far too nervous to provide any fun. Sweat beaded a few foreheads. Hearts raced as my eyes traveled over them.

And then there was *her.*

Bright silver hair pushed out of her face, save for a few strands that fell onto her pale, scarred skin. She was bowed, like the rest, but she was deathly still. There was not a single bead of sweat on her, nor was her chest rising and falling rapidly as her lungs tried to keep up with her pounding heart.

...because her heart wasn't pounding.

I almost missed it in the commotion of the room. But at the very front, off to my right-hand side, there was an *absence.* Her heart was steady, almost silent in the wake of all those pounding around her.

Warm honey eyes met mine as she lifted her gaze. Just like me, she was taking in her surroundings. Analyzing the people who stood in front of her. Her heart jumped, and her heartbeat continued to rise as our gazes locked.

But she isn't scared. Taken aback, maybe, but not scared like the others.

Even after the prince all but threw their lives away, she was calm. The only thing causing any type of reaction was *my* gaze. A thought that only inflated my ego.

A little mouse wormed her way into the prince's ranks, has she?

There was no other explanation. She entered the palace for a reason, and she must have known all too well what her future held... *Unless that's what she wanted?*

I couldn't stop the rise in my curiosity. I needed her close. I need to watch her next move.

She was dangerous. The beating of her heart and the various scars covering her body told me that. *But that's what was so enticing about her.*

After years of being around guards who held no power and vampires who abused their mountains of it, here was a single human who had the possibility to tip the scale.

For the first time in more than a decade, I felt...*excited.* If my slow-pumping heart could, it would flip at the idea of what lay ahead of me.

"Such generosity," my father said, standing and holding his hand out to me. Like the perfect primed princess I was, I placed my hand delicately in his and let him lead me down the stairs and to Icas. "Of course we would be more than happy to accept your proposal. Isn't that right, Princess Aurelia?"

His tone gave no indication of how angry he truly was since the meeting, but I could feel it rumbling underneath his skin. The urge to rip my hand away from his as the volatile emotions trailed through our contact was so strong, I couldn't stop the flinch.

I smiled at Icas as my hand was placed in his.

"I'm honored, Prince Icas," I said, bowing my head to him. When I lifted my eyes again, I had to hold in the shudder.

He had already leaned forward toward my hand, but instead of kissing it, he flipped it over to bare my wrist to him.

"I shall drink from your vein to seal our proposal," he murmured against my skin, his gaze daring me to pull away.

In front of everyone? He would dare?

Anger exploded inside me, only to strengthen when his fangs brushed across my naked wrist.

Never. *Never* should a vampire take blood from a royal unless for a blood bond. A blood bond I had no intention of forging with him. And it definitely wasn't something that was done in front of an audience. It was sacred. Private. *Personal.* It was supposed to be my life essence. My power. *Me.*

And he is just taking it.

I averted my gaze as his fangs pierced my skin. I had long since stopped believing in Krae's powers, but the sight of her image in the glass on the other side of the room caused a stray thought to rush across my mind.

And you will allow this insult to just go unpunished?

She didn't answer, of course.

Pain traveled up my arm and to my shoulder. He hadn't left his fangs in long enough for the venom. Just a deep enough prick before pulling some blood and licking it from the wound.

All pain and no pleasure.

The venom for vampires was nothing compared to what it did to humans, but his meaning was clear.

He was in control of the pain and pleasure that I would be receiving from him. If he wanted it to hurt, it would, and if I wanted pleasure, I would somehow have to earn it.

I hadn't meant to look toward her, but again, our eyes met. *The little mouse.*

She was watching with hardly concealed disdain as he took my blood.

When he was done, I gave my attention back to him and his bloodstained lips.

"Princess Aurelia will show you to your room for your stay here. The guards will be taken by Henry, and he will explain the rules and get them accommodated," Father announced, his hand coming to squeeze my shoulder. Another warning. *Behave.*

Icas gave him a beaming smile and linked his arm with mine. *Disgusting.*

"The silver-haired one," I told Melia as I ran the brush through my hair. "I want her assigned to my personal guards."

I flipped my hair over my shoulder, the smooth column of my neck reflecting back at me in the mirror. There was not a single thing out of place. The skin on my neck was still as unblemished as it had been just a few hours ago, but the phantom pain from his bite was still there.

I narrowly got away without forging a blood bond with him, but that didn't mean that he wouldn't drink from me whenever he wanted. As soon as he was seen to his room I was called upon.

If I was any stronger I wouldn't have allowed him to sink his fangs into me a second time.

Vampire blood wasn't even as good as human blood. It was bland, sometimes even dirty-tasting, in comparison. If he was thirsty, he had hundreds of humans to choose from, including the ones he brought himself.

But that wasn't his intention. It was control.

He was still below my family in status, so the only way that he could feel comfortable entering an agreement like this with my family was to make sure I knew he was above me in every way.

I would allow it, even if the price was my dignity. Because there was nothing more powerful than letting a cocky vampire believe he had control when, in reality, I was the one holding it.

I'll kill him one day. I swear it. Slowly, painfully, and without remorse. If not to get back at him for sinking his fangs into me, then for the humiliation of what he did in front of my own people.

I jumped as Melia's cold fingers brushed against the spot his fangs pierced. For some reason, the act caused my eyes to sting. I blinked away the feeling before the blood could pool in them.

"Shall I go get her now?" she asked. "You must be thirsty."

I hadn't even noticed the dull ache in my throat until she mentioned it.

God, why is she being so nice? It's not like we were actually friends, and we both knew she was just here to report on what I was doing to *that bitch.*

The same *bitch* who was probably crying laughing knowing that she had one-upped me.

I swallowed thickly, fire coating the insides of my throat. *When did it get this bad?*

It was nowhere near the risk of the craze, but it was enough to pull my attention fully away from what the prince had done to me.

It was tempting to get her to call on the silver-haired one. Especially after I saw the look in her eyes when Icas's fangs pierced my skin.

Would her face look the same when my fangs pierced her skin? Would the hate and disgust she held inside her be directed at me instead?

It was so easy to hate others. It removed the responsibility from yourself. All the anger and pain could be projected onto any object of your choosing. I wanted to see it. Wanted to see as she tried to fight the disgust as it took hold of her.

Or would she somehow be able to surprise me again? *I hope so.* I wanted her to hate me as much as she wanted my fangs to pierce her. Unlike the prince, the willingness was what made it worthwhile for me. But maybe too similar to him, I craved to watch humans give into something they wanted yet hated so deeply at the same time.

What did that make me, then? I met my own gaze in the mirror. Hate was brewing there too. But hate for what?

Hate for the prince? Of course...but also for myself. A violent, uncomfortable weight unfurled in my chest. It took *real* strength to hate yourself.

I couldn't move my gaze away. The mask that I had been so carefully putting together threatened to crumble. *Strength...right? Is that what they call kneeling for a monster while he drains you and thanking him after?*

I stood up, unable to handle looking at myself in the mirror any longer.

"No, send a regular feeder, please."

Melia hesitated for a moment. "Now," I hissed when she didn't move. She looked like she wanted to say something but scurried away regardless.

Good. She'd probably make a pit stop in my stepmother's room to give her an update about the prince.

I stiffly walked to my bed and waited for the arrival of my feeder.

The feeling from before grew stronger as the moments passed. Traveling from my chest and settling in my belly. *Hate.* So hot and heavy, it threatened to pull me to the floor.

Hate for myself. For Father. For Icas.

But through it all, images of her warm brown eyes broke through. *Who is she? Why does she have such an effect on me?*

I wanted her. *Needed* to understand what on earth was going on in that mind of hers. She was an obsession I couldn't help but latch on to.

My musings were cut short as the feeder arrived, knocking twice before letting himself into my dimly lit room. It was a man this time.

I didn't have to tell him to sit on the bed. I maneuvered myself in front of him, trying not to look him in the eyes. I didn't want it to be him. In my mind, it was her sitting on the bed, hate brimming in her eyes.

"No touching," I warned. He gave me a stiff nod. "If it's too much, say something. Make a noise, anything. As soon as I hear a peep, I'll stop."

Another stiff nod.

He tilted his head to the side. Swallowing thickly, I leaned closer and, without hesitation, sunk my fangs into his neck. I paused before drinking, letting the venom work its way into his bloodstream.

It never took long, but the ache in my throat was pushing me to go faster. To drain him even before it had a chance to work through him.

When he relaxed against me, I began. The blood hit my tongue, and sweetness exploded across my taste buds. Blood was the single most powerful and addictive thing in this universe. I couldn't help but moan into it.

It changed based on who you drank from, but it was sweet, sometimes tangy, and, oftentimes, the single most delectable thing a vampire ever tasted.

The liquid traveled down my throat, coating it and chasing away the ache before settling in my stomach. It calmed the hate, even for just a moment, because of its sweetness.

His legs opened, allowing me to get closer to him as I gulped down mouthfuls of his blood. I shouldn't have entered his space, but I was so lost in the taste of it that I forgot myself.

It had been weeks since I drank from the source, days since I had blood at all. I had been too careless.

When his hands grabbed my hips, I pulled away, ripping my fangs out of him.

My hand gripped his chin, and finally, I got a look at his dilated pupils and flushed skin.

"No touching," I hissed. Before pushing him away, I licked my bites, making sure to coat them with my venom so they would heal faster. It was too nice of a gesture from me, especially since he went against my orders. This was the type of human I was tired of. "Get out."

He scrambled out of my hold, his heart pounding in his chest and the smell of fear permeating the air as he left.

And then I was alone again, with no one but my bird to keep my company.

Maybe hating myself was the easy way out.

VESPER

Why? *Why the fuck did it have to be **her** I had to bunk with?*

I would've taken anyone. The stupid, beefy football team reject who laughed too loudly at jokes. The man with the psychopathic tendencies who stood at the back of the room, his eyes intently glaring at whoever even brushed past him.

Anyone.

Anyone who wouldn't give a fuck about what I needed to do here. Someone too hung up on the excitement of working for the family that they wouldn't even look twice at me.

And then they gave me a room with *her*.

My hands paused as I spread out the wrinkles on the thin sheets the family assigned me, trying desperately not to give in to the urge to turn and look at her. She had been silent since the assignment, not giving any indication of how she felt about bunking with me.

That's what I hated about her type the most. You could never tell what they were truly thinking. Not unless they wanted you to. Everything else was just a carefully curated mask held in place with barbed wire instead of strings.

It wasn't long until I gave into the urge to look. The tingling in the back of my head told me she might have been looking at me, but when I did finally turn, she was too busy looking at her own bed.

The room itself was small, with only enough space for two twin beds, each of us having a dresser and a nightstand. The bathroom was at the foot of my bed, but the inside was lackluster. The stone was water damaged, and there was moss growing in the corners of it. No doubt there was also a fair share of mold hidden in the cracked floors.

The family was well off—this was a fact based on how they showed off numerous times, even in the short span that I had been here. The floors on the upper stories were furnished with thick, expensive, and most likely imported rugs. Each surface shined, as if it had been polished for hours by some poor maid. And the vampires themselves were decked out in jewels the size of my fist. The family wanted to show the rest of the world what they did with all of the money they accumulated throughout the years. Even the floors smelled of roses.

Even the windows seemed to be made out of crystal and sent shimmering rainbow refractions across every surface.

But it all changed as soon as you reached the guards' quarters. The shimmering windows were barred. If there were rugs, they were worn and frayed. Stone covered the floors, walls, and ceilings, many of which were cracked, and chunks had fallen out. Even walking down the hallway to this room, I had almost gotten hit with one of those stray chunks as it fell from the ceiling.

It became clear what the family truly cared about, and it wasn't us.

The family cared about image.

And then, when you got down to the basement where the guards spent their time, everything looked as if it hadn't been updated in the last century.

As if the conditions weren't bad enough, the universe decided to play one last trick on me and assign her and me to the same room.

The person in question was still hunched over the bed, her

sheets were already spread out across the small mattress, and she started to meticulously empty her backpack.

The bright red hair was hard to miss. She wore the same clothes that had been assigned to me, but she decided to embellish them with two leather weapon straps that crisscrossed on her back.

The weapons were missing, but they seemed to hold daggers.

As if sensing my stare, she turned slowly, her bright green eyes meeting mine. A small, feral-like smile spread across her lips.

It was one I'd seen many times over when we were training at the prince's compound, and the exact reason why I didn't want to get near her. It was the only slip of her mask I had ever seen.

She straightened up and turned before closing the space between us. She got way too close for me to think that her actions were anything but threatening.

And she is taller than me.

She looked down at me, her smile widening. I took note of her shaggy haircut, half up, half down, and showing her pierced ears, both of which had daggers in the holes. Her skin was littered with freckles, some seemingly arranged in a pattern I couldn't recognize.

But what was dangerous about her were her eyes. They were sharp. They saw everything. Maybe even the thing I wanted to hide.

"I don't think we had a chance to introduce ourselves," she said, her eyes searching my face and then slowly narrowing in on part of my neck. The exact part where my tattoo was currently being hidden by magic.

A chill ran through me, and I took an involuntary step back.

She cocked her head at this.

"We will have to do something about that," she added in a teasing tone.

And then, quicker than I could react, her lanky hand reached out and brushed across my neck. Heat hit me right where the tattoo was. *Magic.* Pure, powerful magic.

I had never felt anything like it before. Everything I had encountered up until that point had been a watered-down version of what she possessed.

But that alone wasn't enough of a red flag to quell the anger her touch had ignited.

My hands snapped out, grabbing her shirt and pulling her to me.

"Don't you fucking mess with me li—"

"Or what?" she asked, cocking her head. "You'll tell on me?"

Her blasé attitude caused my brain to short-circuit.

What could I do? I just entered the castle, I couldn't kill her just yet.

A better question was, *What would she do?* Her eyes had a fucking twinkle in them. Like she was just daring me to do something to her.

I pushed her away, trying to put some space between us before I did something I'd regret.

"I didn't know the family accepted witches in here," I grumbled, my hand coming up to rub where the magic had hit me.

She let out a chuckle and placed her hands on her hips. My entire body was ready for attack, but hers seemed right at home. "And I didn't know they let vampire hunters in here."

Vampire hunters. We hadn't been referred to by that name in decades, according to our history. Maybe that was once how my family's organization started, but those days were long gone, and the meaning of the *hunters* had been sullied by some of the atrocities committed by the previous organization.

Another reason for the secrecy of the leaders and the families involved.

"My family handles contracts that are not limited to vampires." The defensiveness in my tone was hard to mistake.

Shit. The smile on her face widened, and I knew I had fucked up.

"And is the Castle family a part of these...*contracts*?"

She brushed past me and went straight to my bed as if to find evidence to prove that I was here for that sole reason. Just as her hand reached out to touch my bag, I slapped it away, but instead of looking at me like she was offended...she looked amused.

"If I can sense magic, then you should be careful what you have hiding in there," she said, moving away from my bag. "If you slip up, some rogue vampire may just...sniff it out."

"Are you threatening me?" I asked, my spine straightening and my blood rushing through my veins.

Could I really get away with killing her now? My hands itched as the urge to reach for my magically forged knife I kept hidden in the bag shot through me. It would do some damage before her magic could get to me, but there was no guarantee that I would win.

Normally, in this scenario, I would have had weeks, if not months, to make a decision, but not here. I had just these few moments between us.

But she seemed not at all affected. She seemed...calm. Comfortable.

"I had us put together because I saw what you were hiding on your neck," she admitted, her eyes trailing back to my tattoo. "If you're hiding something, there's less chance that you'll rat me out for doing the same."

The stiffness in my body was replaced with curiosity. *So I'm not the only one who decided to take on a job in the family.*

This job was the thing I had been created for. All my life led up to this moment. But instead of feeling like this was a threat, I couldn't help but be curious about the type of people who came here with me.

Did they, too, have a prophecy that controlled their lives?

Then a semi-panicked yet relieved thought flashed through my mind: *Would they get to the princess before me?* No, she didn't seem like she was after the same thing I was.

"Vesper," I offered, but didn't bother reaching out my hand for her to shake. If she was giving me this information, she was likely not my competition.

"Cedar," she replied, and slapped her hand on my shoulder so hard I fell off balance. Hot magic shot through my shoulder, and a pained groan slipped from my lips.

"What the fuck—"

"Use those herbs you have stashed in your bag. My magic is more discreet to prying eyes," she said. "Come see me in a few days for a recharge, though."

I looked up at her narrowed eyes.

"Prying different from yours?" I asked. "Should I be worried about a band of witches here?"

She gave me a sidelong look and went back to her bed.

"If someone like yourself made it in here, what makes you think there aren't more?"

AURELIA

"This is enough, you really don't need to—"

"Oh, hush now," Henry said, his wrinkled hands pushing a fur-lined cape into my hands. "Julie worked on this with you in mind."

He was kneeling at my feet like he always did, but as the quarter-human aged, I couldn't help but feel pity for him. His aging knees were no match for the cold castle floor.

The vampires in the palace deserved my wrath. They were good-for-nothing heathens who only cared about a fresh blood bag and their ring-stacked fingers.

But not the humans. Not the people my mother had welcomed into this family with open arms.

They came here based on a promise. A promise that neither my father nor I could deliver.

I wished to kneel down and help him to his feet, but Father would see my inability to take this poor old man injuring himself to gift me with something I didn't need as an insult.

If anything, taking things from a man like Henry should have been an insult. A real king would have showered his followers with presents instead of accepting them. He should have celebrated his only blood heir being married off.

But instead, he used it as yet another way to make money.

His eyes burrowed into my back, a reminder to keep my mouth shut. He might be more lenient with my attitude when we were alone, but if I so much as even looked at him the wrong way while in front of our people, there would be hell to pay.

I was tempted to refuse the gift again, feeling almost disgusted at adding another to the mountain behind me...until I felt something hard hidden inside the bunches of fabric. His deep brown eyes met mine with a silent message.

He was pleading with me to take it. And for me to be silent.

A dangerous lick of curiosity ran up my spine. *And here I thought the only thing keeping me entertained would be the silver-haired guard.*

The same guard who had yet to be assigned to me, even though I had already asked.

Per the head guard, they were letting the new arrivals get situated, so instead of having her by my side, I had Melia and one other random guard I had never seen in my life.

The need to open the cape was almost unbearable.

"There are others who wish to see the princess," Father interrupted, his voice breaking the connection between us. *Right.*

My eyes wandered to the line of our people waiting to see me. It ran down the stairs and out into the hallway. All of them coming to wish the late queen's daughter a happy marriage.

When will this stop? At this rate, I would be here for hours before we even reached the end of the line.

That was what happened when you never turned anyone away for years, then subsequently focused on trying to bring in as many people to our family as possible.

If I had half the power Mother did, I would have been able to put a stop to this. We had no need to accept these gifts. Most couldn't afford them, not after the taxes my father forced on them.

But Henry...I looked down at him once more, remembering his young age when I was a child. He had been so carefree back then, but after so many years, his skin had started to wrinkle, his hair grayed, and once again, he was missing teeth, but there were none pushing in to replace the lost ones.

He was dying right before my very eyes, and I had barely noticed.

Father had never wanted him here, but Mother had insisted. Humans, vampires, even witches were allowed to be a part of the family in her eyes. They all had a place. Even if they never so much as acknowledged Krae.

"Thank you, Henry," I said with a smile, holding out my hand for him. *Fuck, Father, I wouldn't let the old man suffer. It was embarrassing and cruel.* "I have not forgotten the day you were accepted into our family. Thank you for your continuous love and support. I can't tell you how much it means to me."

His smile caused a burst of warmth to spread across my chest, but just as he was about to reach his hand out to grasp mine, guards were at his side.

"Be carefu—"

"Next," Father called as the guards pulled the old man away with far too much force for his brittle bones.

I bit my tongue, not caring about the splash of metallic-tasting blood that spread across my tongue. I turned to the pile of gifts, shooing Melia away as she tried to grab the cape. Anger exploded inside me. It was *mine* to handle. I could deal with my stepmother stealing any of my other gifts, but not this one.

If they thought I couldn't see the small pile they kept for themselves off to the side, they were fools.

"Leave this one for me," I whispered to her. "It's special."

And like a good little princess, I stood back in my assigned spot and greeted the next person.

But it was obvious that this one wasn't like the others. I hadn't seen him over the line of people, but as soon as he made it to the front, the anger rolled off him in waves.

He was a younger vampire, maybe not much older than I was. His brown hair was slicked back, and he wore a clean suit.

He didn't have a gift in his hand, nor was he looking at me. He was just looking at Father.

"The queen would have never agreed to this," he said, his words causing everyone in the room to silence.

"Excuse me?" Father asked, raising his brow.

"Her mother wanted her to marry for love," he continued, his voice getting louder with each word. "You think we haven't heard rumors of what the prince does in his free time? Think we don't know that this is some power play?"

This was not the type of entertainment I wanted. The guards were frozen, unable to make heads or tails of what was happening. No one had dared to talk to Father like this before. He also hadn't given them the signal to move in and cut off his head.

He was just...watching. His face showing none of the anger I knew must have been broiling underneath his skin.

"I can object to my own wedding," I said, rolling my shoulders and moving closer to him. "But I haven't. Half the family saw me accept him—"

"We saw him disgrace you," he said, cutting me off. "And Krae. The attempt at a blood bond has never been taken lightly. We worry for you, princess. We, just like your mother, only want what—"

Guards were at his side in seconds, wrestling him down and forcing him to his knees. Another one came up in front of him and painfully forced a gag in his mouth before tying it in place with a knot at the back of his head.

There it is. My gaze traveled to Father, who was already looking at me. It hit me then.

He knew I hated this arrangement. He knew I would do anything to get out of it.

That bastard wants to see if I would shame him in front of the entire family.

It was a test. And there was only one way to pass it.

I tilted my head to the side and raised my brow as if asking him, *What's the holdup?*

The slightest smile pulled at his lips before it disappeared completely. He stood, holding out his hand, only for a diamond-encrusted gold sword to be placed in it by a random guard.

Most kings didn't like to do the dirty work themselves and instead had their right hands do it. But Father wasn't like most kings.

Father liked to send a message.

The sharp sound of the sword flying through the air was all the warning we got before it sliced clean through the man's neck. I forced myself to watch as the light left his eyes and his head fell to the floor.

A rotten, dark feeling blossomed in my chest. It held tight on my throat and threatened for blood to pool in my eyes.

I blinked it away.

"A little dramatic, Father," I muttered under my breath, aware that he and half the room could hear.

"What else does my princess deserve on the day of her engagement?" he asked, a light teasing to his tone that shouldn't have been there after brutally murdering one of his own family members.

"Gifts," I said, and gave the nervous line a smile "Who's next?"

It had taken us hours to get through the people that had arrived. For most of that time, the guards had left the vampire's dead body bleeding out on the carpet as a show of what would happen to whoever else decided to intervene.

After a while, they moved it, but never cleaned up the blood, even when it started to stink.

Just another reminder of how different it was now that Mother was gone. She would have never let it happen.

But she also would have never let you get married.

Unfortunately, the man had been right. And for some reason, he, and I guess others, saw it as their duty to try to save the queen's only daughter from a life of misery at the prince's hands.

Though only one dared to actually stand up to him and try. And his death was enough to put a stop to all other mentions of it.

After that, it was all smiles and congratulations. The line continued, and so did the gifts.

But there was one thing about the vampire's words that caused disgust to settle in my stomach.

It was all for the queen. They did it because they had a duty to the queen.

Not me.

If their duty was to me, they would have protested the situation I was in long ago.

But yet here they were, lining up in droves just to show how excited they were for my marriage, ignoring everything else that came before it.

The first thing I did when I was dismissed was to carefully take the cape and hidden object with it to my room before the stepdevils could take it. For good measure, I left the rest and even told the demon spawn to pick whatever she liked.

After all, I'm the one lucky enough to get married while the bitch herself never even got so much as a second glance.

Now *that* comment probably did more harm than good, but fuck was her face worth whatever punishment might be awaiting me.

The cape was heavy in my hands, the weight just adding to the excitement of seeing what was inside.

I had waited for some time. Even though I was locked up in my room, there was no telling when Melia might just pop in for a visit. But when it was time, I slowly peeled back the layers, and then when I saw the folded-up paper and what was written within, my heart dropped.

May my love for the queen set you free.

The note was written in elegant handwriting and attached to a vial of shimmering liquid I knew all too well.

The queen. Always for the queen, a bitter voice said in the back of my mind.

But louder was something far sweeter.

It was for Father.

Henry was truly the one who decided to protest. *Maybe that's why the next person created such a fuss.*

I had spent too long on his gift, looked at him too kindly, for Father to just overlook it.

It was poetic. The villainous king's downfall is a mirror of the late queen's.

How he even got this past the border of the palace grounds was beyond me. If there was even a rumor of it, he would be done for.

I leaned closer, inhaling deeply. It smelled fresh, like...*river water.* I couldn't help the laugh that burst from my throat.

The image came to my mind easily. The old man, furious at the king for the death of his beloved queen, kept this bottle in the river on the far edge of the property for months, maybe even years, to hide the smell of magic within.

He would no doubt be disappointed with what I decided to do with it.

Father was one route, yes, but the most pressing thing was not his control over me.

It was Prince Icas.

I had learned how to deal with Father over my lifetime. I created a sort of comfortable life, even among the hell the stepdemons put me through.

But there was no way I would allow myself to be taken by Prince Icas.

I didn't have what they needed to fulfill their wish. To put an end to Father's rule. I didn't have hope.

I had *desperation.* And that was much stronger than hope. It had a bite to it.

The hope had been siphoned away from me, year after year, until nothing was left. I *could* fight Father...but I would never win.

At best, I would be locked in my room until Prince Icas decided to take me back to his palace.

At worst...I shuddered to think of what it meant to be at the receiving end of my father's rage.

It wasn't anything new, but the fear of him keeping me on the brink of the craze was enough to cause my entire body to freeze.

I couldn't do it...not again.

With a shaky laugh, I held up the potion as it glimmered in the setting sun. There wasn't hope brewing in my chest—it was something colder. Something crueler.

With this, I could change it all. It would hurt like a bitch, but it would make even Krae proud.

"You better fucking work."

VESPER

I rolled my shoulders, the pain from sleeping on the hard Castle-family-provided mattress still embedded deep within my muscles.

Not only was I tossing and turning because of the bed, but Cedar turned out to be a snorer. You would think that, as a witch, she would have found a cure long ago instead of having everyone around her suffer from the earth-shattering throat noises she made.

The only good thing about the day was that it was my first official day assigned to the princess.

But what I had thought would be a day by her side, getting to know all her habits and possibly some dirty secrets, turned out to be a lesson in patience.

Patience was never my strong suit.

My family was known for their efficiency when it came to all contracts. Because happy clients meant more money, and the quicker we finished jobs, the more we could take.

But something like this couldn't be rushed.

Still, I never expected it would take this long.

It had been hours since I had gotten the news hand-delivered to my room that I would be starting with the princess. A part of me had been shocked that it had truly worked, but my suspicions over the entire situation were much stronger.

My job that first day was simple. One of the many at her side. Yet she had picked me to be the closest to her, standing *right* behind her, listening as she and some other royal chatted for *hours*.

The other small vampire girl had shimmering blonde hair braided around the top of her head before it cascaded down her back and shoulders. She was about half the size of the princess, with an even smaller personality.

The powdery pink dress she wore gave her an air of innocence that was only shattered whenever she brought a glass of bright red blood to her lips.

This obviously wasn't a normal appointment. They were close. Spent hours chatting about nothing and somehow everything. They even had the royal seamstress come and fit them for gowns for their next ball.

It went on. And on. And on. And with it, whatever ego trip I was on after she picked me so suddenly disappeared into thin air.

But the more she talked, the more I couldn't help but listen.

Is the royal life just gossiping, talking about shopping, and drinking blood?

"He'll be upset when he realizes how long I was gone again," the princess's friend said as she attempted to stand.

Finally.

The three other guards at my side seemed to relax at the notice that the vampire girl was finally leaving. The two at the door had an obvious look of relief on their faces. *I can't blame them.* This was a special kind of torture. Even if the princess's voice was nice to listen to.

The princess was by her side in seconds, helping her up. She was gentle with her, gentler than I'd ever seen a vampire be with someone, and I was definitely not expecting it from *her*.

The rumors of the beheaded man at the engagement offerings had spread far and wide, reaching my door before the news of my post did.

I couldn't help but compare the gentleness of her actions, the carefulness of her smile, to what she had done yesterday.

She didn't even blink.

Even got annoyed at her father for causing blood to be spilled so close to her!

I heard she even laughed at the man.

The guards had no problem gossiping in the hallways as I passed, causing our quarters to feel more like a university dorm than a highly coveted position in a ruthless vampire family.

"With the goodies I'll send you home with, he will be in a good mood for weeks," she said as she motioned for one of us to take her spot holding the small vampire.

Of course I was the first to reach them.

"Allow me," I offered, and gently held onto the lady's arm. It was frail. No doubt that if she were on the other end of the contract, she would be much easier to get rid of than the crueler royal by my side. Princess Aurelia's gaze on me was heavy, but when I met her reddened gaze, I couldn't make out what emotions lay beneath.

Was this not what she wanted?

"Let me know when you get home, Elora," she said, her gaze still holding mine. A sultry smirk pulled at her lips.

Elora. That was it. I turned to the smaller girl and gave her a smile.

"Shall we?" I asked. She gave me a polite nod and smiled back.

I motioned for her to follow me out of the room. She waved goodbye one last time before doing so, and I looked back one last time at the princess.

She was watching us leave.

She wants something. I made a note to try and get her alone after I dropped off her friend.

Elora was silent all the way down the hall and grand spiraling staircase. The palace was buzzing with life. Maids, guards, and vampires were all walking the halls, looking carefree. Except for one teenage human staff member, who was shakily holding a tray with crystal glasses of blood. He was so preoccupied, he all but bumped into us.

I quickly maneuvered the royal vampire away from him, taking her in my arms and pulling her close. A move that caused her to let out a hiss.

I sent a glare at the boy before turning my attention to the vampire.

"I apologize," I said quickly and gently removed my hands from her. "I didn't mean to use so much force."

The issue wasn't that I used more force than I would for a human—it was that she was a *vampire* and still hurt by my movement. Their bodies were supposed to be superior to humans, yet such a little move hurt her?

She shook her head, but didn't meet my eyes. "Forget it, please."

I swallowed all the words on my tongue and, without another word, saw her to the front of the palace, where her car was already being piled high with trunks and trunks of what sounded like jewels and even coins.

Coins in this day and age?

The staff still had quite a few to load, so instead of turning straight back and returning to the princess, I lingered.

Maybe it was her frailness. Maybe it was the way she hid from my eyes. Maybe it was the way she let out a pained hiss at even the slightest touch. But there was something bothering me about the vampire at my side.

"That's a big gift," I commented, looking down at her. "Is Princess Aurelia always so generous?"

For the first time that day, Elora looked at me unflinching.

"I've been where you are," she said, her eyes traveling back to the car. "It's a disgusting amount of wealth to be flaunted, isn't it?"

Shock burst through my system. *Yes it is,* I wanted to say, but instead I gritted my teeth. Something that was so alien to me was so normalized within the walls of the palace. *Didn't they have better things to do with their immortality?*

"I used to think she was doing it on purpose," she continued, a bitterness in her tone. Whatever she was showing me in those moments alone was nothing like the person that had been in that room. "I came from a poor family, married off to the highest bidder. I took her actions as a way to remind me how much more she had than I. But soon after, I learned what she was doing for me, and I couldn't help but feel like an ungrateful bitch."

There was a pause, long enough for me to take a good look at her. To realize just how weak she was. How pale her skin was. And just how many bruises were peeking out of the sleeves of her dress as she crossed her arms in front of her chest.

What was the ice queen doing for you?

I had been too busy being annoyed with my situation to even notice the girl's arms.

"Vampires are supposed to heal themselves," I said, unable to keep the words inside.

Her eyes darted down to her arms before covering them up with a bitter sigh.

"Healthy vampires," she said with a bit of venom in her tone. "Vampires who have enough blood to support the creation of their venom. Just like humans, our bodies can weaken. And when it does for long periods of time, it has to make some tough decisions on how to keep me alive. But even this is better than the *craze*."

The craze. I had heard of it but only saw it once when I was called to clean up a scene local law enforcement couldn't handle.

The vampires weren't themselves. Due to lack of blood, they turned into the monsters the myths made them out to be.

She paused before flipping her arm out to show me the slowly healing bruises on the underside of her forearm. What normally took a vampire seconds was taking her minutes. Starting from the outside of the bruise, the blackened skin was turning yellow before disappearing.

"Visiting Aurelia is the break I need to help me," she sighed, a sort of crazed look spreading across her face. She was a vampire who had been pushed to her limits.

Dangerous.

"You shouldn't be telling me this," I said quickly, fixing my eyes on the staff loading the final trunk. *I don't need to get involved in this.*

"No," she whispered. "But everyone knows. You'll understand soon. When you have more experience with the family. Things like this are usually the worst-kept secrets around."

I opened my mouth to speak, but the staff called for her. I bowed my head to her as she left, and she spared me not one single glance.

She dropped all that on me and didn't even blink.

Vampires are more fucked up than I thought.

"Princess!"

Chaos.

That's the only thing that could describe the small room I had left not ten minutes before.

No one had come running, but every single guard in there was hunched over the princess. All of them yelling, but none of them truly helping.

I pushed through the door, my heart pounding in my chest.

How the fuck did this happen while I was gone?

The Castle family home was supposed to be one of the hardest to break into, and yet on my first full day at the palace, the princess was already hunched over on the floor, dry-heaving, and looking like she was about to lose her fight to keep on living.

It wasn't hard to push the panicking guards away—they were too frightened. Not surprising since none of them had the actual experience to think on their feet.

Just like the princess, they had been sheltered, spoiled by the easy life they had in the palace.

It only made me angrier.

"Get the head guard!" I growled at one of them. "Another one of you useless idiots inform the king."

Two guards left, leaving me with the remaining three idiots. All of them were staring at us, unmoving.

I gripped the princess's clammy face, forcing her eyes to meet mine. They were bright red and filled with bloody tears that stained the skin of her cheeks.

Black vine-like veins throbbed across her temples, and her skin had paled significantly. *She was dying.*

This wasn't just any attack. It was magic. That was the only thing that could do this.

But the witch—*Cedar*—was assigned to the perimeter and far away from the princess. *It couldn't have been her, could it?*

The princess's gasps were painful. As hard as she tried, there was no getting anything into her lungs.

Vampires are supposed to heal themselves.

Healthy vampires. Vampires that have enough blood to support the creation of venom.

The venom could help fight the magic, right? Assuming it wasn't too potent?

I looked at her face, her neck, any visible skin I could. The amount couldn't have been enough to kill her instantly. Probably half the dose of what was needed to truly bring her down.

We are dealing with an amateur.

"When was the last time she drank blood?" I asked. No one had an answer. She hadn't been drinking much, if at all, the entire time her friend was here. She had been too focused on healing the girl.

"She just got some delivered," a guard behind her said after a moment. "Then she started—*this.*"

Too long. This is taking too long. If I don't get her blood, then I may really lose my chance.

It shouldn't have made me panic like it did, but when her hands gripped my shirt and her mouth flopped open as she gasped for air... Something else overcame me.

"Drink," I commanded and pushed up my sleeve for her to

drink. I pushed it toward her mouth, but all she did was stare at me. Those bright red eyes held some type of message in them. She was telling me to do something. *To do what?*

I cursed under my breath before looking around the room. I didn't want to use the sword strapped to my back for this. It wasn't meant to pierce my skin…it was for *hers.*

Next to us were crystal glasses, once filled with blood, now shattered, allowing blood to seep into the floor.

I grabbed one of the cleaner shards and brought it down on my wrist, deep enough to draw blood for her. I barely registered the pain, too concerned that I might truly lose my chance to fulfill the prophecy.

Turning back to the princess, I tilted her head up and forced my bleeding wrist to her mouth.

"Drink, princess," I whispered to her.

She didn't listen at first. The blood filled her mouth to the point that it was spilling over at the corners, but then, as I brushed my fingers down the column of her throat, she took her first gulp.

Then she changed. Her hands were no longer gripping my uniform but my wrist, forcing it closer. Her gulps were getting quicker. So quick, the blood flow wasn't enough.

I hadn't expected her fangs to pierce my skin. The groan that forced itself past my lips was evidence of that. And it was the clarity I needed.

I should have let her die.

But I couldn't because then it wouldn't be *me* who killed her, right? Then what would have been the point of it all?

It didn't explain why I continued to rub small, comforting patterns on her throat. Or why I held her gaze even as the warm vampire venom worked through my veins.

I had heard of the effects, but nothing prepared me for the way it caused my belly to clench. For the *need* it started in me.

"Keep going," I whispered as the veins started to disappear. Her eyebrows pushed together, the red in her eyes flickering to show the blue hidden behind all the bloodlust.

She tried to pull back, but my grip on her throat was tight. For good measure, I tangled my hand in her hair, forcing her against my wrist.

"You were poisoned, *princess*," I said in a low warning tone. The heat was becoming too much. It traveled through my body, down to my core. "You will drink until your body has enough to heal."

A low growl sounded from her throat.

I couldn't help it. For the second time that day, I learned that my mouth was much harder to control than I anticipated. I leaned forward, my lips brushing against her ear.

"You may be able to push your daddy around with that attitude," I whispered. "But it won't work on me. Drink the fucking blood and stop whining about someone saving your life."

In response, she bit down even harder on my wrist, pulling a shaky moan from me. The pain mixed with the venom was too much. I craved more of it. Craved more of *her.* My body was getting embarrassingly reactive, even when my mind tried to remind me where we were and what my purpose was.

Stay centered. Breathe. Breathe. Hold it in. Breathe.

I heard the sound of the head guard rushing into the room behind me and yelling orders. One of them was to stay where I was. *Fuck.*

I needed to get away from her. Get her teeth out of me.

He leaned down beside me, getting a look at the princess.

"She's almost done," I reported, trying to keep my voice neutral. "Black veins, unable to breathe. Weak and clammy. I had to puncture a wound and stimulate her throat to make her drink."

"Magical in origin, it would seem," he commented. "You'll need some blood replenishers after this—"

"I'll be fine," I said quickly. I did not want any palace magician near my body. "The magic didn't seem potent enough to take her out right away. Or maybe it was diluted."

Just as he was about to fight me on my refusal of help, the princess pulled her fangs from my wrist and gave me a glare.

Seriously? She is pissed I saved her?

Arousal shifted into a different heat. *Anger.* It coursed through my veins and reminded me that the vampire in front of me didn't deserve my help.

"If I didn't want to drink—"

"You would have di—"

"And you had no right to interfere," she said and pushed herself to her feet, shoving me in the process.

The princess folded her arms across her chest and sent a scathing look at the guards, who were still frozen at her feet.

"Well?" she asked. "Don't you have anything better to fucking do?"

I shared a look with the head guard.

"I know who did it," I said after a moment of silence. He gave me a stiff nod.

"Get yourself cleaned up," he ordered. "The king will need to hear this."

You had no right to interfere.

The words rang loud and clear in my head as the princess glared at me. Her father was sitting on his throne again, his lips set in a strong frown. His daughter was a spitting image of him, the only difference was the roundness of her features and her lithe frame. Even without seeing her mother, I could imagine what she looked like.

What would she think if she knew you wanted this to happen?

The man I passed while taking Elora to her car lay at my feet, his hands bound. His sobs filled the silent throne room.

Why me?

I had one job here and one job only, and I fucked it up on my first day.

Kill the princess.

I had her right in my fucking hands, and I *saved* her life. *Why?* Just so I could be the one to do it?

How was I even going to move with all this attention on me now?

I grabbed the man's hair and forced him to face the king. Hate boiled underneath my skin.

I shouldn't be killing humans for these monsters.

My gaze met the princess's. *This is your fault,* I wanted to say. *You're the reason he's going to die, and for what?*

"Do it," the king ordered. "I'm tired of this."

I reached for the short sword attached to my back, the one I was reserving for *her*. Now it was going to be stained with human blood.

This wasn't the first time I killed a human. Just because my family specialized in vampires didn't mean we weren't contracted for *other* beings. But there was something so bitter about this. About having to take his life while the vampires stared down at me with their red, shimmering eyes. Their bellies were full of blood, their slow-beating hearts speeding up as much as they could because of the excitement of the bloodbath that was about to take place.

But there was one thing I knew to be true.

I might have fucked up. Might have lengthened my stay. Might have garnered unwanted attention on me...

But I earned their trust.

I placed the blade at his neck and, with one motion, sliced it open. I held his head up so they could watch as he bled out. His gasps turned to gurgles as he drowned in his own blood.

It took a few minutes for him to die, but when he did, I let his body fall to the floor and bowed to the king.

"Get this cleaned up," the king ordered and stood. He looked over at the corpse with disgust.

We were dismissed with a wave, but I didn't move, the princess still resting her eyes on me. Then she gave me a sinister smile before tilting her head in her own informal bow.

AURELIA

S he was watching. *The little mouse was always watching.*
       She thought her little stunt would keep her safe. That I
       wouldn't take it like the shot it was.

The air was cold outside. Cold enough to chill my face but
not enough to penetrate the fur coat. Underneath was nothing
but a satin dress that would do nothing against the world
outside.

I had a role to play, and with that role came the outfit. It wasn't
my normal attire and maybe something I would have worn when I
was younger, but the place I was going required a certain type of...
attitude, so I was forced to look the part.

And act it. Something I was looking forward to even less.

It was late at night, the sun had long since fallen, and thousands
of stars lit the sky above my head. I let myself linger in the fresh air
and silence, trying to clear my head and the anger that had been
boiling underneath my skin since the prince had sunk his fangs
into me.

I wasn't sneaking out, per se. Father liked to look away when it
came to these *outings,* but he and I both knew just how beneficial
they were to his ruling. Relationships formed behind closed doors
were the strongest in the world we lived in and sometimes were the

only thing stopping an all-out war with some of the families involved.

But there was no getting without first giving. I had been in attendance at these events time and time again, but this was the first time I would go as a newly engaged woman.

They would want to see me. Would want to make sure that I wasn't going to leave them and take all their secrets with me.

That deserved something big.

I paused at the limo door, motioning for my guard to stop. The weight of someone's eyes on me was still present.

Looking up at the darkened palace, I felt the weight of her gaze. Most of the windows were dark, but the moonlight shone into the palace just enough that I was able to catch where the eyes were. And *whose* eyes they were.

Fifth floor, west wing. I could barely make her out in the distance, even with vampire sight, but damn could I feel her.

It was a surprise that the little mouse had made it so far up before realizing that I wasn't even there.

Looking for me, huh?

But would she be so bold as to try to find me in the middle of the night when every other human was sleeping? Her actions excited me so much it felt like my insides were buzzing.

"Bring the silver-haired one to me," I ordered. "She will be accompanying me tonight."

I got in the car first and shut the door, enjoying the way the warmth felt against my skin.

She had the perfect timing. If she wanted to be around me so badly, I might as well just take her with me.

Because of her, the plan had ended in disaster. Instead of being able to use the poisoning attempt as a way to force Father's hand for my freedom, I had to watch as my newest guard killed a boy, an innocent human boy, in front of me.

Why did she have to save me? Why couldn't she have waited until Father showed up?

If she had just waited, there would have been no reason that boy had to die. Prince Icas would have been the one to blame, and I would have been out of this stupid engagement faster than he could run away with his tail between his legs.

Father would let a lot slide, but murdering his only blood daughter? *Not likely.*

It was no more than fifteen minutes later that the silver-haired guard was pushed into the back with me. She gave me and my guard a hesitant stare, as if waiting for instructions.

The back was spacious, but I motioned for her to sit next to me. She took one look at the empty seat beside me before moving.

The bastard decided to sit a whole five feet away from me instead. *Annoying.* It took everything in me to keep the smirk on my face instead of twisting it into a scowl.

Her eyes stayed planted on the floor, and her arms were crossed. *Annoyed? Pouting?* A picturesque image of a child not getting their way.

My guard gave me a lingering look before shutting the door and joining the driver up front. The loud slam didn't even have her flinching, but she did give the guard a side-eye.

Just how long is she planning to sit there in silence? But as the seconds passed, it seemed that she had no intention of speaking.

The car rolled forward, causing her to look out the window as we pulled away from the looming palace. *My home.*

It looked so beautiful under the darkening sky. The palace stood tall over everything in the area. The images of the hundreds of roses reflected on the lower floor's windows.

There was no mistaking its presence...or Father's importance.

"Kidnapping now? They better give me my weapons back."

I couldn't stop the light chuckle that spilled from my lips. *So she had a little bit of a bite.*

Someone must not have liked it when I almost sucked them dry. *Or maybe she liked it more than she was letting on.*

I wouldn't easily forget the noises that came out of her mouth. The snarled look she gave me as the venom lit her body on fire.

"My father and the prince told me I could do whatever it is I wanted with you," I said, crossing my legs and sinking into the heated leather seat. "I decided that, as a reward for your *heroic* actions, I'd like to take you out."

"Too late to say no now," she muttered under her breath. Her golden eyes shot toward the divider between us and the driver.

Still not looking at me?

"They can't hear us," I confirmed. She merely shrugged.

I enjoyed the attitude she put on, and it made me want to get back at her even more. She couldn't possibly understand what she caused me to lose in there.

"You're going as my plus one." I inched closer to her, pulling her gaze toward me. "A small *party*. More than a few vampire family heads. Lots of blood. Dancing...and *other things*. Guards aren't allowed in, but tonight you're just there as my human companion. Which means you and I have a role to play."

There it is. The anger. It flashed so quickly across her face that I almost missed it. She had been so good at concealing it, but all her efforts were thwarted by that single slipup.

"If it's what I think it is, I will refuse."

I clicked a button on the side of the door that connected us to the front.

"Stop. Pull over."

The silver-haired guard steadied herself at the sudden jerk of the car. When we came to a full stop, I gave her a shit-eating grin.

"We aren't that far," I said and motioned to the door. "You can get out."

Obviously, she hadn't been expecting my offer. Suspicion was heavy in her gaze, and I could hear the grinding of her teeth.

"What do you think it is?" I asked her, tilting my head to the side. Her jaw clenched.

"Something I shouldn't be going to. Why are you bringing me?" she asked.

Why was I bringing her? I lifted a brow at her. Why wouldn't I be? I already told her that the prince and my father told me I could do whatever I wanted with her.

Not many guards would have the balls to ask. I was well within my rights. But I liked the little mouse's fire more than her compliance.

"You ruined things for me. Interfered with something you had no part in," I reminded her, leaning forward and running my eyes down her form.

She was lithe, but surprisingly muscular, underneath her uniform. If I were any crueler, I'd ask her to strip for me so I could see just what she was hiding underneath her clothing, but I would save it for another day.

"You mean when I saved your life?" she growled. "You were going to *die* if I didn't save you. All while those other guards just stared at you, doing *nothing*. Is that what you wanted? For your last moments to be you begging for breath while those fuckers watch—"

I pushed myself to the floor in front of her, placing my hands on her knees and leaning up so our faces were centimeters away.

Her skin was warm, even through the pants. It had been so long since I allowed myself to indulge with a human that I forgot just how much their blood warmed their skin.

"I had a plan," I whispered, my eyes trailing down her face to her neck, where I could see the veins pulse with fresh blood. My mouth watered just remembering the taste. "Father was going to find me. The blame would be placed on the prince, but now that poor boy died because of *you*."

Her hand shot out to my throat, much like it had when she forced me to drink her blood. Hot, unbridled fury twisted her face into a snarl.

"That was all you, *princess*," she whispered. "You did this as some type of ploy to get what you wanted? It was immature. Stupid. And honestly embarrassing for someone of your stature."

Krae. Her words felt like lava running down my skin, warming every possible inch. I never took myself for much of a masochist, but fuck did her words cause my cunt to flutter.

"That was at first..." I murmured, leaning into her hold on my neck.

I couldn't breathe. The air in the limo was too charged. The hate in her eyes was too intoxicating. I wanted it all. Wanted to feel how much she hated me.

"...but now I realize that you'll be the perfect cover."

She raised a scarred brow, her grip on my neck loosening.

"Are you in?" I asked.

Her jaw twitched.

"I can't agree to something blindly." She took her hand off me and leaned back into the seat with her arms crossed over her chest. I let myself get distracted by the way her muscles jumped in her uniform. Even if she annoyed the shit out of me, it didn't mean I was going to miss out on the eye candy.

"So you're interested?" I teased and lifted myself up to the seat at her side. "It's a sort of *secret gathering* of—"

"Rich vampires," she finished for me. I tried to lean into her, but she shifted away from me with a scowl.

"And powerful," I added with a wink. I trailed my fingers up her thigh. "But I'm an engaged woman now"—I created mindless patterns on her thighs that caused her heart to jump—"and oftentimes, you can't trust them. *Especially* if they marry into powerful families. So, I'm bringing you to give them a little *assurance* that they can still trust me."

She paused for a beat, her eyes shifting back and forth.

"You want to blackmail yourself?" she asked.

Ah, the little mouse is a bright one, isn't she? I knew she would be. Makes it all the more fun.

"You could say that," I confirmed in a low murmur. "To be honest, after tasting your blood, I can't get it out of my mind. So if there is one person I want to be seen acting as a blood-crazed fool for, I want it to be worth it. I want it to be you."

"You trust me with these vampires' secrets," she said, crossing her arms over her chest. "Aren't you the least bit worried I'll use them for my own purposes?"

"I hope you do. Bring a little *excitement* into the palace," I said with a shrug. The response obviously surprised her, her eyes widening and the tenseness in her shoulders dropping just a smidge. "I do have a request, though." When she didn't respond, I nodded. "I want some of your blood before we arrive. I am willing to *act* like a blood-crazed fool in there, but not *be* one."

Her jaw clenched, all the implications of what I was asking her plastered on her face. She was unhappy about it, but maybe if she could get something out of it...

"*Fine*," she spat out, and in seconds she had assumed a position much like I had previously. She kneeled in front of me, her hands placed on the seat on either side of me. I spread my legs so she could get closer. The flaps of my coat fell to the side, exposing my legs and the small piece of cloth that was covering what was between them.

She leaned in and tilted her head to the side, exposing her long, toned neck. It was one of the only places that wasn't marred by a large scar.

"Light petting is okay, even preferred, so we can sell it. I'm not particularly fond of being finger-banged by a human in these scenarios, so stay above the underwear if you get handsy. I won't say no to a bit of head, though," I explained as I gently brushed the hair away from her neck. The light shiver that ran through her caused my excitement to rise. "If you're comfortable and feeling it, I can make you feel goo—"

"No," she interrupted harshly, her narrowed eyes cutting to mine in warning. "I will be in control of that part. No touching from you."

I bit my tongue. "Very well," I said, leaning toward her neck. The pulse point there was calling to me. The blood was so close under the skin that the scent was already mouthwatering.

I didn't hesitate this time. I sunk my fangs into her, pausing just enough for the venom to travel through her before drinking my fill. One, maybe two gulps. That was what I told myself. But then the little mouse just had to touch me.

I don't think she meant to. She was probably trying to steady herself on the seat, but my legs had been spread so wide that her palms came into contact with my bare thighs.

I didn't let anyone touch me during feeds. Not only because of what the venom did to them, but also because they were usually selfish lovers, only seeking to find their own pleasure while they rode out the effects of the venom.

But not the little mouse. *No.* She was different. She gripped my upper thighs. The feeling of her warm, calloused hands sent shocks through me and had me tangling my hand in her hair, pulling her closer.

Does she hate how this is making her feel? How warm her body is getting? How needy? *I hope so, after what she did.*

The car jerked forward, forcing her to fall further into me. If I hadn't been so preoccupied with her, I would have been angry that my driver disobeyed me, but maybe I should have been thanking him instead. Her hands were forced up my thighs, her thumbs just teasing my underwear.

The blood was delicious. *Her blood.* I couldn't deny it, but there should have been no reason why I arched into her. Why I moaned against her.

I couldn't remember the last time I *wanted* someone to touch me, let alone a human.

Feedings were always the same. Cold, hard walls forced between us, and as soon as those boundaries were broken, I ended it. Never giving into even an ounce of the warmth that blossomed in me as the blood settled in my belly.

But it was different with her. I wanted her to feel it. Wanted to get back at her for what she had pulled in the room. And I was failing.

I forced myself to pull away from her. Both of us were panting. Her golden eyes were hooded, and her mouth was open, giving me a sinful peek at her pink tongue.

I want to kiss her. The thought alone enraged me.

Who is she to make me feel this way?

Her eyes roamed my face before settling on my lips. She brought her hand up to my oddly steady lips and wiped away the blood that lined them.

"Vampires," she uttered with such disgust it shocked me. "Do all of you have such awful fucking table manners?"

"If you wanted me to clean you up, all you had to do was ask, little mouse," I purred and jerked her head to the side so I could run my tongue up the length of her neck. I paused when I got to her ear. "Or maybe there is somewhere else you'd like me to *lick*?"

"Vesper," she growled and pushed me away. The desire was clear in her eyes, but so was the distaste. "You call me Vesper. Not *little mouse*."

"Aurelia," I murmured. "But you can call me princess."

VESPER

Nothing about the princess should have caught me off guard.

Not her cruelty. Not her bloodthirstiness.

Not even the way she was trying to play me.

But for some reason, the way she treated me after she was done was something I never expected.

She treated me like a lover, not an object.

Her teeth had brought a searing pain, but her hands were gentle, even as she tangled them in my hair. And then there was that pause as she tore into my flesh to allow the venom to enter my system.

It would have been better if she had treated me like the piece of meat she thought I was. It would have made it easier to hate her and not fall victim to the way the venom made my body feel.

After her comment, I couldn't help but let out a scoff and forced myself back into the seat beside her, whatever happened during the feeding long gone.

But if *that* was supposed to be a glimpse of what would come... it caused my unease to worsen.

Going to this *event* would only help me. Even when the princess died, the type of blackmail material I could gather here would be a powerful tool for my family's future.

I didn't know exactly what that future would look like. My entire life had been spent preparing for the moment when I would shove my sword into her chest, and that moment alone. For me, there was no talk of an after.

My siblings would get yearly plans. Each of them getting jobs and contributing to the family in ways I never could. I was lucky if I got assigned jobs, and most of the time I had to go out searching for them myself.

But after this?

I snuck a peek at Princess Aurelia as she fixed her coat. The blood had been wiped from her mouth, and her skin had a nice flush.

My body was still buzzing from her venom. Heat curled in my belly at the remembrance of her hand in my hair. Of how she arched into me.

You can think of the future after you complete this job. Stay focused.

My inner critic's voice was my father's. Reminding me just how vital this job was. Not like I didn't already fucking know it.

But for the first time since I was a teenager, I pushed him to the recesses of my mind. As much as I didn't want to do this job, I would need to if there was any chance of a future for me. And there was no way in hell I would lose my life to the spoiled brat of a princess who had trouble keeping her fangs to herself.

"Will they be watching?" I asked. Her eyes shot to me before a small, feral smile spread across her face.

She likes the attention.

"Me, yes. Everyone wants to see a princess embarrass herself," she said as she shifted her body to face me. Her fingers worked quickly against the buttons of my uniform coat. I shimmied out of it for her, leaving me in nothing but a tight black tank top that showed off the scars on my arms. "They don't care much about the blood bags. So just look pretty and try not to scare people off with that mug of yours."

A smile threatened to pull at my lips at her comment. *So she does find me attractive.*

The car came to a stop, and, moments later, her original guard was opening the door for us. Cold air rushed through the car, causing my skin to prickle. The princess got out first, and it took me only a few moments to regain my footing as I followed her.

I didn't miss the way the guard's eyes narrowed at me. How he looked at me with a disdain that could only mean I had stolen his place for the night.

The princess placed her arm through mine and pulled me along toward a house that spanned stories above us. Not as extravagant as the Castle family residence, but it was still a magnificent show of wealth all on its own. It was well lit, with a multitude of guards standing outside, all wearing different uniforms and looking bored as hell.

"They're not allowed inside, so they wait out here," she murmured to me.

"What a waste," I said under my breath.

Many of them looked at us as we approached, some of their hands going to their weapons. One even had a gun. She let out a light laugh.

"Sometimes they stay till morning," she said. "But don't worry, I only have a few people I need to speak to, and then we will do our thing and be off."

"Is this something you like to do?" I asked, looking down at her. "Having strangers watch you get off?"

She does. I could see it in her face when she mentioned it. How her pupils dilated, and her mouth fell open just slightly.

"Ahh," she breathed out. "*That's* what you're worried about. Sweetheart, no one asked you to get me off. Not that I have much faith a human would, woman or not."

Her jab only caused my resentment for her to grow. It was a stupid, petty comment, but it was enough to severely bruise my ego.

Her smile told me she meant for it to do just that.

Fine. I slipped my arm around her and pulled her closer as she led us up the stairs.

"We'll see about that, *princess*," I whispered in her ear. "I'll play your game, but don't come complaining to me when you *really* embarrass yourself tonight."

She all but puffed up at my words, but there was no more time to discuss. The doors were opened for us, and what I expected to be an empty foyer was actually a hallway packed with humans and vampires in various stages of undress.

Many were couples, sometimes three or more people touching and kissing each other. Fangs were buried deep into necks. Hands shoved between legs.

But what took me aback was the potent smell of magic in the air.

Vampires could smell it easily, but if a human could pick it up as much as I did, that meant the place had to be *filled* with it.

"Very lively tonight," the princess said from behind me, a small teasing tone in her voice. I followed her gaze past the entrance and farther into the house, where there was a large opening. Right in the middle was a stage with multiple vampires rubbing a human's blood all over their skin before licking it up.

The inside of the house was bathed in red.

Red drapes. Red carpets. Red lights. What wasn't red was a shade of black, and whatever clothes people decided to wear showed so much skin, it was a mystery why they even decided to wear clothes at all.

That was when I saw it. When my eyes were roaming across the people surrounding us. A bright pink glitter-like substance was being rubbed on the bodies of humans before the vampires bit into them. As soon as they did, the vampires' eyes went wide, and black veins started to form on their foreheads.

Magical...drugs?

Was that why the princess hadn't been worried when she poisoned herself?

A vampire threw her head back, the blood dripping from her

mouth shimmering with pink magic before falling onto her naked chest.

My attention was drawn to the princess as her coat was taken from her. She was dressed in a satin dress that had a plunging neckline and showed the top of her belly button. She wore no bra underneath, a nipple poking through the deep red fabric. There were slits on both sides of her body, leaving only a small cloth between her legs as coverage.

My mouth dried at the sight, need attacking my entire being. *Stop,* I ordered my body. *It's the venom. Get a hold of yourself.*

I swallowed thickly and averted my gaze to look at the rest of the party. It was hard not to get overwhelmed with the sheer number of vampires in the room, all of them either with bloodstained lips or actively drinking.

"Party favors?" I asked.

"I think I have had enough of that already, don't you?" she retorted before she slipped her arm through mine again and gave me a sly smirk before pulling me farther in.

Bodies pressed against us, only moving when they caught the scent of her. Even through their bloodlust and magical haze, they made sure not to invade her space.

Mine, on the other hand, they had no problem invading. I wanted to snap at the wandering hands that touched me like some prized meat ready to be sampled. A hand caressed my shoulder as we passed, another tugging my tucked-in shirt out of my pants.

"*Aurelia,*" gushed a woman as she came up from our right. Her eyes were bright red, just a shade off from her long hair. She wore a see-through, open-chested robe that showed off a matching sparkling bra and panty set. Shimmering blood stained her pearly white teeth, and what I mistook as lipstick at first also happened to be blood.

"Dalia," the princess greeted and untangled herself from me to meet the girl with open arms. They embraced only for a moment before Dalia pulled her back and made a show of complimenting her outfit.

This was a different friend from the blonde one. Dalia was care-free and, just like the princess, seemed to like the attention she was getting.

Do you help this one, too? Maybe it was the opposite in her case. Maybe the princess owed *her* something.

In that case, I would need to pay extra attention to this vampire.

"I almost thought I'd never see you after that proposal," Dalia whispered, her eyes shooting to me before going back to the princess. "Daddy told me Icas is—well, I'm sure you know."

The princess gave her a smile. "You won't get rid of me that easily. Is he here? I'd like to say hi."

"Not the kind of *daddy* you thought he was, huh?" the princess whispered to me with an all-knowing smirk that showed off her left fang. "It's her *husband's* father."

I couldn't sneer down at her, not even if I tried. I was too taken aback by the scene in front of me.

No, he was not the daddy I was expecting him to be.

Instead, what I came face-to-face with was a burly vampire sitting comfortably on one of the all-red couches in a room off to the side of the main area of the mansion. It was smaller than the rest but more intimate and allowed for only a handful of other people to be in the room at the same time. Though that didn't stop people from trying to look in through the door.

The red wallpaper looked to be made of velvet and had intricate, shining swirls. A large chandelier swayed above our heads due to the pounding of feet on the roof. There were lamps placed on all walls, but they were dim and only shone just enough light into the space.

The man had the power to suck up all the attention in the room without even so much as changing positions. As soon as you stepped in there, there was a sort of force drawing you to him, making it impossible to look anywhere else.

He had to be old.

His white shirt, already stained with blood, had many of the buttons missing—probably popped off, based on the way his shirt was straining against his muscles. Red eyes, salt-and-pepper facial hair, and a grin that told me he owned this place. Though the flock of girls, both human and vampire, hanging all over him could have told me that instead.

Dalia had no problem plopping herself in between his legs, her petite frame looking almost comical in front of the huge vampire.

His hand wrapped around her neck before forcing her against him so they could share a heated kiss. The women on either side of him ran their hands through his hair and helped Dalia undress without a care for us as onlookers.

Dalia moved to straddle him, letting the girls take off her bra at the same time.

"Aurelia's here, Daddy," she whispered as she pulled away from his kiss. "I can't believe she's being sold to that brute. He's gonna make it hard for us to play together again."

Sold. What a nice way to put it.

His reddened eyes traveled to the princess at my side, assessing. There was something about his stare that made me uneasy. His hands came up to cup Dalia's breasts without breaking eye contact, his thumbs running across her nipples.

"A pity," he said with a sigh. "He has no tact. No care. Treats women's bodies—" Dalia let out a content sigh and fell against him, her eyes meeting mine. "*Like trash.*"

I couldn't help but stiffen under his gaze.

"That's why I'm here, is it not?" the princess asked with a laugh and leaned against me. "He was so kind as to give me such a skilled guard that I decided to make *full* use of our time together. If not, I might just go mad."

Cue the attention. Princess Aurelia's hand slid across my back before spreading out her fingers. Then she gave me not one, but two, pats.

What is—is she trying to get me to relax?

Annoyance pricked at my senses.

I know how to do this. I don't need her to guide me.

I let an easy smile fall across my face and reached my hands behind me to grab hers and use it as leverage to pull her closer.

"It's an honor to serve you, princess," I purred, dropping my voice low.

Her nails dug into my palm, but the look on the faces of the group in front of us told me I played my part well.

"Well then, Aurelia," he said, his eyes trailing down her form. "Why don't you join us? I'd love to see the way a mere human makes you squeal. I'll even lend you Dalia, for old times' sake."

"You seem to be enjoying her plenty," the princess said and looked up at me. "But why not take my new toy out for a ride?"

VESPER

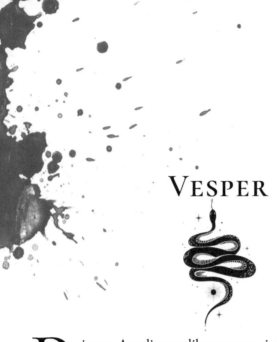

Princess Aurelia was like a queen sitting on her throne with the way her presence overtook the red velvet love seat. She was all-consuming. A woman who knew her worth and knew the power she held over every single person in the room.

And then there was me. Her obedient guard. *Her peasant.* Kneeling right between her legs and ready to serve.

It wasn't a position I found myself in often. My whole life had been spent in servitude to my family and the secret organization that employed us...but never did I allow myself to be degraded in such ways. *Especially* in front of others.

The princess knew this. She looked down at me with a sly smirk, her eyes taunting me into the *challenge* she thought this would be for me. She thought I would crack under the pressure. Thought I would make a half-assed attempt at this and come to regret my actions with her little magic mishap.

I could hear the teasing sound of her voice weaving through my mind. *Come on, little mouse, show me what you got.*

But little did she know, this wouldn't be a challenge for me at all. She could gloat all she wanted, but she wouldn't be faking anything here with me. Like I said, I never degraded myself in such ways.

But bringing pleasure to a woman? *That* would never be something to be ashamed about. I agreed to accompany her tonight knowing what awaited us behind closed doors. That solidified me as her partner tonight, no matter the circumstances that brought me here.

And the only thing that would be shameful about our interaction was the spoiled princess *faking* it.

I could feel the eyes of the others on me. The older male vampire from earlier was still sitting on the couch right behind me, his stare heavy on the back of my head. I think they said his name was Fredrick but in all honesty, remembering his name wasn't important in the moment. His partner Dalia's stare was a lighter one that I could feel bouncing between me and the princess. I could hear her rapid breathing. Feel the tension rising in the room.

The longer I kept eye contact with the princess, the more the voices around us turned to whispers.

So this is what the vampires do in their free time. This is the type of blackmail they use against each other.

But what I didn't understand was: If there were so many vampires in this house, then how could it be that this served as a purpose for blackmail? These vampires didn't seem all that nervous about the things they did behind closed doors.

Maybe that's it. Maybe it's not the fear of blackmail that keeps them doing this...but the excitement.

Vampires lived for hundreds, if not thousands, of years. What else was there to look forward to other than sex and drugs? Adding in the excitement of blackmail only heightened it. The possibility that at any moment someone outside would find out what they did here and call them out on their shit.

But that too was just a boring facade put on by the vampires. Just like the princess.

I bet your father knows you're here, I wanted to say as I leaned into her with a smirk. *I bet he **asked** you to come on his behalf. Get close to these people in exchange for the worst-kept secrets in the vampire world.*

I let my hands wrap around the princess's ankles, squeezing them before I began to rub small circles on her calf as I traveled up her smooth legs.

Her breath hitched at this, her eyes widened just the tiniest amount.

That's right.

"So tense, princess," I murmured as my hands reached her upper calf. "Did someone forget their massage today?"

Annoyance flashed across her features, but she hid it quickly, settling back into the chair and spreading her legs further for me. The sight of her wet underwear bared to me had my heart skipping a beat.

The remnants of the venom were still fighting in my system, begging to be noticed. But it was the challenge she so kindly provided for me that pushed me forward. The *need* to prove her wrong.

Normally, I would have let it go, but there was something in her stare that wouldn't allow me to. A cockiness that told me how little she thought of me.

The dress fell on either side of her thighs, the thin material that had been keeping her somewhat modest, gone. Her thin red lace underwear left nothing to the imagination and gave me a perfect look at the wet folds of her cunt. A sight that caused my mouth to water—when it shouldn't have.

"It's because you've been a little tease," she said with a breathy sigh as my hand traveled up and over her knee and to her thigh. I dug my fingers into the muscles, enjoying how she jumped. Her legs widened even more, her movements enticing me closer.

I was so close, I could almost taste her on my tongue.

"Oh, but isn't that what you love most about our time together, princess?" I asked with a sly smirk before turning my head to the side and brushing my lips against her inner thigh. With careful hands, I slipped her leg over my shoulder and licked the skin I had just kissed. Her hips gave a slight jerk. "Better than what that *brute* can do? A two-pump chump, I think you called him?"

There it is. The true anger I had been waiting to see flashed across her face.

Her hand shot forward to tangle in my hair, her leg fell off my shoulder, and I was forced up to her for what I *thought* was a kiss until she yanked my head to the side and buried her teeth into my neck.

I couldn't stop the groan that fell from my lips. Searing hot pain moved through my neck and shoulder as her fangs ripped through layer after layer of flesh. Even without the venom fully catching up, the pain settled sweetly in my belly.

"Impatient, are we?" I forced out. The only answer I got was a large gulp of my blood. Heat ran through me, causing my core to clench. The venom was working fast because of how deep her fangs were inside me. There would be no fighting it, and sooner rather than later, the same need I experienced for her in the car would overtake me.

I wrapped my arm around her waist and hoisted her closer. Her body melded against mine, her breasts pushed into my chest, and her hips ground against me, reminding me of my duty.

She was unrestrained. Using the pain and heat from the venom to put me in my place.

But it fanned the flames of hatred I had for her. I let the heat control my movements. Let myself fall into the uncontrollable lust for the person who had single-handedly held the puppet strings over my and my family's lives.

I skipped trailing my fingers against her inner thigh like I wanted to and went straight to the small fabric covering her cunt. *Wet.* She was so unbelievably wet. But it wasn't disgust that ran through me. It was need. The need to get her off. The need to watch as she lost herself in front of all these vampires. As she embarrassed herself by calling out for her guard while her rich vampire prince was waiting for her at home.

Need so strong that it had me slipping my hand into her underwear and running my fingers through her wet folds. She gave a hard jerk against me, trying desperately to force me to slip my fingers into her cunt.

Didn't want to be finger-banged by a human, huh?

But her movements told me the exact opposite. She was pulling me closer. Holding me tighter. Even pausing her drinking as I got close to where she wanted me the most.

Needy. Just as needy as she was making me. Her light moan had the thin straps holding me back snapping entirely.

I placed my thumb on her clit, circling it while my fingers teased her entrance. Forcing two of them in to give her just a taste before pulling them out. The whine she let out was nothing like what I had heard from her until that very moment. High-pitched and wanton.

Is she acting? She couldn't have been. Not when she tried to inch closer and closer each time my fingers pushed into her.

"So wet already, princess?" I asked, my voice coming out hoarser than I intended. Finally, I sank two digits into her. She stopped her feeding and froze against me, allowing me to fully fit my fingers inside her. I pushed the heel of my palm against her clit, grinding against it as I rocked my hand between her legs.

There was a noise from behind us. One not too dissimilar to the ones the princess was making herself.

Heavy breathing. Light moans. The sound of fingers fucking a wet cunt.

Her friends decided to have a little fun too.

"Are you watching them while I fuck you, princess?" I whispered. "Seeing how much they enjoy hearing your wet cunt as you greedily suck in my fingers?"

Her grip on me tightened, and she took another gulp of my blood. Her groan came from deep in her chest.

"*Fuck, daddy,*" Dalia moaned from behind us. "I want to share her. May I, please?"

"Let her have her fill, Dalia. Afterward, maybe," he replied.

Being reminded there were people in the room should have jolted me, but instead I began to pound my fingers into her cunt to match the pace of the couple behind us. She had me in a vise, gripping me so hard I feared she might come right then and there.

"Don't tell me you're going to come already?" I asked with a light laugh. "Is it all the people watching how bad you're being, or have you truly been so deprived since our last meeting that you've been—"

The moment was broken. No longer was the princess bending to my will and grinding on my hand. She needed to remind me who was in charge.

Her fangs were ripped out of me, and she used her inhuman strength to force me between her legs, my fingers still in her sopping cunt.

"You talk too much," she growled and planted her leg on my shoulder. "Make your mouth more useful."

I couldn't help but laugh at her actions. *The princess was realizing how it felt to lose control.*

"Your wish is my command," I purred.

Without hesitation, I all but ripped her underwear off before diving straight in.

AURELIA

F uck.
Her lips went straight to my clit, licking and sucking, before I had a chance to force her to do it.

I wouldn't be able to handle it much longer. As angry as her comment had made me, she was right. With the taste of her blood running through me and warming up my body, combined with being able to watch Dalia and her partner *and* have her fuck me like she actually knew my body...I was going to come in no time.

I shouldn't have egged her on. Should have known that the little mouse had something up her sleeve, and all that confidence back in the car wasn't for nothing.

But for some reason, I still expected her to chicken out in front of the people watching her. That maybe the seriousness of it would turn her off.

But not this little mouse.

Even though I told her she didn't really have to do it, something had changed between the time we stepped foot into this place and me burying my fangs in her neck.

I wanted her to try her damnedest to pleasure me all while knowing my cries were fake. I wanted her to suck. I wanted her to be the worst possible human in bed.

But, fuck, she is too good at this. It only made me hate her more.

There was no gentleness to her caress after I forced her between my legs. The time when she was massaging my calves and causing an addicting swirling heat in my stomach was long gone. Instead, I was left with a ravenous beast hell-bent on making me embarrass myself in front of all these people.

I was no stranger to public sex. These parties happened as often and whenever bored vampires felt like it. And for those who had been alive for more than a hundred years...Well, let's just say they had been to things like this far more times than they could ever count.

I saw my time in the house as more of a chore. I showed up, gave them just enough to hang over my head, and got on my way. But I would be a liar if I didn't admit that these parties excited me in a certain way. Seeing beautiful women get fucked. Hearing their moans and cries of pleasure. All of it had once caused heat to settle in my core.

It was intoxicating to see them lose themselves. Seeing all the hung-up vampires, forced to abide by royal vampire law during the day, finally let go and be introduced to a side of themselves they didn't know.

I wanted that for myself too.

But the time with Vesper was different. Seeing the way their eyes moved over me with her between my legs had a different type of heat swirling inside me. She was wrong about one thing.

It wasn't just the others who had almost caused me to come.

It was embarrassment. Vesper was embarrassing me because, for the first time after coming here for years, I didn't have to fake it. *And I liked it.*

It was a sensation I had never experienced before. She made me lose myself. Her blood, the way her fingers curled inside me and turned me into putty—all of it broke down the carefully curated walls I built for myself in these scenarios.

I didn't have to fake my moans as she flattened her tongue against my folds. Didn't have to add an exaggerated shudder as her teeth teased my clit. Nor did I have to pretend my body was tensing as it neared an orgasm that was coming on *way* too fast to be from a human.

Fuck, fuck, fuck. I wanted to beg her not to stop, but I wouldn't degrade myself in such a way.

"Good, little mouse," I cooed before I could stop myself.

Her hand shot up to cup my breast, her thumb teasing my nipple. I arched into it, needing more of her touch. Then she pinched it hard enough to cause just the slightest prick of pain.

She kept her mouth fastened on my clit as she slipped two fingers inside me again. I was so wet at that point that they fit easily, and each delicious pump caused my wetness to leak onto the couch.

I was a mess. A moaning, writhing mess...but the orgasm teasing my senses caused me not to care. I let the embarrassment mix with my pleasure. Let it heighten what was happening.

And when Vesper's lips pulled into a smirk and her eyes met mine...I couldn't hold back.

I came with a barely muted cry, all the while holding Vesper's gaze.

That's right. Her eyes seemed to tell me. *And you thought I was all talk.*

I did. I wanted to get back at her, but she turned this into something else entirely. How was I to go back with her to the palace, have her stand by me day in and day out, and *not* remember what happened between us?

I opened my mouth to tell her to wipe the look off her face, but there was a commotion out near the entrance. All vampires in the area stiffened, many looking back to the hallway that led to the entrance.

There was fighting. Shoving. The sound of glass shattering. Voices raised. Grunts. Bodies colliding into each other.

My eyes met Fredrick's as he quickly tried to conceal Dalia.

There's an uninvited guest.

Then, chaos.

Vampires started to filter out of the room and run out the back,

many trying to hide their faces. Crowds passed, none of them daring
to peek inside to see what was happening. The risk of being caught
by an uninvited guest was too great.

They were not held to the same standards as everyone else here,
and if it was a royal who got involved, it was unlikely that we would
be able to kill them for what they saw.

I jolted up, nodding to Fredrick. The night's business had to be
cut short, and I would have to find us some other time to talk.
Vesper was still between my legs, her eyes carefully watching my
reaction.

I fixed my underwear and dress before pulling her up.

"Something's not right—"

"Uninvited guest," I muttered and pushed her along with the
crowd. I ignored the temptation to look at the entrance. "All
vampires heard it. We are now exposed and have to get out of here
before—"

Vesper dragged me closer and placed her arms over my head,
shielding me from any possible view.

Another surprise. Any other guard would be trying to run out
and save their own hide, but she somehow thought to try and hide
me first.

We were pushed by the crowd of panicking patrons, all of us
trying to get out as soon as possible. Bodies slammed into us,
vampires and humans alike. Their voices ringing in my ears.

It felt like an eternity before we finally made it out to the
gardens at the back of the house. All the staff who had been
lingering up front were now waiting at the far end of the garden
wall in a single line, as per protocol. All faces shrouded in darkness.

Vesper spotted our driver before I did and steered us
toward him.

"Jacket," Vesper ordered him as soon as we got close enough.
He gave her a startled look before slipping off his jacket and handing
it to her.

Warmth enveloped me as she placed it over my head and
shoulders.

"Princess, the car is waiting," my driver said and quickly led us out of the mass of people.

It wasn't until we were safely in the car and driving away that I dared peek at the entrance.

Not one but three vampires were forced to the ground with their hands tied behind their backs.

My dead heart lodged in my throat when I recognized their uniforms.

"Looks like the prince is not so keen on finding his wife in a sex dungeon," Vesper murmured.

Of course she just had to fucking open her mouth.

"He was kicked out," I hissed, my eyes darting to hers. Her mouth was still shining with my wetness. When she noticed where my gaze landed, she licked her lips. "A *long* time ago."

"How embarrassing," she said with a sly tone. "Princess Aurelia coming in under three minutes, all thanks to the weak human guard. The prince must really be *awful* in bed—"

"Shut it," I growled. "No one asked you to defame the prince like that."

She raised a brow at me. "Then what do you call spreading your legs for a human in front of all those people? You think my words changed what they thought of you? You think that one remark all of a sudden made what you were doing in front of them any less insulting than if you fucked me right in front of him?"

Her words caused my mouth to slam shut.

"Don't try to act all high and mighty, princess," she said. "Not when that was your intention all along."

VESPER

Was this some type of tantrum?

That was the only word for it. I had gotten a short break from the princess's games, but I guess one could only hold her off for so long until she came back full force.

A tantrum.

Being woken up in the middle of the night and forced to go down in my sweatpants and loose T-shirt to a part of the garden I had never seen before was jarring.

For a moment, I thought maybe I had been exposed. That somehow I hadn't been careful enough. That my tattoo had been seen, and someone reported it to the king.

As soon as my eyes opened, I went through every possible exit procedure I had learned throughout the years.

Fight my way. Run. Last resort, kill myself. But I still valued my life far too much to entertain that last thought for long.

For the first time, I was panicking. Unable to figure out what to do. Any other "contractor" like myself would have jumped into action right away. But not me. There was something holding me back.

I wasn't quite sure what it was, but something felt off from the moment I woke. It had me in a fight-or-flight, trying desperately to put the pieces together and try to make out the dark blobs that resided in my room. All of them murmured, but none of the words registered in my mind.

Until I made out the familiar form of the head guard and heard him utter something I never imagined he would.

He said they needed my *help*.

The sky was dark, save for the brightly shining moon hidden behind a curtain of gray clouds. The light of the intricately woven iron lamps in the garden was just enough to cast a warm glow off the hundreds of flowers that surrounded us. I had gotten used to the sweet smell of them since arriving at the palace, but that night they seemed to smell extra sweet.

Perfectly laid brick muted our footsteps as we approached. I could hear the sound of rushing water from a fountain three times the size of an average swimming pool that stood at the center.

It was beautiful. Made of what looked like marble and had small lights that turned the water bright blue.

The night was calm. No sign that there was actually anything *wrong*. But the number of guards, along with the tenseness in the air, told me there was.

"We've tried everything, but more than once, she took a chunk out of the fountain and hit one of us right on the head," a head guard said from my side. His face was tired, the circles dark under his eyes. "We even tried her handmaiden, but she had an even more violent reaction. If it weren't for one of my men pulling her away at the last second, she might have been killed instead of left with a small concussion."

He wasn't my head guard, but I had seen him talk to mine on occasion. He was human like me and had the years spent working for the prince sewn onto the sleeve of his uniform. More than ten, but my guess was that he had been working in this type of job for longer, given the small wrinkles at the corners of his eyes.

"And why not just leave her?" I asked with a raised brow. "Can't a princess do whatever she wants?"

He gave me a sidelong look before letting out a sigh. I knew the sigh all too well. I had caught myself making the sound multiple times since having to deal with the royal vampires.

We are all too tired for this shit. Yet, for whatever reason, we stayed. We let the vampires beat us down. Let them have their little tantrums. Let them sink their fangs into our skin.

And for what?

"The prince and her father would like to save themselves the embarrassment," he answered, shifting on his feet. *An uncomfortable topic for him then.* It made me wonder just how many times he had done this same thing before. "There will be some guests in the morning, and there's no telling just how long she'll be out here. Last time we just *left* her to her own devices, it was almost a full day before she was back in her room."

So this is a pattern.

Not very like the princess, though. Given what happened at the sex party the previous week, I would assume she hated any type of embarrassment. Including something like what the guards had hinted at.

Up until then, I had done my duties like a regular guard. I had been at her side as she frolicked around the palace. Watched as she met with more friends. Accompanied her to her seamstress appointments.

It was a little boring, in all honesty, but what I assumed was very normal for someone of her status. And there was not a single sign that anything was bothering her. She was still her same spoiled self.

And then I was woken up in the middle of the night.

I couldn't make out where the princess was from our position, but as we got closer, I was able to make out the dark brown of her hair in the water. The long tendrils moved with the light waves the falling water produced.

When I was a child, I caught myself having similar fantasies of going swimming in a fountain, but unlike her, my father would have never allowed it.

And unlike then, my fantasy of joining her in the fountain was pushed away immediately.

"Leave us," she ordered. "Silver-haired stays."

Just like that, she already had the situation under her control. Her voice held a tone that dared the guards around her to disobey. *She must be so annoyed that they aren't listening to her.*

The thought alone was almost enough to make me smile. *A bit of a rude awakening for our spoiled highness, was it?*

"*Vesper*," I reminded her, and shifted on my heels.

She was floating on her back, her eyes closed, and outright ignoring everyone else around her. *I can see why the others worried that she might embarrass herself.*

With a final step forward, the princess came fully into view. She was wearing only a white nightdress that had become completely see-through from the water. Her rosy nipples were hard and poked through the fabric. I tried and failed not to look at the tuft of hair between her legs.

It would be more decent if she were naked. The white fabric clung to her skin, pulling tight against her hips and chest as it tried to sink down to the floor of the fountain.

It was reminiscent of a painting. One of those my parents had ushered me away from when we went to museums. One that my brother would laugh at because of the inappropriateness.

But I always thought they were beautiful.

Even though it was over a week before, I couldn't get the party out of my mind. I regretted going. Regretted what I did even more. But only because of how much I enjoyed what we did. How it *excited* me.

It wasn't how someone of my lineage should feel about their job. Generations of us had been trained, hundreds were out there completing their jobs with calm, cool heads...and then there was me. Getting distracted by a spoiled princess with a smart mouth that felt far too good against the skin of my neck to forget.

The head guard lingered at my side, his gaze heavy. I met his eyes with a raised brow.

"Can we trust you with this?" he asked.

Trust. I wanted to laugh at the ridiculous question. *Yes, you can trust me, sir. You'll leave, and I'll get her alone so I can finally fulfill my prophecy.*

The only issue was that I hadn't brought any of my weapons. My sword was magically enhanced and would make it easier to kill her. It would slow her healing and allow the magic to attack her system, giving me enough time to finish the job if I chose to. But there was little advantage I would have over her. They had rushed me so much that I hadn't even been allowed to change.

I'll figure something out. I had to because, for the first time, I was going to be truly alone with the princess.

"Yes, sir," I said and took the final steps to the fountain. The princess didn't open her eyes until the guards' steps faded.

She sat up, her hair flattening against her head and sticking to her upper body. Her eyes were still blue when she looked at me. *Meaning this had nothing to do with bloodlust.*

But there was something else swimming in them. Usually she had a playfulness behind them, but not then. It was something heavier.

I wondered if she wore the see-through nightgown on purpose. That maybe this had been her plan all along. Just another way to play with my mind like she had in that house.

I wouldn't put it past her. She seemed awfully content to make my life here a living hell, even if only for her own amusement.

"*Vesper.*" My name came out like she was trying to see how it felt on her tongue. I hated how it made a shiver go up my spine. "I like 'little mouse' better."

Annoyance pricked at my senses.

"Is it normal for you to throw yourself into the fountain when you don't get what you want?" I asked, tilting my head to the side.

She let out a scoff and rolled her eyes. Her eyes settled on a faraway target, something flashing across her mind enough to take her away from the present moment. Her jaw clenched hard enough for me to see the way it caused the muscles in her face to bulge.

"Not get what I want?" she muttered under her breath.

Testy. She didn't like that. But why?

"Why else would you be doing this?" I asked and stuffed my hands in my pockets.

She looked up at me with a scowl. I raised a brow at her. It was a challenge, one I didn't realize I was setting until it was too late. I should have known she'd try something when a glint crossed her eye. I should have backed away from the fountain.

But I didn't.

She lunged forward, putting her hand on the edge of the fountain and using it to steady herself as she reached for me. Her hand tangled in my shirt, and I was yanked over the edge and straight into the water.

The icy cold water shocked my system and froze my movements for a few seconds before rage seeped in. *Is she being fucking serious right now?* I pushed myself out of the water, sending a glare to the princess, who looked at me with a satisfied smirk.

Water ran down my body, pulling a violent shiver from me. My hair stuck to my face, my clothing not much better. *A drowned rat.* That's what she wanted to make of me.

"I'm doing this because I *want* to," she said, the smile widening on her face. "Just like I pulled you in because I *wanted* to. And just like you'll do whatever I say because I *want* you to."

I stood to my full height and closed the space between us. My breathing was heavy, fists balled at my sides.

She was shorter than me, and I was forced to look down in order to meet her eyes. But that little fact didn't seem to faze her. She just looked up at me with that defiant look.

"Just because your daddy is willing to do anything you want doesn't mean I will," I growled at her. "Now you're going to get back into the house before you embarrass yourself—"

"Or what?" she asked, a playful light shining in her eyes. Her lips tilted enough for me to catch a glimpse of her fangs.

Or what? I would kill her. That was the correct answer. But I was stranded, wet and cold, with no weapons. There wasn't much I could do at the moment. Not only that, but the rest of the guards were waiting for me to finish my job.

Then an idea popped into my mind. A smirk pulled at my lips as I leaned forward. We were close—closer than I ever thought I'd let us be again. Her eyes widened before falling to my lips. Her breath hitched just like it had that night, no doubt both of us remembering exactly what happened the last time we were this close.

My eyes trailed the length of her in the see-through dress. A present I allowed myself, even for just a moment. She was so generously showing herself to me that it was almost rude not to indulge even a little. I committed it to memory. Taking in the way her hands were crossed under her breasts. The way her nails dug into her skin, leaving marks. The way the wet fabric bunched up against her hips.

Too enchanting for her own good.

I forced my gaze back to hers when I realized just how long I had been staring at her.

"Then I won't play with you anymore," I whispered, trailing my gaze from her eyes to her lips, then back up.

Seconds ticked by before understanding passed through her features. Confusion, then realization, then annoyance. I stood straight and walked right out of the fountain, not waiting for her reply.

She sputtered for a response behind me, but I didn't let it give me pause.

The best way to get what you need from a spoiled brat? Just take away the fun.

And boy, did it work. She was at my side in seconds, a pout forming on her face.

"Really?" she asked. "You're just gonna leave me there alone? I picked you as my guard, aren't you worried that I'd get hurt or something?"

"In your own backyard?" I asked with a scoff. "Not likely."

"But it's your duty! And you're just going to walk away? Aren't you even the least bit pissed that I had them wake you up in the middle of the night for this? Aren't humans like super into sleep or something?"

I gave her a smile but didn't respond until we made it to the back entrance of the palace, where her guards were waiting for her. They all perked up when they saw us, some even sharing looks of disbelief.

"After you, *princess,*" I said with a mock bow. The guards were deathly silent behind me, probably waiting for my punishment.

But it never came to pass.

She huffed in response and stormed barefoot into the palace. The head guard gave me a nod, though I could sense the questions in his eyes. Especially when he took in my soaking-wet clothes.

"Just Vesper!" she called behind her. "No one else!"

Damn it.

"I'm thirsty," the princess said as she sat down on her bed, her dress soaking the comforter with water.

She didn't bother turning on the lights, even for the benefit of the human she forced up here with her. My eyes were getting used to the dark with the help of the moonlight shining through the windows, but it was hard to focus on anything other than her reddening eyes as they started to glow in the dark.

My wet clothes were sticking to me uncomfortably, and no matter how warm the palace was, I still began to chill.

"Call a feeder then," I said and leaned against the wall closest to the door. I didn't want to give into whatever she was playing. I could see something brewing behind her eyes, but I hoped to leave and get my weapons before she could enact her plans.

There was a line that I didn't want to cross again, no matter how tempting it was...but the princess seemed to make the decision all by herself. Since we got into her room, she had been looking at me with an expression akin to that of a hungry wolf.

"I want you," she said and motioned for me to move between her legs, much like the night at the club.

I could say no, I should say no. But then it might make it harder to be alone with her again. At least that was what I told myself.

"You're wet," I said instead. "Go change."

"Vampires can't catch colds," she said with a tilt of her lips. But when she saw I wasn't willing to move, her smile turned into a pout. "Fine. But you have to take them off."

I let out a sigh and pushed off the wall. This got a reaction from her.

"Oh?" she asked, tilting her head. "So the little mouse decided she wants to play?"

"Vesper wants to go back to bed," I said as I reached her. "Arms up."

She sent me a smirk before complying, her eyes never leaving mine.

"Isn't it degrading?" she asked as I pushed the wet dress up her thighs and over her hips. It was a bit difficult to get it all while she was sitting on it, but the fabric was thin enough that I was able to pull it out from under her.

I tried to ignore how it felt to be so close to her naked body. How it felt for her breath to waft across my skin.

With my weapons, it would have been easy to take advantage of our position. She wouldn't even see it coming.

"Everything I have done here is degrading," I admitted, pulling the rest off her. She put her arms on the bed and leaned back, pushing her chest out. *An invitation.*

"Just be honest—since that night, you've been wanting to taste me again, haven't you?"

I rolled my eyes and pushed her legs apart so I could step between them. Her bed was high enough that her mouth was right at my neck. She inched closer to me, brushing her body against mine.

She was so soft. I could remember the feel of her skin, and even through my clothes, I knew that as soon as I put my hands on her, I would lose myself again.

"I haven't even thought of it," I lied. I had thought about it way too many times. "You wanted to make me pay for what I did, I wanted to prove you wrong. I won, and I'm not the type to gloat."

I tilted my neck to the side. "Now eat so I can be on my way."

Her hands shot out to grab my wrists and bring them to her body.

"Aw, come on," she purred. "You don't want to play? Isn't this what you meant?"

She placed my hands at her waist, slowly moving them up her wet skin until they were caressing her breasts. They fit perfectly in my hands, and her nipples were calling my attention, just begging for me to put my mouth on them.

Don't react. Don't react. I had to say it in my head for fear my body would give me away. It was already heating. My stomach was twisting with need.

How on earth will I be able to finish my job if she acts like this?

"I didn't want to play," I said through gritted teeth. "I wanted to get you out of that fucking fountain."

"And you did," she breathed. "How about we call it a reward?"

I swallowed thickly, unable to deny the heat coursing through my veins.

I hated how I was reacting. Hated that I couldn't just end it all right then and there. Hated that my mouth watered at her offer.

Most of all, I hated how well she played me. I wanted her. *Badly* and more than I had anyone else in my short, miserable life.

But my job was to kill her, not indulge in either of our fucked-up fantasies.

"Just my job," I murmured, letting my thumbs brush across her nipples. I brought one of my hands up, my fingers stopping to caress her collarbone.

And then, just as I was about to put my hand around her neck, she did something I never expected from the princess.

She flinched.

It was one quick shudder of her body as she instinctively tried to move her throat away from my grasp.

Her face gave her away before she could get a lock on her expression. *Fear mixed with pain.* The princess was afraid and hurt?

I looked her over once more before stepping away. *No, that couldn't be it.* But whatever it was, it shocked me enough to get me away from her. Only then did I realize just how much my body had given away.

My heart was pounding in my chest. My underwear was damp, and not because of the fountain. And *fuck* did I want her to sink her teeth into me.

But I couldn't get the way she looked out of my mind. I wasn't supposed to see it, but even as she sat there, watching me retreat, I knew there was something that had caused her to act like she did that night. And I was afraid to find out what it was.

"Good night, princess. Don't call me for something so foolish again."

AURELIA

And Father was worried I'd embarrass myself.

It was a laughable notion. He and I both knew no matter what happened the night before, I would be dolled up in the finest jewels and clothes to meet guests.

It was a given in our family. There would never be a time where it was acceptable to show up with even a hair out of place. If I could dream, I would surely have nightmares about the one time I embarrassed him in front of his guests.

The memory of my parched throat and sore wrists from being bound and starved was pushed far into the recesses of my mind and buried under the rubble. *Where it belonged.*

I never made that mistake again. I was young then. Naïve. I knew better now.

The prince, on the other hand, and his lack of trust had been annoying. He came into this palace, not knowing anything about our customs, and still had the audacity to doubt me. Even if it was his fault.

I gave him a side glance as he shifted next to me, his hand coming to touch my thigh under the table. His touch left a slimy feeling on my skin. I jerked my leg away from him and sent him an innocent smile when he turned to glare.

The place where he all but ripped open my neck the night before still ached. *Phantom pain.* My venom should have taken care of even the worst of the damage sometime this morning, but that didn't mean the mental pain was gone.

I can't wait to pay him back for it one day.

If he thought I was just going to sit here and take it for long, he was wrong. I didn't care about what my father would do. I would get out of it one way or another.

"From France, princess, age twenty-two," said a human to my right. His wrist was facing up, and there was a stark white towel under it. I grabbed my glass and held it near his wrist, smiling as he removed the towel and brought forth a golden knife to slash his wrist open.

"Thank you," I said once there was just enough blood in my cup for a few sips. He took his dismissal with a light bow, going right to Prince Icas after me.

He didn't use his glass and opted to sink his teeth right into the man's wrist like the animal he was. The man's bright red blood leaked out the sides of his mouth and stained the white towel below. I didn't avert my gaze fast enough to avoid seeing the blood seep into the towel and spread across its surface. It reminded me too much of a blossoming flower.

I tried to ignore the pained intake of breath from the young man.

I pulled my gaze away from the violent act and looked across the table at our guests. Some royals from across the country. I didn't remember ever seeing them in my life, but the man and his wife were somehow important to my father.

They had three children, all of them over the age of fifty, and making quite a mess of their clothes as they too opted to take a bite out of the human tasters instead of using their cups.

I glanced behind me to see Vesper in all her glory standing right between my and the prince's chairs. The sun from the windows hit her just right, her silver hair glowing in the light. Her gaze was on me, and she was as serious as ever. Her scars were highlighted against her skin, all except for the one that went through her eye and was interrupted by a purplish bruise under her eyes. The dark circles were a prominent reminder of our night.

I can't believe the little mouse rejected me. It was impossible to believe that she could annoy me even more than she had. But somehow, she still kept surprising me.

I wonder what she thought of this show. Did it disgust her?

I hope it fucking does.

The embarrassment of her rejection caused my face and my entire body to heat. And it was nothing like what she had shown me at the party that night.

This one was wounding, but it made me that much more determined to figure out what the little mouse's motives were for being here in the first place.

She wasn't like the rest who had signed up, that much was painfully clear. The others wanted the status or the money that came with working for a family. But the way she watched me when she was on duty was not at all like a guard.

I was more like a hunter watching her prey.

I sent her a wicked grin and watched with satisfaction as her eyes narrowed at me. *That's right, little mouse, let that anger brew, and then maybe finally I'll get another taste of whatever it is you're—*

The painful squeeze of my thigh caused my gaze to snap to Prince Icas.

"Watch yourself," I hissed under my breath, hopefully low enough for the guests not to hear, and tried to shake off his hand again, but he held on tight.

His grin was a slimy one.

"Too busy watching you, my love," he said and lifted his hand from my leg to push my hair behind my ear and expose my neck. The same side he bit last night. It was hard to smother the urge to flinch away from him.

I gave him a smile for show but turned my head to look at our guests so I could get his disgusting hands off me.

The oldest daughter was looking at us with a grin that more

closely resembled a sneer with the way she bared her bloodstained teeth at us. She wore a stark white sweater that had bloodred rubies sewn into it, making it look like she had accidentally spilled her tasting on herself.

"If only the Castle family had a son," she said with an exaggerated sigh and plopped her head on her hand with a pout. "Maybe then we'd be talking about marriage plans to merge the families instead of this back and forth."

Her parents and Father both paused. I almost thought Father was going to explode with the way his jaw tensed, but instead he let out a laugh. The two older vampires relaxed at the sound of it.

"Trust me, if I could have a daughter as cunning and ruthless as you, I would marry my son to you in a heartbeat," he said, his eyes cutting to her parents. "I heard Priscilla alone is in charge of family punishment, is that right?"

As cunning and ruthless as her? He said it like I had never actually killed for him. Like I hadn't plotted with him on the various ways to take over other small families and even a clan here and there.

I had done everything he expected of me and more.

His words were a burning insult. I calmed the anger that was coiling in my belly by taking a drink of the blood. I tried to focus on the heat that it sent through me instead of the anger that threatened to unravel my perfectly crafted control.

Her mother sat up at this. "Yes, actually, and she—"

"Is that your plan, Icas?" Priscilla asked, her gaze still locked on the prince. "But last I heard, there was no plan to merge the families. Weird."

She took a sip of her blood, the look in her eyes daring me to say something. As if it were my place to try and defend whatever motives the prince had for marrying me.

I won't. I don't want to fucking be in this situation in the first place.

"No. Unfortunately, Aurelia will be leaving us. My dealings with Prince Icas's father have been a secret long before Aurelia was even in the picture," my father said, a warm smile still on his face. "So yes, we would like to unite the families, but not in that way."

His comment was news to me. *Not in that way? Then in what way?*

Obviously, Father had to have been bluffing for Prince Icas's sake. For someone like Father to marry me off to Icas's family and *not* get any of the people under their rule in return...it was unheard of.

But when I looked at the prince, his expression didn't change. As if he already knew the supposed *secret* that had been decided by them so long ago.

What the hell?

I tuned out the noises of Father and his guests talking, urging the prince to look at me. But when he finally did, he met me with another one of his slimy smiles, as if to say, *What, something Daddy's favorite didn't know?*

Prince Icas leaned back with a satisfied grin and wiped my blood from his mouth.

His room was bright, the curtains thrown wide open and letting the bright daylight seep through. There was no hiding what we were doing. No pretending it wasn't happening.

"Add something else to sweeten the deal, Aurelia," he commanded, his eyes trailing down the front of my dress and lingering on my chest. He tried to make his voice come out like a purr, but it sounded terribly forced and cringy. It took a lot to not visibly grimace at his words. "I promise I'll spill all of Daddy's secrets."

"Let's start with how they are uniting the families," I purred and placed my hands on his knees, sensually massaging up his thighs, the evidence of how much he liked it already showing in the front of his trousers.

So easy. And here the male vampires thought it was the women who gave their bodies up so freely. Prince Icas was a perfect example of a male who thought more with his cock than his head.

He was a simpleton. I just needed to figure out how to use it in my favor and get over that overinflated ego of his.

My neck was still painfully sore. My venom did what it could to heal the deepest holes, but I hadn't drunk enough during the day for it to heal fully. If I wasn't careful, the lack of blood would have me spiraling.

"Come on, baby," he said, running his hands down my arms. "The engagement announcement was a long time ago, and we still haven't done anything. Maybe if you show me how grateful you are, I'll spill."

Even my blood was more than I should have been forced to give. And I only kept it up so he wouldn't go squealing to Father that I wasn't fulfilling my duties.

Worse. There was a chance he could go to the stepbitch, and she would use it as her way to pit Father against me.

I knew her game too well, and I wasn't going to let her get her way.

But his request? It was too far. There was no way I'd be fucking him.

I leaned forward, getting as close to his face as possible, before grabbing a handful of that offending thing between his legs and squeezing.

The panic and pain that flashed across his face were immediate. The pained groan was more satisfying than anything I'd ever experienced. I wanted to rip it off. Wanted to watch as he screamed bloody murder and begged for me to save him.

It was easy to get drunk on the power...but alas, I had to keep up appearances.

"Tell me now, and you get to keep this," I warned in a low voice. "What does your father want with me?"

"You're gonna pay for this, you bitch," he growled and tangled his hand in my hair, attempting to get me to let go, but I only gripped harder.

"Cooperate, *babe*," I said in a sickly-sweet tone. "What does your father *want*?"

"He wants an heir! One with your mother's bloodline!" he answered in a pained voice. "Your cheap father wouldn't give any of his family over, but he had no problem handing you over as a bargaining chip. Do you know how many people your child would bring?"

If the confession wasn't this shocking, I might have let myself feel proud of how easy it had been to get him to spill.

My mother's bloodline?

"You're his heir," I spat. It didn't make sense to me.

He let out a bitter laugh.

"An heir who brings in no people and no new money," he said. "Did you know there's a bet going around the palace as to who will knock you up first? Him or me?"

I jerked away from him and slammed the palm of my hand into his cheek. The crack of his bones was almost for sure a sign of fracture, but I didn't care.

The horrifying image of what was to come as soon as I left the palace did enough damage.

What the actual fuck?

That couldn't be true. Father wouldn't allow that...would he? That was a new level of cruelty, even for him.

I never expected my father to actually protect me, but it was a new level of betrayal I didn't see coming.

I had bitterly joked that I was nothing more than a broodmare, but they were serious.

Memories of the way my stepmother's spawn looked at me and whispered those exact words with an evil grin on her face hit me like a slap in the face.

Did they know too? All this time...Had I been the only one who didn't know?

I had to ball my hands to stop them from shaking.

"His heir," I repeated. "His, not yours."

Prince Icas looked up at me with a spiteful smile. "That's right, so I suggest you work on opening your legs for me, or else he'll fill the space for me."

It was too much. The red was seeping in, and the only thing I could think of was letting out the murderous monster that had been festering behind the locked cage I kept in the back of my mind.

I wanted to slit his throat open. Bathe in his blood and paint the walls with it to send the message that *no one* could ever say such a horrific thing again.

"Remember who you're fucking talking to," I threatened, backing away from him. My body was shaking with rage. My eyes turned fully red, and a low growl rumbled in my chest. "You think I'll just sit around and let this happen?"

"You have no choice," he replied, leaning back and looking over at me with a disgusting look in his eyes. "Face it, babe. Your days are numbered."

Fuck that. Fuck him. And fuck Father.

I never expected much out of the man who sired me. He was cruel and always lived up to his name. *Did I really think he would treat his favorite daughter differently?*

Fuck him.

I turned away from the prince and rushed out the door. I would make them pay.

I would make *all* of them pay. Even if it meant going up against *him*.

VESPER

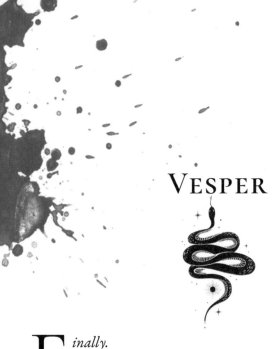

Finally.

After all the mind games, the night had finally come where I would fulfill the duty set upon me by my father.

I had to stand there and watch as the princess goaded me. Like she knew *just* how close I had been and was reminding me of my failed job.

The image of her completely naked and waiting in her bed had been a memory that haunted my every waking moment.

I didn't want to think of her that way. I didn't want to remember what she tasted like on my lips. I didn't want to remember what she sounded like when I made her feel better than that prick of a vampire prince did.

When the guests came the other day, I had already had enough of him. He looked at me like I was some competition. Like he could already clearly see a relationship between us that didn't exist.

Or, well...that I didn't want to exist.

I couldn't deny that, even after the vampire venom was gone, I still had a need for her. Instead of the violent one the vampire venom incited, it was more like an ache that made itself known at the most uncomfortable times.

Like when I was sneaking out to finally fulfill what I had come here for.

I had planned it perfectly.

After the night in the fountain, the princess hadn't called on me. She gave me a few glances here and there when I was working, but never again were we alone.

Almost like she was avoiding me.

The guests stayed for three days, and after that, the house was quiet. Everyone recovering from a negotiation well done. Or at least that's what the whispers in the guard quarters were about.

So I took my chance. When it was quietest and when there was the least chance of me getting caught.

It was late at night, all the human guards were dead asleep in the rickety beds provided to us by the family. There were a few out patrolling, but most had fallen into the false sense of security the mundane life at the palace provided.

It wasn't hard to sneak out of the room after Cedar was asleep. One would think that a witch of her caliber would be wide awake at the slightest sound, but her beastly snores drowned out any possible sound I could make, even the bed that creaked with every move.

She had been the same when I was all but kidnapped from my bed at the princess's request.

Or maybe she just hadn't wanted to get involved.

The path up to the princess's room was a different thing, though.

It wasn't just the guards sent by the prince—the family also had their own guards patrolling. After all, the guards were a show. Fresh blood. They hadn't actually put them in any position of importance.

And luckily for me, because of my new role at the princess's side, I had been taken off the nightly patrol schedule.

But that didn't mean I hadn't memorized it. Cedar had caught me when I was reading it in the dead of night once, when she woke up to go to the bathroom, but never said anything. Instead, she just gave me that irritating, all-knowing look.

I paused as I shut the door behind me, her snores darting out through the closed door. It was late enough at night that most who were asleep were in deep, and hopefully the vampires had their own priorities to take care of.

This time, I made sure not to forget my sword.

When I was sure it was clear, I silently walked down the stone hallway before pausing at the end of the corridor. Taking a breath and counting to twenty in my head, I peeked around the corner just in time to catch the back of the guard rounding the long corner past the stairs.

I need to work quickly to climb the stairs before he turns back around.

My heart was pumping wildly, fear gripping my chest. This was it. Everything that I had been working toward down to these few moments.

I forced one foot in front of the other, cursing when one of my steps sounded a bit too loud against the stone. The boots were too thick for something like this. Instead of letting it deter me, I forced myself to work faster. I slipped around the railing and pulled myself up just as the guard's footsteps sounded throughout the hallway.

I waited again. Forcing myself to hold my breath for fear I would be caught.

No one can see me. At least not one of the guards. Not if I want any chance of getting out of here alive.

Waitstaff and the feeders were different—they would mind their business. But the guards would be forced to report anyone they saw walking the halls. Even one of their own.

When he finally turned the corner again, I pushed myself up the stairs. The flight I had chosen was for those who wished not to be seen. Mostly people like myself and feeders. The higher floors weren't guarded all that well, so as I ascended, the weight on my chest got lighter.

By the time I reached the fifth floor and home of the princess, I had seen only one other soul. A feeder who had looked far worse for wear and probably was too out of it to even look twice at me.

Easy.

Besides the princess sticking her fangs in my neck and the tantrums...the whole job had been *easy*—textbook perfect. I had done the hours, *years* of prep, and mixed with a little luck, I got to where I wanted to be on the first day.

Maybe it was all luck. Maybe all the time and effort I had put into it didn't mean anything as soon as I stepped through the palace doors.

Why had I caught her eye? It had been my goal all along, but I couldn't understand it.

The unknown answer was making my skin itch. She treated me with a passive-aggressive disdain mixed with playful curiosity, as some sort of pet she could play with, and pouted whenever I didn't play nice with her.

Yet she didn't get rid of me the moment I rejected her...*So what gives?*

Images of her writhing against the couch, her eyes hooded and her lips open flashed across my mind. Seeing my own blood coating her mouth should have disgusted me. It usually would have. But when I was there between her legs, making her feel the things she assured me I never could...it felt more like a claim.

I shook the thoughts from my head and looked out at the rows of windows overlooking the palace grounds. A dark, inky sky was beyond, but the stars and moon were so bright even to human eyes that the hallway was clear to see.

Plush carpet concealed my footsteps. The air was warm, *pleasant*. A stark change from what we were forced to live with on the floors below.

I calmed my heart and forced it to go still.

She would be awake in there. Vampires never slept. Constantly forced to roam the world without even so much as a moment of rest. Yet she hadn't called for me or, hopefully, anyone else.

She will be bored. May even welcome the distraction. But I expected it. Expected her to fight back.

It's why I chose nighttime. So no one could hear her. No one could hear *us* as we fought. And when I was done, I could sneak back into my room and act like it never happened while I prepared for my exit.

When I reached her door, I hesitated. Wrapping my fingers around the crystal doorknob, my mind stalled. *This is it.* The most important moment of my career and the thing that would make my and my family's name go down in history.

Fuck it.

I pushed the door open and slipped in, shutting it softly behind me. The click was like a thunder crack in the silent room. She was there, I could feel her presence in the room, but she made no movement to greet me.

I hadn't taken a good look at her room the last time I was here, too preoccupied with trying not to give into the ache for her. But even in the darkness, it looked fit for a princess of her status.

Large, fluffy bed against the back wall. Floor-to-ceiling windows letting in the moonlight. A fucking crystal chandelier hanging over the center. The dimly lit candles that were placed all over the room caused light to bounce off it and sent beautiful reflections all over the floor and walls.

Next to the bed was a bird cage covered by a blanket, an odd addition that made me pause.

But then there was a motionless lump in the middle of the bed. *Vampires don't sleep,* I reminded myself. She had to be putting on a show.

You don't want to play? Her words from that night played again in my head, the teasing tone sounding all the more sinister when I was trapped in a room alone with her.

She must have heard me coming down the hallway or smelled the familiar scent of my blood.

But this time, I would play along. I walked forward, one foot after the other, my eyes never leaving the bed.

Isn't this what you wanted? That *damned* voice. I couldn't get it out of my head.

I wanted this...more importantly, I wanted this phase of my life to be over. I wanted to turn the shitty cards I had been dealt around and go back to save my brother from the abuse my parents had forced on us.

There is no other way. And all it took was killing a single *spoiled* princess.

I could do it. I had killed for less. I had killed for money.

Fucking move, I commanded my frozen feet. They were as heavy as lead as I closed the last few steps between me and the bed. Where just a few nights before she had been sitting, *naked,* and spreading her legs for me.

All the while never knowing that *this* was my true plan.

She didn't move, not even when I was right at the foot of the bed staring at her. *Another game.* She wanted to see what I would do.

I grabbed the short sword from my back, ready to pull—

"I knew there was something interesting about you, *little mouse.*"

She had moved in an instant. Her vampire speed was too fast for me to catch. She had thrown back the covers and was before me, on her knees and in nothing but a frilly lace nightgown that floated around her sides. It was light pink and see-through, giving me a look at the matching underwear she had on underneath.

It was a sinful image. One that almost made me believe she had been waiting for the moment I would show up.

Her face was inches away from mine, her fangs peeking out of her lips as she gave me a smirk, telling me that she wasn't disappointed with the turn of events.

She is amused.

My brain took a second to kick into motion, but after all that training, my instincts were faster.

"No hard feelings, princess," I said as I pulled the sword out of its sheath and pushed it down on her. It had magic woven into it. Even if I had to use it on a human before this, it should still pack quite a punch when it came to vampires.

But her *fucking* vampire speed meant that my sword came down onto the soft bed cover, splitting it and causing a burst of feathers to shoot up into the air.

"Aw, too slow," she teased, her voice inches from my ear. One of her hands caressed my neck, almost like she was ready to choke me, but the touch was so featherlight, it felt more like the touch of a lover than a vampire who was about to murder me. The other grabbed onto my hip, hard enough for me to recognize the pressure but not to keep me in place. "And here I was just thinking of how bored—"

I twisted around, bringing down the sword where her voice was, but she was gone.

She let out an annoyed huff, calling my attention to my right. She hadn't moved far and just stood there, looking down at her nightgown, which was now slit at the side.

I got close.

It was enough to give me some type of hope. Assurance that it wasn't all ruined.

"This is one of my favorite night—*ugh,* can you stop?!"

My attempt to stab at her stomach was thwarted by her sidestepping, then lunging at me. My back hit the carpeted floor with a hard enough impact that it forced all the air out of my lungs. My vision blurred. The ceiling multiplied. A ringing sounded through my head.

She made quick work of forcing the sword out of my hand and throwing it across the room while I was trying to regain my composure. The hard thud of it embedding into the wall echoed throughout the room.

Her hand was around my throat, her red eyes shining through the night. This time, she meant business. Whatever fun and games she had been playing were over.

It wasn't the pleasure-fueled stare that she had given me that night. There was no teasing in her eyes. It was anger. It was hurt. It was feral. It was...so much better than any of it.

There was something so breathtaking about her anger. It was so unrestrained, and for the first time, it felt like I was finally seeing something real from her.

The need was back in full force. I couldn't deny it. I couldn't blame it on the venom.

It was all me, feeling something I wasn't supposed to for a person who was supposed to be my sworn enemy.

Her nostrils flared and her eyes searched my face. She was caught off guard by my body's reaction.

But I wasn't. I had denied it, but I wasn't surprised. Her reaction was the in I needed.

I grabbed the knife at my thigh, and with one thrust, I—

Her hand caught my wrist just as the blade was about to pierce her ribs. The sword wasn't long enough with her arm extended.

Fuck.

"Never have I ever seen someone act with the utter careless confidence you have," she whispered, her face coming closer to mine. Her breath wafted across my lips, daring me to close the space. She was smiling again. "Was this your plan all along, little mouse? If so, you should have at least fucked me when you had the chance. How *boring.*"

Anger burst through me, and I couldn't help but bare my teeth at her. I had just tried to kill her, and she was saying I was...*boring*?

She's crazy. Completely and utterly insane.

She forced my wrist to the floor, squeezing hard enough to force me to let go of my grip.

I had never been overtaken so easily before. Not by a human, witch, or vampire. And yet she had me pinned down in minutes. *Maybe it was me who had underestimated her.*

She shifted against me. Her legs had been on either side of me, but for the first time, she pushed her body against mine. Melding us together, just like at the party. I had the foolish thought that she was going to kiss me...until she leaned to the side, her tongue licking the pulse in my neck. My heart skipped a beat and heat traveled through my body, starting right where her wet tongue met my skin.

"I have also never been so turned on by an assassination

attempt," she whispered against my skin. "I guess the same could probably be said for you."

She let me flip us. Let me put my hand around her throat. This time, she didn't flinch. All she did was wrap her legs around my waist so I couldn't separate us. I had all the power. Was in the perfect position.

Yet her legs around me felt like wrought iron bars, rendering me incapable of moving.

"Regardless, I'll be the one to end your life tonight," I growled.

She let out a breathy laugh, her hands coming up to run down my chest. My heartbeat skittered under her touch.

"Then why don't you?" she asked. "In fact, if you were so serious about it, why didn't you just let me die that first time?"

I hadn't realized how close I had gotten until our lips were centimeters away. Hadn't realized how my heart pounded in my chest. But *fuck* did I realize the heat that settled in my belly and the need. The need that I thought only existed when her fangs were deep in my neck.

"I wanted to be the one to do it," I whispered, unable to tear my eyes away from her lips. "Who knew you'd be stupid enough to poison yourself?"

"*Lies,*" she whispered.

I couldn't stop what happened even if I wanted to. I should have sensed it from the start. We were two unstoppable, chaotic forces bonded by opposing goals that were on a predestined path to collide.

It was only a matter of time before we met. *But who could have predicted it would be like this?*

Our lips were fused together, the hand I had locked around her throat keeping her in place as I ravished her mouth. The low moan she let out traveled through me, and wetness began to pool between my legs.

My other hand gripped her hip, and I forced myself into a kneeling position so she could sit flush against me. I couldn't let her go. Couldn't give us even so much as room to breathe for fear that it might bring me to my senses. I needed to feel her against me. Needed to know what it felt like for her to grind her wet cunt all over me.

I wanted her to make a mess of me, stain my uniform.

Immediately, she straddled me, her arms wrapping around me and pulling us impossibly close together. Clinging to me just like I was to her.

I couldn't breathe. I couldn't think. The only thing I could focus on was the heat running through my body. The need to get as close to her as possible. The need to hear the sound that she made at that party again.

It was dominating my entire being. Making me forget about the true reason I had come here. My dagger lay just a few feet away from me, where I could easily reach it to punch it into her chest while she was distracted, but instead, I grabbed her hips. Instead, I let my hands slip into the sides of her gown and teased the edge that covered her breasts.

She kissed me like she had nothing to hold back anymore. Vicious and unrelenting. I felt like she was punishing me for taking so long to get us to this point. Her teeth scraped against my bottom lip, hard enough for blood to pool between our mouths. She greedily drank it up.

"Don't think this means anything," I mumbled against her lips. She let out a gasp when I slipped my hand into her panties. She was so unbelievably wet, even more so than in my daydreams. "You were just waiting for me to come in here and fuck you, weren't you?"

"You're so full of yourself for a human," she spat back bitterly. "You think just because you performed well at the party that I'll just forgive your attempted assassination?"

"No," I said, with a dark chuckle as my fingers ran through her wet folds. "But I think you'll let me do whatever I want to this pussy because this is the most turned on you've been in years."

To prove my point, I slipped two fingers into her entrance. She reacted with an immediate sharp inhale and ground down on my hand. I didn't even need to pump into her. She did all the work

ETERNAL CAPTIVE 123
riding my hand like some depraved, unsatisfied being who hadn't orgasmed in years.

I pulled back to watch her. To get a good look as she threw her head back, her arms wrapped around me and using me for balance as she fucked me. She was so determined at that moment. She was going to force her orgasm, whether or not I participated.

But *fuck* did I want to be the one to make her feel that way. I used my thumb to rub her clit, my breath catching as her pussy clenched my fingers. She was so responsive. So willing to take all the pleasure I could give.

Who exactly has she been with that refused to pleasure her in such a way? It was so satisfying to think of all the people she fucked before me, none of them even getting close to what this mere blood bag could offer her.

"I think you like being fucked by a human way more than you let on, *princess*," I teased, trailing open-mouthed kisses down her neck. When I got to the place where her shoulder and neck met, I sunk my teeth into the pale flesh.

She can't tune me out, not now. I'm gonna make her pay attention to me. I'm gonna make her remember the one that makes her feel like this.

"Harder," she demanded.

I did as she asked, biting her as hard as I could. Of course, with my teeth, I couldn't break the skin, but as I pulled away, I saw a satisfying bruise just before it disappeared.

I wanted to mark her like she had me. Even if it was temporary. It would make what happened just that much harder to dismiss.

I pulled down her flimsy top, freeing her breasts. *Perfect.* They sat there, so patiently waiting for their turn. Her nipples were erect and just begging for my mouth on them, just like the night in the fountain. But this time I let myself pull one into my mouth, sucking on it before teasing it with my teeth. Her whole body shuddered against me, and she rode my hand even harder, slamming her hips down onto me and getting more unrestrained with each movement.

Her pussy was clenching tighter and tighter around me, and I knew within moments she would be coming.

So fast, with so little effort...it was enticing.

She pushed me down, causing us both to fall to the ground. She was straddling me again. She slapped both hands onto my chest, forcing me down as she continued to ride me. I anchored a hand on her hip, forcing her to stop so I could be the one pumping into her hard and fast, the heel of my palm hitting her clit each time.

She froze above me, her eyes meeting mine as her face was overtaken by pleasure. And then her lips, still stained with my blood, formed into a snarl. As her orgasm ran through her, she was at my neck, and in an instant, her fangs sank into my flesh.

Aurelia

Hot, sweet, delectable blood filled my mouth. It was even more delicious now that she was this aroused.

There's something about blood and sex. Venom intrinsically tied the two, but I never let myself be as much of a glutton as I had with her. Her fingers were still inside me, pumping as if I hadn't come as I sliced open her neck with my fangs.

She moaned against me as the venom took hold of her. Since our fight, I could smell her in the room. I could smell the arousal pooling between her legs. All I wanted was to taste it. *Fuck,* bathe in it. More than I wanted to bathe in the blood of my enemies. More than I wanted revenge.

My entire mind was filled with only *her.*

I had never been one of those vampires who took to draining their blood bags so they could lounge in a pool of their blood...but if all blood was like hers? I don't know if I could help myself. She might just be the one to turn me into one of those crazed rogues.

She was annoying, stuck up, and never acted the way a normal human should, but it just made her all that more addictive.

What else would the little mouse show me? The curiosity itself had the ability to send me into an obsessive spiral.

I should've been furious that she tried to kill me. But from the moment I saw her, I knew the little mouse had something up her sleeve. I just couldn't quite place it. Couldn't understand why she stuck to me like she had without trying something like the other guards. Why her eyes never left me.

A part of me was so excited for this outcome. To finally be on par with someone. To be able to fight and talk back. To be around someone who didn't want me as a status symbol.

Sure, the other part of me was pissed that she had gotten so close to wounding me. *Offended.* But the excitement outweighed all of that. I didn't care how annoying she was or how she had literally almost brought down an entire vampire family.

All I cared about was making the little mouse eat her words. She was right—whatever happened between us wouldn't mean anything, but *she* decided to start this back at the club, and I was going to finish it.

Her pants were buckled tightly, but I made quick work of them before pushing my hands inside and between her legs.

I pulled away from her neck, licking the wounds her blood still dripped from. She hadn't given up. Even as I forced my hand between us, she had moved from pumping to the sort of rocking motion that caused my eyes to roll into the back of my head.

"Seems I'm not the only one who came here looking to get fucked," I said as I teased her clit before running my fingers down to her entrance. *Wet.* She was completely and utterly drenched, and she sure as hell wouldn't be able to blame it on my venom.

She wants me, just as much as I want her.

"I didn't say you could touch me," she spat.

"Then tell me to stop," I told her, my eyes meeting hers. Her face was adorably flushed. Her eyes still held the hatred, but they were clouded by lust. "Tell me that you don't wish that I was between your legs right now—" I said, slowly pushing two teasing fingers inside her. "Lapping up your cunt, letting you ride my face as you try so desperately to pretend that you aren't enjoying yourself."

She cursed under her breath and averted her gaze.

"Nuh-uh," I whispered and used my free hand to force her to look at me as I continued to pump slowly into her pussy. "You're gonna look at me as I make you come."

Rage flashed through her eyes, pulling a laugh from my lips.

"Tell me to stop, little mouse," I purred and copied the same rocking motion she had used on me. I jerked my hips against her hand, reminding her that I wasn't quite done yet.

I wanted more, and I wouldn't be satisfied for a long while. Not while she still looked at me with such anger.

"I fucking hate you and your whole kind," she growled.

"Say it again," I murmured, leaning down to run my tongue across her lips. Her slow-but-steady movements were causing heat to run through me. It wasn't rushed like the orgasm that was pulled from me earlier—instead, we were watching each other's faces, seeing exactly who would be the first to lose this little bet we had. "All while you come for the *spoiled little princess* you seem to hate so much."

The venom had done its job prepping her to come. Her cunt pulsed around me. Her reluctant moans filled the air. She tried to hide them, but I only curled my fingers inside her and forced them to come out.

She bucked against me, trying wildly to get me to stop. As if she could somehow still get away from admitting her defeat. But she was too close. The orgasm had already worked its course, our fighting being all the foreplay she needed.

Then, she threw her head back, her mouth open and her body freezing as her orgasm finally ripped through her.

It was beautiful, uncontrolled, chaotic. Her harsh moans sounded more like sobs as it moved through her. Over and over again, the orgasm was assisted by vampire venom and forced her body into a pleasure I doubt she'd ever known before.

I want to see more of it.

I wanted to see her try to fight it. Adamantly try to stay in control. All while we both knew that the orgasm would come eventually.

What a fun game. The most fun I'd played in a decade.

"Taste yourself, human," I ordered and forced my wet fingers into her mouth. "Doesn't taste so much like hate, does it?"

Her teeth bit down on my fingers, and just as I was about to pull away, her thumb started with those intoxicating hard circles on my clit again.

"What are you—"

"Shut up and take it," she growled around my fingers. "Fair is fair, and I won't have you complaining about my bedroom skills because you decided to cheat."

I was left shocked by the little mouse, but she was right. Fair *was* fair, and if that meant getting an orgasm from her, I wouldn't complain.

Our heaving breaths filled the silent room as we lay side by side, not bothering to fix our shredded clothes.

The ceiling was in perfect condition, but I knew as soon as my eyes wandered around the room, I would be met with destruction. There were more orgasms. Again and again until we were too tired to go on.

Fair was an excuse—the reality was that both of us wanted to one-up the other.

"You're not gonna kill me?" she asked, her voice breaking through the post-sex haze.

Kill her? I scoffed aloud. I should've killed her hours ago. I should've killed her when she forced me to drink her blood when all I had wanted that day was for the poison magic to kill me.

No. There would be no killing.

"You're much too interesting for that," I admitted. I turned to look at her, taking in her still-flushed face. At some point during our fucking, I had sliced her shirt open, and now her entire chest lay open and bare to me, her nipples swollen and red. They were tempting me again.

"That doesn't change what I need to do," she said.

I turned over on my side, propping my head on my hand, and sent her a smirk.

"Tell me who sent you," I requested. "I can double whatever they pay."

Her eyes narrowed. "This was never about the money."

Her words struck me as odd. *If it isn't about the money, then what is it about?*

Sure, my father had made a bunch of enemies during his existence, but I hadn't. I was well-known among the various royal families, and I stayed in my lane. I attended one too many blackmail parties, but they had information on me too, so there was no reason to send an *assassin* after me...

So, who did I offend to have them go to such great lengths?

It was unnerving to have such a calm conversation with her after everything. To look into her eyes and realize that, no matter what, she would still gladly put a blade in my heart.

I was bargaining for my life. As much as I tried not to let the panic show on my face, there was a sort of fear that gripped my throat.

"What else can I offer you?" I asked. "The prince's head on a stick?"

She let out a laugh and shook her head.

"He holds no value to me. If anything, that would help you more than it would me."

I thought for a moment. She wanted blood. *Royal* blood. Though I didn't fault her for not wanting the prince. He was all but useless. Even his family name at this point had been destroyed by his actions. My father's motives for selling me were still unknown, so the prince would not be a bargaining chip, but...

An idea popped into my head. I had been so overtaken by her attempt to kill me that what my father had done had fallen into the recesses of my mind.

I can use her. She didn't know about my hatred for him, so to her, my offer would look too irresistible to pass up.

"Then my father, and in return, you're my personal feeder. I'm not talking about light work. We've been doing that with you as my guard. I want you here every night with me."

Her eyes widened, and at first, I thought she would grab her dagger and plunge it into my heart right then and there, but instead, she surprised me.

She laughed. Uncontrolled, pure amusement.

It caused anger to boil underneath my skin. *Does she think I'm just some sort of fucking joke?*

"I'm serious," I hissed and leaned closer to her. She wasn't at all intimidated.

"I'm sure you are, *princess,*" she said through her chuckles and pushed herself into a seated position.

I shot my hand out, grabbing at her ripped shirt and forcing her face close to mine. I bared my teeth at her, hoping that her blood was still staining them. But instead of gawking in fear, she merely smirked at my actions.

"There is no one in a better position than me to get you the king's head," I said. "Why would you stop at a princess who's about to be married off? I am of no use to you. I cannot control anything. I do not have any power. I will never have any power, but I can give you the keys to toppling this family."

Her smirk faltered for just a second.

"And how am I to believe that you hate your family so much you would allow me to kill the only one of your parents still left alive?" she asked. Her words were hurtful, her tone even more so. I pushed her away.

"Then you haven't been paying much attention," I hissed and stood up, trying to straighten my clothes. She did the same, trying to cover as much of her skin as she could with the scraps she had.

I almost offered her a shirt, but that would be going too low, even for me. She was a guard. One who tried to kill me and insulted me.

It was embarrassing. I had let myself fuck my assassin-to-be and then concocted this crazy plan in hopes of saving myself...How low was I willing to go?

That familiar sense of shame was playing on my senses.

Maybe it was the years I'd been locked in that cage I kept hidden in the back of my mind. The years of having to obey my father as he continued to look down on me. The last-ditch effort at trying to avoid becoming a Solei plaything. Maybe it was the heat I had seen in my stepmother's eyes that was finally pushing me to do something as insane as trusting her.

But nonetheless, it was more of a plea than a bargain. And for her to deny it so abruptly...it hurt.

"Get out before I'm summoned," I ordered. "If anyone asks, just tell them that I requested you."

"Worried about me, princess?" she asked as she walked toward the far wall, where her short sword was sticking out. She grabbed it by the handle and pulled it out, looking it over and nodding with satisfaction when she realized there was no damage to it.

"Well, you have proven interesting," I said with a shrug. "Even if you're a coward. At least we'll have a bit of fun until you can sneak back up here again."

Her jaw clenched, the sound of her teeth grinding together hitting my ears. She then let out a huff before bending down and grabbing the dagger as she made her way toward the door. She didn't pause until her hand was on the crystal doorknob.

"Next time, it won't end like this," she vowed.

"I'll be waiting," I said, trying to muster as much of that fake confidence as I could.

I hated her. I wanted to hate her for the hurt she caused. She had a job to do and probably wasn't reading into everything that went on with the family. But I had run out of options.

And she'd taken the last sliver of hope I had left.

AURELIA

"When have I ever let you down, Father?" I asked, turning my head back to look at him.

He sat back in his desk chair like he did in all of his seats in the palace, making it look more like a throne than anything else. His dark hair was pushed out of his face, the same exact eyes that looked back at me in the mirror staring at me.

Vampires really didn't age, or if they did, it was so slow it would be thousands of years before any of it showed on their faces. Father had little signs of age besides a few wrinkles by his eyes.

He reached forward and pulled the papers that I was sitting on out from under me with a sigh.

"Off the desk, Aurelia," he grunted.

"*Father.*"

He gave me a warning look. He *hated* that whiny tone that seemed to work so well on him. I had seen the stepmonsters use it more than once to get their way, so it was only a matter of time before I implemented it myself.

I jumped off the desk and went around it. He let out another sigh before leaning back in his chair to watch me.

"It's just a little tantrum," I said in a low voice, fully aware that he surrounded himself with vampire guards and not the normal human ones he assigned to the rest of the family.

Since he's the most important one, he can give us the scraps. Even ones that try to kill us.

Anger and embarrassment flashed through me again, even if just for a moment before I could push it deep down.

It was foolish to think I could utilize someone. I had never been able to rely on anyone in my entire life—*why would that change now?*

Her reaction had been the wake-up call I needed. A well-aimed slap to the face that reminded me the only person who could change this was *me*.

"A tantrum that could call off a wedding," he said very matter-of-factly.

Prince Icas was less than happy about my performance when he finally spilled what the plan was for my marriage. Maybe it was the viselike grip I had his cock in or the subsequent silent treatment after I realized what he was truly after.

He did quite enjoy my blood, but over the last two weeks, he hadn't gotten so much as a taste of it. *He deserves it.* If he couldn't trap me with a blood bond, it seemed his next idea was a baby. And my guess was that he was annoyed that his father was trying to hold me in front of him like a sweet, forbidden treat he couldn't have.

But it would all change when I officially joined their house, so I had to work fast.

"He gets more out of this deal than you do," I reminded him, and grabbed a stray strand of hair to circle around my finger. "And we both know his father coddles him too much. He hasn't gotten used to what it means to deal with a *Castle*."

His pause was all the answer that I needed. He was hiding something. Even if his body language didn't give much away.

"It's important for our future," he said after a long moment. "Just do what he asks and try not to fight him too much. If he is happy, his father is happy."

It's important for our future.

"How so?" I asked and snuck to his armrest, sitting on it and putting my hand around his chair. "I know nothing about what was negotiated, and yet I'm being asked to do the unthinkable."

"Unthinkable?" he asked with a huff. "This is your duty, Aurelia." His tone held annoyance but not anger. *He is softening up.*

"Then let me in, Father," I whispered and leaned against him. Something I used to do when I was younger and wanted something. "I want us to succeed. Know my loyalty. It will always be to you. How can a snake enter their nest if it doesn't even know what to expect?"

His hand came to grab mine. An action I thought was supposed to be a comfort until his nails dug into my skin.

"What did he tell you?"

Ice-cold fear froze my veins. Panic clawed at my throat. I was too close to him. Memories of punishments flooded my mind.

My fight-or-flight response was begging me to run, but I couldn't. Running would tell him I had done something wrong. And he would sic the guards on me before I could get to safety.

"Nothing I wasn't expecting, Father," I said, trying hard to keep my voice steady. "But it does seem it's his father who is more interested in what I can offer than he is. It begs the question: Why not just marry me to him?"

His grip loosened, and he let out a huff of a laugh.

"He's already been married for longer than you've been alive," he said. "The family would riot."

I let his words sit between us.

"What do you owe him, Father?" I asked.

For the first time, he froze against me. It was so slight, I almost missed it. Would have if I were not leaning against him.

"I don't *owe* him anything," he muttered. "But you can say I... stole something from him."

My head swirled so violently I thought I might throw up all over his desk.

"Something or someone—"

The door was pushed open by none other than the fucking devil's son himself *with* the stepmonster.

She gave me a fucking knowing smirk when she saw our position. She knew exactly what I was doing because she and her spawn had done it hundreds of times to get what they wanted.

Prince Icas, on the other hand, looked a bit miffed.

"Prince Icas offered to give us an introduction to his feeder sourcing consultants. We came to propose it to you, but if you would rather spend ti—"

"We need to relish in some feeders," he said and stood up, pushing me off the arm of his chair. "This is more important."

He gave me a look that told me to get going. I bit my tongue and bowed to him, forcing my feet to move me across the space as they all stared.

"Oh yes," the stain on our family said just as I walked past her. "Prince Icas shared something interesting with me. Be sure to find me tomorrow so we can...*talk* about it."

Krae. Was this how he was going to play this? Complaining to Father was bad enough, but to *her*? He must have been annoyed with how long it had taken for Father to get around to calling me into his office for punishment.

My gaze cut to his, only to catch a disgusting fucking smirk playing at his lips.

Bastard.

I pushed out of the room only to come face-to-face with the handmaiden I thought I had gotten rid of. I clicked my tongue and turned down the hall.

Her footsteps followed me.

"If you need some blood, princess—"

I turned on my heels to confront her, closing the space between us and grabbing her face.

"For the last time, leave," I hissed. She tried to avert her gaze, but I forced her to look at me. "I know that bitch sent you. I want nothing to do with you, and I don't give a shit about what she will do to you. If I find you near me one more time, I will officially make you vacate your post. However I can. Do I make myself clear?"

She nodded shakily, her eyes filling with tears.

I let out a noise of disgust and pushed her away from me.

I couldn't trust anyone in the fucking palace. The little mouse had gotten far too close and almost killed me. I couldn't take the risk of having a known spy by my side.

Against my better judgement, I found myself wishing the little mouse was on my side.

VESPER

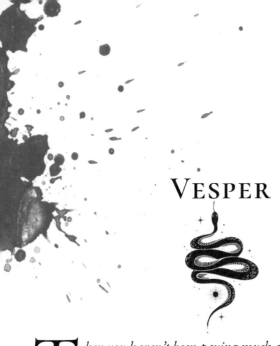

Then you haven't been paying much attention.

I had been. I had seen it all.

I had seen the way her father made her stand by him, as if she didn't deserve to have a throne for herself. Always standing in his shadows. Growing up to be a miniature cruel version of him. It was all part of his control tactics.

Because if he didn't put her in her place or constantly beat into her how much he was to thank for her current existence and life, she might just fully forget about her mother's blood roaring through her veins.

As if the queen wasn't the one everyone wanted.

That's what the little princess didn't get. I didn't want her father. No one wanted her father. He was just some vampire who had gotten lucky. Married the right girl. Started a vampire family. And somehow managed to make it into something that caused other vampires to foam at the mouth with envy.

He was rumored to be cruel. Violent. But he wasn't the truly dangerous one. He was just a vampire who liked to wear a mask of importance and walk around like he was the shit. The only person who thought he was dangerous was himself.

What was dangerous was her mother's blood.

The one who caused hundreds of vampires to join the ranks of her father's kingdom just so they would have a chance to protect their newfound queen. She toppled clans. Families. Vampires left in droves to join her when they heard about her marriage to him. She was the single force that pulled the vampires together. *And controlled them.*

And the princess didn't even realize the power she held.

It was my family's job to make sure that type of power and control would be gone for good. It started with a long line of us, all hand-chosen for the secret organization that sent us across the country to kill vampires and witches alike.

The families it employed never questioned why. They only knew whatever prophecy had been handed to them by the powers that be. It didn't matter how many generations had gone by or how many hundreds had joined since the conception of the organization, they would follow it until it was their time to die in battle.

I thought I had been paying attention. *But maybe she is right.* Especially if *that* was what I had been missing this entire time. And just because it was my job to learn everything about the princess and *still* kill her didn't mean that I had to like what I saw.

The slap of her stepmother's hand coming into contact with her cheek reverberated throughout the room. Her little mini-me of a daughter was right by her side, not even attempting to hide her smile behind her hand.

I hadn't had much time to prepare for this meeting or to decipher what it meant when the princess called for me bright and early in the morning to accompany her on some "errands." Obviously, when she pulled me to the opposite wing of the palace and straight into her stepmother's sitting room, it was a hint the day wouldn't be filled with trying on dresses and gossiping with fellow royals.

I almost wished it had been. At least then I could hide under the annoyance of following a spoiled princess around instead of the... pity? Guilt? I didn't quite know how to describe the feeling that weighed down my chest and only got stronger as the day went on.

The vile vampire had hit the princess so hard that there was a dark purple bruise immediately forming on her cheek. I counted the seconds it took for it to disappear.

Eight.

Twelve.

Thirteen.

It took fifteen. More time than it took when I bruised her skin, and the entire room sat through the silence as we all watched it fade away.

There were other guards here, some leaning against the doors, and even more outside. All of them kept a cold face in response to the abuse they witnessed. I looked at them, attempting to see into their minds.

How often did this happen? Was this the norm?

Their faces gave no answer to my question. They merely stood there, their black uniforms blending into the dark-red walls and black doors.

But this is my first time coming face-to-face with it.

I had been so desensitized to the murdering of people for contracts and had seen more than my fair share of fucked-up creatures and humans alike.

But there was still something so raw about the way the princess just took the abuse.

"I told you the *next day,* you insolent brat," the stepmother hissed. "What about that did your brain interpret as almost a whole fucking week later?"

"It's been four days," Princess Aurelia said, her tone bitter. She threw her hair behind her shoulder. A defiant move that caused my chest to swell.

She looked down at the small table next to her. It held hardened blood cubes that shined like rubies. She took a few, popping them into her mouth as her family looked at her, enraged.

"Your father has gone soft on you. Because he thinks no matter what, this deal will go through. But I know better," her stepmother said. There was an air of seniority in her tone. Like she was the true mastermind behind the vampire family she got lucky enough to marry into. "You're lacking. The prince is unhappy."

"The prince seems *very* happy here," the princess answered, reaching for another blood cube. "At least that's what I can tell from the dozens of feeders who have been summoned to his room in the middle of th—"

It was the stepsister who stepped forward this time. She raised her hand and brought it down quickly, smacking the blood cube out of her hand.

"Do you know what he told us?" she spat, a wicked grin pulling at her lips. "He told us *exactly* what he plans to do to you when you're shipped off to his family home. You have no room for that attitude of yours there, and if you're lucky and please him enough here, he said that *maybe* he'll be good to you when the time comes."

I expected a slap. I wanted to see it. But Princess Aurelia raised her hand but paused. The little demon flinched, her reaction pulling a smile from the princess before she wiped her fingers on the girl's white dress, staining it with blood.

"And here I was, thinking you knew all about it the whole time."

"Remember the time Father almost pulled out your fangs?" the stepsister said with a smirk. She was trying to keep as much power as she still could. "Maybe we need a reminder. After all, it's a fitting punishment. Can't run your mouth without being subject to the shame of it all."

"Don't be so jealous," the princess all but purred, unfazed by her threat. "I'm sure if you begged on your knees and flashed him a bit of that rotten cunt of yours, he'd bed you in a heartbeat. Maybe then you'd finally learn your place here."

"Aurelia—"

Her stepmother tried to intervene, but the princess wasn't done. She stepped forward, grabbing the girl's dress and yanking her closer.

"Because I'm his blood daughter, I get married off to the wealthy and powerful," she said. "But you? No one knows what sewer you and your bitch mother crawled out of. No one wants you. No one will pay for you. So here's a bit of advice: say some shit like that again, and I will make sure none of the vampires in our circle will *ever* bid on you. Meaning you'll have to spend the rest of your life begging for attention from a lowly, poor vampire who probably got you for half price."

I couldn't hold back a snort, nor could the guards at the door stay totally silent. They shifted, one even trying to conceal his laugh with a cough.

"Aurelia, you will go and do whatever it is you need to do to make the prince happy!" her stepmother raged. If vampires could die of an aneurysm, she would certainly be close. Her eyes were wide, and her entire body was shaking with the intensity of her anger. "Now go, before I make you regret ever stepping foot in this room!"

Princess Aurelia paused for a moment. I could see her mind whirling, but her facial expression remained neutral. Then, the smallest smirk pulled at her lips.

It was the kind of smile that told me she was ready to end everything. Told me that what she had said was just the beginning, and if she wanted to, she could burn this entire place down with just a couple more sentences.

It was an even more dangerous power than her mother's. The elder vampire commanded love and adoration, while her daughter was the bringer of chaos and drew people in just close enough so she could slit their throats when they were least expecting it.

She invoked anger. Rage. Volatile emotions that could end a fight before it even started.

I stepped forward, not saying anything to the stepmother but merely reminding her of my presence. She gave me a look. A dismissive one that told me I should probably back off, but instead, I placed my hand on the princess's elbow and murmured, "Shall I escort you out?"

"You're right," the princess said, her smile widening as she met the gaze of her stepmother. "I think it's time that I go visit him. Thank you for the reminder."

Shock froze me in place. This was not the vampire I had been fighting when I tried to assassinate her the other night. The uncontrolled, burning anger that seemed to take over the entirety of her small frame seemed to have just vanished into thin air.

I had been waiting for her to unleash on them like she had on me. She had the power to. I could feel it building up inside her.

But like a switch, she changed completely, and back was the picture-perfect vampire princess who obeyed every command and still managed to hold her head high even after all the insults hurled at her.

It was like a completely different person.

She didn't say anything else as she made her way to the exit, though I did spare one last glance at the mother-and-daughter duo who stood there fuming. I almost expected one of them to come flying at her, given how poorly they were holding in their anger. It had my fingers itching to grab the weapon I had stationed at my back.

But they did nothing as we passed the threshold. The door closing behind us didn't hide the frustrated screams from the vampires.

"Going back on your word?" The princess asked as soon as we were down the hall and far enough away from the others that they couldn't hear us. She was leading me to the prince. I already knew from the direction we were headed.

A bit of a disappointment. I almost wished she'd just agreed so she could ditch him again.

"I hate all vampires equally," I retorted, sneaking a look at her. But this time she wasn't looking at me with one of those smiles of hers. This time, her gaze was straight ahead, her mind a thousand miles away.

"I know you're tied to him," she said, her pace coming to an abrupt halt. This time, she looked at me without anger. There was a plea in her eyes. "But when we're in there, your loyalty is to me. If he loses control, remember that."

Loses control? Does everyone in this palace like to beat up the princess?

"You trust me that much?" I asked, unable to find the words for anything else.

"If not you, then who else?"

It was worse. Much worse than I thought.

I stayed still and watched as the princess fell to her knees in front of the prince. He had already been gorging himself on the blood of multiple feeders, all lying dazed in various places around the room. Many of them were half naked, some not even wearing clothes.

How the fuck could the prince get away with this?

I knew he was a bastard. From both my experiences in his kingdom and the rumors surrounding him, I knew that there was nothing redeemable about him.

But I had expected him to clean up his act as soon as he got to the palace. At least during the engagement. Act like the perfect prince he was supposed to be. Schmooze the in-laws.

It would seem that he had her stepmother on his side...but acting like *this*?

It only made me realize how much they must have hated the princess. How much they wished for her downfall.

The stepsibling's words rang in my head.

He told us exactly what he plans to do to you when you're shipped off to his family home.

If *that* was what he decided to do in her own home, what was awaiting her there? Not only that, but everyone in the Castle family was actively rooting for her demise.

They might as well have just handed her to me.

"It took you long enough," Icas said, his bloody lips pulling into a smirk. "Seems you have daddy dearest wrapped around your finger. Even when I told him how you assaulted me, he still didn't even force you here to apologize."

"If that's what you call an assault, I'm seriously concerned about the damage you took to your brain," she said with a huff. "The stepbitch is annoying. That's the only reason I'm doing this. Cross the line, and next time I'll cut it off."

He let out a booming laugh.

"Yeah?" he asked, leaning forward with a shit-eating grin. "How about finishing our blood bond? Is that crossing the line enough for you? You even brought a witness."

I prayed that my heart wouldn't give me away. *Blood bond?* He had mentioned it since the first day he arrived at the palace, but the princess wouldn't actually go through with it...*would she?*

That's not why we're here, or is it?

That would make my job that much more difficult. A blood bond between vampires was ritualistic and intertwined them for the rest of eternity. They would be able to feel each other; more importantly, he would feel it if she died.

But more than that, the princess obviously didn't want to create a blood bond. I could see it on her face. The hatred that I thought was reserved only for me was starting to make an appearance on her face.

She wasn't pretending in front of him. Maybe that's why he had the nerve to tangle his hand in her hair and force her head to the side, baring her neck to him. She let out a pained groan.

Why does the image of her like this make me angry? I should be happy the spoiled princess was getting what was coming to her.

"You and I both know that's not fucking happening," she growled at him. "Take what you want and stop causing trouble."

"You think this is causing trouble?" he asked, a laugh falling from his lips.

A stray feeder let out a groan as they turned over on the hard floor. None of us turned to them.

"I think you're scared you can't control me," she gibed. "I think you want to get back at me for holding my power over you. I think that you're pissed your daddy forced you into this marriage only to take the prize for himself. That's why you're making up shit. Telling my stepmother that I haven't been *pleasing* you. You're *scared*."

She spat out the word "pleasing" like it was a curse.

"I can count the number of times on one hand that you've been to see me," he said. "Each time refusing my blood bond."

"Don't make me laugh," she hissed. "In the short time you've been here, you drank from me five times. Drained me until I was weak. So don't lie to her and tell her I haven't been to see you."

My blood ran cold. Vampires, especially the rich and powerful, would do anything to assert control. That's why the hierarchy between clans and families existed. Why those at the top forced their followers into a bond they could never escape.

I'd known that, known it my entire life. I'd seen them all, and the prince barely scratched the surface of the worst ones out there.

There was just something so despicable about the way he treated her. But that was not what angered me. What angered me was that she refused to fight back. I knew she could. I had experienced it. I knew she could at least teach him some kind of lesson.

So why is she hesitating?

The more I watched them, the more it angered me. I didn't like how he handled her. Didn't like how his response was simply to smile at her before viciously digging his fangs into her neck. It was a gruesome attack. He sliced open her neck, letting his teeth rip into the flesh without a care for what might happen to her.

And then that bastard pulled away. He looked at her with her blood streaming down his mouth and neck and let out a chuckle.

"How does it feel, my love?" he asked. The way his voice took on a fake sweetness caused my skin to crawl. My hand had already shifted to my sword. I was ready to slice his chest open.

Princess Aurelia just sat there. Her eyes narrowed at him. The wound on her neck was healing, but not fast enough.

She fed on me too long ago. Has she had nothing since then? The blood cubes didn't count. They probably wouldn't have been able to sustain her if needed. Or maybe the wound was too deep. Blood poured out of it, streaming down her neck and soaking her dress.

"Fucking peachy," she muttered.

Her response did not amuse him. He leaned forward once more and drove his teeth back into her neck. He wasn't in the same spot, nor did he leave his fangs in long enough for her to get the venom.

He is hurting her on purpose. Something shifted inside me, the weight in my chest becoming painful. My fingers twitched, just begging to grab hold of the sword on my back.

"A reminder to be gentle to Princess Aurelia," I said through gritted teeth. "While you may be her intended, her father would not like her body battered and bruised before the ball this weekend."

This was not the intervention she wanted or the one that I had planned. I don't know how the words forced themselves from my head to the back of my throat, just begging to get out...but I couldn't stop them.

His eyes darted to me before he ripped his fangs from her neck. "She'll heal."

And then his mouth covered the wounds, and he began to suck. I hated it. Hated him more than I thought I would. I couldn't see her face from my position, but I could hear the pained noises she tried to hide.

He wasn't giving her any venom. I couldn't tell which was worse —having to watch him make her feel things she didn't for him or for him to hurt her like he was.

Pity. Anger. All of it swirling inside me and not directed at her... but for her. I had killed so many in my time on this earth, but this was the first time that I had ever wanted to *save* someone. Let alone a vampire.

This time, when he pulled away, I closed the space between us and grabbed the princess's arm. He wasn't going to stop me, I could see it in his eyes. It didn't matter that he had feeders around him— he wanted to make a point that he could do whatever he wanted to the princess.

"That's enough," I commanded.

His eyes snapped to me, and he was up in an instant, his hand wrapping around my throat and squeezing so hard, I feared it would snap.

"You work for me, you *bitch*," he hissed. "If I want some time with my wife, I can fucking take it."

The princess forced herself up with far less strength than I'd ever seen in her, and pushed him away. He let himself be moved by the pitiful display. His hand unwound from my neck, and I took a big gulp of air that stung my lungs.

"I'm not your wife yet," she reminded him. "And she's right. Father would be displeased. We're leaving. I'll visit you at the scheduled time."

Icas glared at me but didn't say anything as the princess pulled me away.

As soon as the door shut and we were out in the hallway, she leaned against me. Her breathing was heavy and her skin clammy. She needed blood.

Instead of going straight to her room, I walked us back down the hallway and into a random closet. It wasn't glamorous, and the princess probably would've complained if she wasn't so out of it, but I didn't want anyone to see this.

It was cramped, filled with cleaning supplies, and forced us closer together than I ever would've liked. I pulled her to me and positioned her near my neck.

I shouldn't be doing this. I should separate myself. My mind knew clearly what I *should* have been doing, but I couldn't stop my actions.

"Princess, drink," I ordered. She shook her head.

"I have some blood back in my room. Just get me there," she murmured, but her voice was weak.

It caused a panic to burst through me. *Is this how she would die?*

The killer in me already had a plan. To leave her in the closet, wound her while she was weak, and leave without a trace.

It was my chance. She couldn't fight back, even if she wanted to. *But she trusted me to save her from him...and foolishly, I did.*

"Just drink, goddamn it," I growled. "You think I like offering myself as a feeder? I wouldn't do it if you weren't on the brink."

"You could kill me right now," she noted. "A dark closet; no one comes down this hall except for the feeders and the prince. It would be a while before they found me."

She was leaning against me, unable to hold herself up. Her breathing was getting weaker. *I need to move quickly.* Instead of tangling my hand in her hair like he had done, I placed it on the back of her neck and positioned her face against my neck.

"*Aurelia,*" I forced out. "Drink."

Please. The wretched word was almost out of my mouth in my panic.

I held her there, and at some point the hunger must have gotten to her because it wasn't long before I felt her fangs sink into my neck. It was gentle this time. She wasn't ravenous like when I cornered her.

She was calm, careful. She wasn't trying to hurt me like he did to her. The stark difference between the two made the feelings in my chest even more confusing.

You're doing this because you still need time to prepare, I lied to myself. Even in my own mind, the excuse sounded absurd.

I tried to focus on anything but the heat running through my body, igniting everything I had tried to forget from that night. Tried to focus on how my hand felt on her hip. On how my blood felt as it soaked my shirt.

But then her hands were grabbing my hips, pulling us closer together, a moan spilling from her.

A flashback to our night together consumed my mind. The feeling of her wetness against me. Of her lips on my neck and breasts. Of the way she rode me.

A mistake. A deadly one. But still, I couldn't stop myself.

When she tried to pull away, I gently pulled her back.

"Keep going," I whispered.

There was desperation in the way that she gripped me. Pain in the way that she reluctantly drank my blood. But no one else could see it, not when we were alone in the closet. And that made it so much easier to live in denial.

Her hands made quick work of my zipper, and before I knew it, her cold hand had slipped between my legs.

"This is not why. You don't have to—*ah.*"

My protest died on my tongue as her finger slipped inside me, and she used her palm to rock against my clit.

My hands gripped her hips, and I closed my eyes, losing myself to the feeling of heat that I had tried so desperately to ignore. Molten lava licked my spine, and my core clenched. Just as easily as it had started, she was going to make me come with minimal effort. There was something about the gentleness of it mixed with the intensity of the venom. I couldn't ignore it, couldn't get lost in it like I had when we hate-fucked.

I felt everything. The way her lips felt against my neck. The way her body melded against mine. She played me so easily, making me bend to her will.

And then she paused. She pulled her fangs out of me and ran her tongue up my neck.

"You help me," she whispered. "I help you."

"I told you, you don't need to—*fuck.*" I couldn't speak as she leaned forward, her mouth somehow finding my nipple underneath my clothing and bit—*hard.*

"You didn't like watching him do that to me, did you?" she asked.

In the haze of pleasure, I didn't even consider not answering.

"I was going to kill him," I admitted. *But I shouldn't have even felt that way to begin with. I was fucking losing it.*

And then her mouth was against mine. The taste of my blood spread across my tongue. I moaned into her, letting myself fall into the rocking of her hand between my legs.

I was close. *So close.* She pulled back.

"He would throw a fit if he knew what I am doing with you," she whispered against my lips.

Good. I wanted him to know that, while he may force her to kneel for him with empty threats and the backing of her step-mother, she would do it for me without an ounce of hesitation.

"Only because he knows you will never act like this for him," I forced out between moans.

She gave me a sinister smile.

"Come for me, little mouse," she purred. "Claim your reward."

I couldn't hold back. My orgasm unleashed in me like a tidal wave. I placed my forehead against hers, needing it to center me as wave after wave rocked my core. I bit my lip to stifle the moans.

She didn't stop, even as my orgasm subsided. She fucked me through it slowly, and as I came back to earth.

"Let me know about that deal," she said, pulling her hand from between my legs only to plop her fingers into her mouth.

I was speechless as she opened the door and motioned for me to come out. It took far longer than I'd like to admit for me to button up my pants and collect myself before I stepped out into the hallway.

I shouldn't have fucking saved her...Maybe I truly am losing it.

AURELIA

T he chaos of dealing with the prince and the would-be
assassination attempt almost made me forget how
mundane the cycle of my life was.

Board meeting with Father. Decompress at the club. Save face at
the gala.

Over and over again for years and years. The only time anything
was worth noting at one of these things was a marriage or, if we
were lucky—*an affair.*

But this time was different. Because this time, *I* would be the
one providing the entertainment.

People were invited from all over to celebrate the engagement.
And to put it frankly, I was the chained animal put on display for all
to see.

The family took special care in preparing me for this event.

My hair had taken hours to complete and felt heavy on my head
with all the diamonds and rubies they pinned throughout the braids
that crisscrossed over my head. Of course, they couldn't skimp on
the tiara.

It was my mother's from when she got engaged. Apparently, it
had been a gift from my father to her, but I had a hard time
believing my father would have done anything nice for her.

The gown was brand new. I hadn't even had time to try it on or pick any of the fabrics that went into making it. Father and the step-bitch did that for me. Both of them carefully crafting it with the knowledge that hundreds of vampires would remember the occasion, and *me* in it.

It was a deep red with velvet accents all around, and luckily it covered most of my skin. A nice pick, though it was hard to move with the way it constricted my chest and arms. I was dressed up like a pretty little doll, ready to be gawked at, while Prince Icas had on a normal suit.

He gets the easy part, of course. No one really came to see him anyway. Just like when I joined the same type of gala in other families, they were just foaming at the mouth for a chance to see some high-profile royals embarrass themselves.

Holding the gala at our palace was nonnegotiable. We had a room reserved for this—multiple, actually. It was the same setup every single time. A large ballroom, decked out in glittering gold, multiple crystal chandeliers, floor-to-ceiling windows that showed our thousands of bright red roses surrounding the palace, and more blood than any vampire could consume in their entire lifetime in both the pitchers and with humans walking around, offering their wrist to whoever wanted.

I recognized a few of them from the blood tasting we had not long before.

Extravagance was the name of the game. My father didn't want to just *tell* people that he was a king among vampires—he wanted to show them. He wanted people to leave this place not questioning his wealth or his right to power.

I had blurry memories of when I was a child, when my mother could still quell him. Instead of these lavish balls, we would have small parties in the garden. But only for those we cared for, and most of the party was spent bonding with them, catching up, and just laughing. One of my clearest memories of that time was when I caught my mother laughing at something a family member had said.

She threw her head back, her laughter echoing across the garden and drawing all attention to her.

She radiated such happiness, even if no one knew what was happening behind closed doors between her and my father.

That was something I could never live up to. After being locked in the gilded cage for so long, I had lost any softness she had instilled in me. All that was left were the sharp, cracked edges my father left after trying to mold me into what he thought was the perfect daughter. Strengthening relationships looked different after she died.

If she were here, I wouldn't have to marry the prince. If she were here, the old men scattered among the crowd wouldn't look at me and lick their lips as if they knew that no matter what my marriage status was, if they offered a big enough sum, I could be theirs too.

With her, I could be free.

Icas squeezed my arm tightly, bringing me back from my melancholy daydream. His grip was hard enough to bruise, but it would disappear in seconds. I almost wished it didn't. Almost wished he had broken me down like Elora's husband did to her so that everyone would see what a disgusting prick he was.

I blinked my eyes rapidly, the two withering vampires in front of us both looking at me. I had forgotten their names, but I did remember the distinct black veins that ran across their faces and necks.

Those weren't left from too many fun nights on magical drugs. Oftentimes, those would fade and wouldn't harm the vampire. The ones they had running along their faces were deep-set, painful-looking. Intentional.

They pissed off the witches. It wasn't often that a vampire got away to tell the tale, but if they did, they usually ended up looking something like that.

All I could think was, *They deserved it.*

"Sorry," Icas said. His voice for once actually sounded something like an aristocrat's. "It's been quite a night for Princess Aurelia."

They both gave me smiles that caused my skin to crawl.

"Well, yes, not surprising. The royal women of this age aren't like their mothers. Spoiled. Disinterested. They should be grateful we still let them attend these things."

The jab was unexpected and enough to cause my insides to broil with fury. It didn't help that the humiliation and anger from forcing myself to my knees in front of Icas still resided in my body, just waiting for the opportune moment to come out.

"How dare you—"

Icas shut me up by pulling me closer, his grip on my hip hard enough to leave another set of bruises. "We won't bother you any longer, gentlemen. Thank you for the chat. I'll follow up with you later about what we can do about those witches."

His promise to them made them entirely ignore what I was about to say. I let him pull me off to the side before I launched into my questioning.

"What *we* can do about the witches?" I asked in a hushed tone.

The witches were not to be messed with, every vampire knew that. They had the power to destroy us. Every single one of us, if they amassed enough people. And they were known to travel in close-knit covens, tighter than any vampire family out there. So if you fucked with one, the rest would come.

He gave me a look before flagging down a waiter with crystal flutes of blood.

"Yes, Aurelia, what *we* can do," he said and sent a smile to the waiter after snagging a drink for himself only. "You think all I want out of this marriage is your blood and body?"

The flames of anger licked at my insides. *All he wants?* He said it like my body, my entire fucking soul, wasn't sold to him to be a sex slave whose only purpose was to be passed around and shoot out an heir that could do what *he* failed.

"You told me your father wanted—"

"You know, you were right about one thing," he interrupted, leaning close. The music was loud, loud enough to drown out any conversations around us besides our own. "If my father thinks he can use me to get back at your father for a decades-old revenge, he has another thing coming."

I stole something from him. Father's voice ran throughout my mind. A sick feeling twisted my stomach.

"Are you suicidal?" I hissed. "Not only are you trying to piss off *two* vampire kings but also waging a *war* with the witches over something that was hardly *their* fault to begin wi—"

"Not me," he said, slipping an arm over my shoulder before turning us straight to look at the man of the hour—*my father.* He was sitting on his throne at the very back of the room. The platform he was on was elevated and gave him a clear view of what was happening at the party. My stepmother was at his side, chatting with a guest, but Father seemed woefully disinterested. His eyes were searching the crowd...until they came to us. "Name goes a long way here, darling."

Not for the first time, fear clawed at my heart.

"War with the witches will bring you nothing," I whispered.

He let out a huff of a laugh.

"They started it," he said, rolling his shoulders to stand straight. "Those little parties you go to, the ones where you whore yourself out—"

"Watch yourself," I growled, stepping closer to him. I looked around us, hoping no one heard him. While the parties were not totally secret, they weren't something we discussed out in the open.

"The drugs were laced, princess," he said. My eyes snapped to him just in time to catch his wicked grin. "That's right. Instead of giving you a high, they just about killed a handful of *extremely* powerful vampires. In my mind, that calls for retaliation."

But from him? What gives him the right? Not only that, but he wasn't a savior on a white horse riding into town to save everyone. His motives were corrupted and just as ugly as his dead heart.

"Is that why you tried to get in?" I asked.

He let out a huff. "Let's call it a happy accident," he replied before taking another sip of his blood. "You still don't get it, do you?"

I looked to him for an answer but was interrupted as he waved down another couple in the sea of vampires. *Smile for the people, Aurelia.*

It was torture having to act like I was enjoying what he was putting me through, but with the weight of my father's eyes on me the entire time, I couldn't help but play my part. Laugh when I was supposed to. Insert a well-timed information snippet. Charm them. The works, until they were tired of us.

But the entire time, I couldn't get what he said out of my mind. *He is going to get me killed.*

Prince Icas had grown up much like me, in the comfort of his father's money. But all that did was give him the illusion that he could do anything. I, on the other hand, knew that he was walking a dangerous line, and he wouldn't be the only one to pay.

If he was using my father's name to wage a war on the witches, there would be no saving myself. It didn't matter that the drugs were laced—as horrible as it was, we all knew it was a risk. Working with witches always carried the same risks, just as it did when they worked with vampires.

But none of us could survive an all-out war.

Maybe I can use this. Instead of falling victim to his plan, maybe I could tell Father. Maybe it would be the key that I needed to finally get rid of this god-awful man.

I just needed to wait. Just needed to get more information. *I can do that.*

The chess game he was playing continued for what felt like hours. We moved across the room, mingling and chatting, until the center of the room cleared for the dancing.

It wasn't until then that I finally got a glimpse of how fucked his plan truly was and how bad it was for me.

"You're not the only one who's had trouble with them lately," Icas said as we were all pushed to the sides of the room so couples could dance. The sound of the live band filtered out the conversation from prying ears. But not mine.

"All I wanted was a little taste, really," the woman pouted and crossed her arms over her chest. "How was I supposed to know he was high-ranking in the coven? And it's not like I would have killed him if they didn't show up."

I grimaced at her words. *Disgusting.* How she even cornered a witch was a miracle, but actually killing one and escaping before the rest of their coven got involved?

Something else was going on here.

"We'll take care of it," Icas told her as he held me closer, his grip bruising my shoulder. "Consider it a wedding gift. *To the family.*"

Family. My family. I recognized the woman. I had seen her around the table at my father's gatherings previously.

Her bloodred lips twisted into a sinister smirk.

"Keep treating me this well, and I'll have no choice but to stick around longer."

Icas let out a laugh that chilled me to my bones. "Well, you're not the only one. Many people have already pledged their loyalty to Aurelia here. Where she goes, so do they. You'll be in good company."

Blood rushed to my ears, drowning out the music and voices around me. My feet became unsteady. And quicker than ever, the fire that was burning at my insides became an inferno.

My family. My mother's.

Were they really going to follow me? *They couldn't.* This wasn't in the plan. Father made it very clear that there would be no transfer of people.

He was stealing them. Getting on their good side with false promises and using my name for it.

Not even my name—my mother's. That's why they stuck around. Many of them making it clear even at our engagement announcement.

My mother's black-veined face hit me like a ton of bricks, reminding me just how much she gave up for them. For me.

Can I truly let them go like this? Knowing what he will do to them? Knowing they will turn into nothing but his slaves? Knowing that when Father finds out, there will be an all-out war between the families?

He wouldn't take this lightly.

Henry, the man with a weak knee who gave me a chance to end it all, would never make it. The vampires who had nothing to their name, being taxed into poverty, could offer nothing to him...What would he even do with them besides making them work off their "debts" to his family?

No.

I pushed him away. He had the audacity to look shocked.

"Aurelia—"

"He'll kill you," I warned. "You think just because you've concocted some batshit crazy plan, he won't see you are stealing our people?"

He placed his hands on his hips, puffed his chest, and gave me a sinister grin.

"They're coming for you, princess," he cooed. "You're the one who's stealing your own people. And right under daddy's nose."

"I never—"

"You didn't have to. Not when we have the next best thing," he said. He turned his head to the side just as a person strolled up to him. *Melia.* She stood by his side and bowed her head to him. "I think the princess is tired, don't you? Take her to her room."

She merely nodded and lifted her gaze to meet mine. The shock of it was like a slap in the face. *Since when did she ever listen to him?*

My eyes darted to my stepmother, who was still by Father's side at the head of the room. This time, it was her who looked at us. Her smile chilled me to my core.

She's going to get me killed.

The puzzle pieces started to click into place, each painting a more gruesome picture of what they had done right under my nose.

"You'd get your own wife killed?" I spat, turning back to him. The dress felt too tight. It constricted my movements and my breath. The longer it stayed on me, the more panicked I got.

"You're not my wife yet," he said with a shrug. "You made that very clear when you refused my blood bond. It could have saved you from all this, Aurelia."

He didn't get his way with me, so he decided to just...get me killed instead? But, of course, not before he could get what he needed out of me.

For once, the prince had outwitted me, and I could think of nothing other than the need to slaughter him.

But my hands were tied. I needed to retreat. Needed to get out of the stifling ballroom before I caused even more of a scene.

I needed to escape.

I backed away, running into the sides of the vampires around us. He tried to follow, but I held up my hand and turned away from him, beelining to the door.

VESPER

"Don't let her leave," Cedar said, the first words she spoke to me all day.

I jumped at them, but my eyes were already on the runaway princess as she pushed through the crowd.

I had been watching her the whole time. Watching as the vampire who had sunk his teeth into her neck paraded her around the room.

It caused a nasty feeling to swirl in my stomach. Especially when I caught her multiple times looking like she might just kill him right then and there.

It shouldn't have. Just like I should have never felt enough pity for her to intervene when they were in his room.

What the hell is wrong with me?

I couldn't wrap my brain around how I had gone from the good little contractor my family created to some sort of caring, lust-filled teenager that couldn't keep her hands off the royal vampire.

I hated it. *Hated her.* Hated how she made me feel. Hated how she was making me rethink things that had been taught to me for over a decade.

...but if that were the case, would you even have covered your tattoo when you got here? The small voice that whispered the damning

statement had been far too loud after the night of my failed assassination attempt.

Nothing in my training demanded it. Nor was it deemed appropriate by the secret organization's standards.

It was *supposed* to be visible at all times. But even if they assumed the general population wouldn't connect the dots between my tattoo and my job here, it was too risky.

And I valued my life too much for that. *Hers too, apparently.*

Enough to not kill her. Enough to not be able to take my eyes off her.

But in a situation like the gala, it wasn't strange. Others were watching too. The room was filled with vampires, highly important vampire councilmen, politicians, billionaires, some of whom I had only heard rumors about. All of them gathered to watch the new couple.

Those on the lowest rung tried to smoke them. Tried to hold their attention as long as possible before they were forced to be handed to another.

But she handled it. Maybe poorly at times, but it was likely no one else noticed and instead just saw the perfectly dolled-up, well-behaved vampire princess Aurelia wanted everyone to see.

"Don't tell me how to do my job," I grumbled to Cedar. We had strict orders to watch the perimeter, regardless of what our previous stations had been.

That's how Cedar and I got stuck together. But still, I hadn't been able to stop watching the princess.

Curiosity burned at me from the inside. I wanted to know what the bastard said to make her flee like that. It even angered me a bit, knowing what he had done not long before.

But I couldn't control the princess. If anything, her fleeing would help me. And no matter the confusing feelings and thoughts happening on the inside, I couldn't let myself continue to fuck up the job.

There were so many things at stake.

For me. For Tate. For my entire family.

"I said stop her," Cedar growled, her side brushing across mine. I didn't realize what she was doing until heat spread across my side, where her body met mine. Painful spots burst across my skin as a warning.

Panic ran through me, and I froze against her. *Could vampires smell magic?*

The place was packed, but there were so many in here at once, it was possible that the scents mingled together in a way that would hide it.

But it wasn't guaranteed.

"If you let her leave, you'll need to find yourself another contract," she said, her voice low. Finally, I met her gaze. Her face was cold and her eyes clear.

What the fuck? Was she saying what I th—

"What do you know?" I said in a harsh whisper, my hand shooting out to grip the side of her uniform. Now was not the time for this cryptic bullshit.

"Remember what I said in our room," she said in a low voice, her eyes traveling over my face.

If someone like yourself made it in here, what makes you think there aren't more?

Impossible. I had been here far too long not to catch anyone else, unless...*she isn't one, is she?*

It was all the push I needed. She had made the decision for me. *I needed to be the one to kill the princess.* And my chance was about to slip through my fingers.

I jerked away from her and rushed after the princess. She was nearing the exit far faster than I was, but she was constantly slowed by the vampires around her, all trying to chat as she passed.

Luckily, one grabbed her attention for a bit too long, and I was able to slip my arm around her waist. She shot me a look and tried to push me off, but I ignored her.

"Excuse us," I said, sending a smile to the vampire she was talking to. "But isn't it a crime that the princess hasn't danced to a single song yet?"

He merely laughed and waved us off, but as I tried to drag her to the dance floor, the princess pulled us to a standstill.

"What do you think you're doing?" she hissed. "I'm trying to leave this godforsaken party."

"Because of the prince?" I asked her. "Did he say anything? Is he the one pushing you to leave?"

All the impatience seemed to leave her body at my questions, and she looked up at me with a raised brow. There was a tenseness to her I'd never seen before.

Almost like she'd seen a ghost.

"What's happening?" she asked. Slowly, her eyes started to move around the crowd until they fell on the vampire in question. My eyes followed hers. He was staring at us, and next to him were Aurelia's handmaiden and her stepsister.

That doesn't look right.

I leaned down to whisper in her ear. "Something feels off. Stay with me for a bit. Somewhere visible."

I looked back to where Cedar had been standing guard, but she was gone, and a new person was in her place.

Alarm bells went off in my head. *It couldn't be her, could it? If so, why would she give me a heads-up?*

There was no time to waste. Aurelia was getting more and more impatient by the second, and the more I looked around us, the more it felt like everyone was staring. And there was no way that I could make out which stares were the ones of a true enemy or of just another curious onlooker.

You should leave her, a voice in my head said as Aurelia tugged at my hand in a poor excuse to get free. She could have distanced herself from me with minimal effort, but there was something about the situation that rang differently to her as well.

If I left her and something bad happened, I would be absolved of my duty. I could leave and never look back, see my little brother, and then...*what?*

Father would no doubt hear about how she was murdered and sooner or later would find out what I knew. He wouldn't be happy if I showed up at the house after that. Better a runaway than a child who failed her mission.

But he wouldn't be the only one looking for me.

The secret society that ran our lives wouldn't like the information I had. Wouldn't like how easily I could topple their organization. It didn't matter if they kept their head people a secret. I knew too much and gave them too little.

But more importantly...there was something deep inside me that caused me to pause. Something I had never felt before. Something I didn't want to give a name to for fear it might actually become real.

Enough.

She had no time to protest, and I pulled us both to the dance floor. People cleared the way, my action gaining us attention.

The head guard would no doubt give me shit about my actions later. *A guard dancing with a princess right before she is about to give herself to the prince?*

But looking at the stares from others around us, they didn't seem all that offended. If anything, my actions amused them.

Good. Think that way. It didn't matter that they looked down on the human guard attempting to get her last few minutes with the princess. In their minds, this was probably the most exciting part of the night.

I faced her and pulled her to me, trying my best to replicate what I had seen the others do, taking her hand in one of mine and placing my other hand on her waist.

I hadn't touched her like this since the time in the closet, and the dancing wasn't even sexual...So why did it make my heart race?

The skin of her hand was soft—softer than even the velvet accents on her dress. When I pulled her to me, I didn't realize just how close we would need to be to dance. Her face was on my chest, but when she looked up at me, she felt close enough to kiss.

It took my breath away to see her so close in the bright light.

"Did I forget to mention I can't dance?" I said after she raised a brow at my attempt to position us.

She held my gaze for a moment before she forced a smile across her face. It was a little strained—no doubt she still wanted to escape whatever unique torture this gala was.

But it was enough to cause the tension in my shoulders to ease just a bit.

"I'll guess I'll just have to lead then, won't I?" she teased, repositioning our hands. "Try to not embarrass yourself too much."

I didn't want to admit how her sass caused my heart to jump, but her knowing glance told me she had heard it herself, giving me no choice but to come to terms with the fact that the spoiled princess actually caused me to react in *those* ways.

Her hand slid across my back and pulled me closer to her, while the other held our intertwined hands up for all to see.

She then pulled us into the crowd, her strength overpowering mine. I had no choice but to follow her steps as she swayed to the music.

I had no idea what I was doing. My foot collided with hers more than once, but each time she was able to expertly redirect us and make the dancing look smooth.

After a while, it was easy to lean into her. Easier to hold her gaze. Rewarding when a smirk spread across her lips.

She is enjoying herself.

In a bizarre twist of events, the princess seemed to actually be pleased with my company.

"Does this mean you're on my side?" she asked as she spun me around. A move normally reserved for the more femme partner. A move that caused heat to spread across my cheeks.

I didn't chance looking at the others to see their reactions, trying my best to keep whatever bubble we were in for ourselves.

"There are no sides here, princess," I muttered when she pulled me back to her. "If you attempt to dip me, I will leave."

She threw her head back and let out a twinkling laugh. *Is this a show? Or is she truly enjoying herself?*

A light feeling swirled in my chest and chased all the other anxiety-inducing thoughts away.

My job was to keep us here for the time being. Keep us visible. That was the only way we would be safe.

But, after a while, it felt less like I was trying to protect her and more like I was the overly confident guard who just wanted her chance to dance with the princess.

"And leave me all by myself?" she asked with an exaggerated pout. "Maybe you don't take your job very seriously."

"If I didn't, I wouldn't be dancing with you," I reminded her with a fake smile.

She let out a tsk of annoyance, but it was more teasing in nature than actual dissatisfaction.

"Very terribly at that," she said, and twirled us both. "Do humans not do this or something?"

The song was bleeding into the next, the band no doubt seeing how much the princess was enjoying herself and wanting to keep the light mood going. Or maybe they also enjoyed the little bit of scandal they were witnessing firsthand.

"*Rich* humans do," I replied, looking down at her with a smile. "Unfortunately, my humble upbringing didn't get me invited to these things."

"No," she said before leaning in, dropping her voice low. "But they sure taught you how to handle a sword, didn't they?"

"Among other things," I murmured, finally letting my eyes wander the ballroom.

That was until, on our third circle of the ballroom, I met her fiancé's eyes. He was standing next to a vampire who was talking his ear off, but his attention was on us. Though, if I were being honest, I wasn't sure it ever left. His gaze was narrowed, his jaw tight. If he held his glass any tighter, it would be on the floor, shattered.

Only second to his was her father's gaze. But his wasn't one of anger. He was too poised for that. His anger lay hidden there, behind his reddening eyes.

We are embarrassing him.

Maybe one song would have been fine, but I was hogging her, and people were noticing.

Cedar was the next person I saw. She was back in our original position, and when our gazes met, she gave me a quick nod.

Is that some kind of signal? Are we safe?

But seeing how the other high-ranking vampires looked at me, it only felt like I had put us in more danger.

"Was it worth it?" she asked in a whisper. "The disdain of both my fiancé and my father?"

I swallowed thickly before looking down at her with the sweetest smile I could maintain.

"To keep you safe?" I asked. "I would give my life for yours, princess. Shouldn't you know that by now?"

If the princess could blush, her cheeks would have been burning. *I take it as another win.*

AURELIA

At first, it would seem that nothing was off about the room.

The bed was perfectly made.

The cart of blood had been replenished.

There was a light smell of lavender from the maid's cleaning supplies, but that wasn't out of the ordinary.

Nothing should have tipped me off. But there was a certain aura around the place. I felt it as I walked down the hallway, like it was calling to me. Warning me that I was about to experience something horrific.

I've come to recognize the aura. After years of encountering the same thing, I no longer had to guess who would've been inside. I had come to expect something like this. Especially when I had been a bit too outspoken.

And then I saw it. The birdcage that I had so carefully placed near the window had its cover torn off. The cage was empty. The door had been left open, but there was no mistaking what happened.

The blood and feathers left behind told me what they had done.

Mine. She not only took what was mine but showed me exactly what she would do to me if I wasn't careful.

Stepmother had always been creative with her cruelty. Sure, she never shied away from putting a hand on me, but she knew other ways to inflict pain. Pain that would linger. Bruises and cuts healed, but the cruelty of her mind games remained, the painful memories popping up every single time we crossed paths.

She had waited long enough that our meeting about the prince was far from my mind. I'm sure my less-than-stellar performance at the gala wasn't any help, but I knew what this was truly about.

She was reminding me just how trapped I was here. That I wouldn't be able to fight back against whatever plan they had concocted.

One wrong move, and I would be just like the bird in the cage. She easily killed the poor thing, but there was no telling what she would do to make my life miserable.

Fresh pain stabbed my chest and intertwined with the anger that had long since been festering just under the surface. *I hate them.* Ever since they came to my palace, taking over the place of my beloved mother...I just knew what their motives were.

They thought they could take over for her. They thought the people in our family would just accept them with open arms.

But they didn't. And instead, they were haunted by the ghost of her glory, just like I was. And to them, that was a threat. *I* was a threat to their magical rags to riches, so they locked me inside a gilded cage, only to sell me off to the highest bidder when they got the chance.

Melia's opening of the door behind me had my attention drifting, pulling me back to the real world. But the red haze stayed, clouding my vision.

"Oh dear," she murmured. "Not another one. What ticked them off this time? Don't they have anything better to do than kill poor birds?"

I turned to her, but had no intention of forcing a smile. The anger was too potent for that. It was like a deadly virus, destroying my insides and leaving a trail of destruction as it coursed through my veins.

"Like you don't know?" I asked, unable to keep the venom

from my voice. "Like you probably weren't standing out there keeping guard while they did this? What, too afraid to even peek in and take a look at their mess?"

She grimaced and placed a gentle hand on my arm, as if her simple gesture wouldn't enrage me even more. How was she still playing this game?

"I never had a choice," she whispered. "Much like you, princess—"

"Don't try to get pity from me," I growled and slapped her hand away. "Drop the act."

"I don't tell them everything," she said quickly, her eyes darting around the room. *To escape?* The thought of her trying to run away from me only brought the monster lingering inside me closer to the front.

"And you think that's better?" I asked with a bitter laugh and turned to her.

I wanted to end her. Wanted to get back at her for the way she tried to fool me into trusting her just so she could give it all to those fuckers.

I was *tired* of people trying to control me. Tired of being the scapegoat.

I wanted to live. I wanted to be free. *I don't want to die.*

"I understand, princess. The cards you've been dealt haven't been easy..." Her voice trailed off. "If you just cooperate with them, they will make this much easier on you. It's true, the prince has been trying to pull Castle family members into his, but that can only help you. Don't you see what he's doing is only for your benef—"

A hard slap echoed throughout the room, accompanied by a sting against the back of my hand. The red that had clouded my vision had come on so fast, I hadn't even been able to make out my movements until Melia was staring at me, shock abundant on her face.

"Stop talking," I warned, taking a step closer to her with trembling hands. I looked her up and down before letting out a huff.

"My benefit? You know he is using me as a scapegoat? Once Father finds out, he will *kill* me. And all you've done was help him."

"Princess," she murmured, her eyes filling with bloodred tears. "You're his prized possession, the king would never—"

"You don't know shit about what your king will do to me. Stay out of my affairs," I spat. Was she truly that blind? While she was working for them, she never saw what they were truly up to? I didn't believe it. "Don't comment on them. Don't even *look* at me when someone else is near, god forbid you accidentally see something you feel the need to speak about."

She took a step back and opened her mouth to speak again, but a knock on the door behind her caused her to pause.

Go away. I wanted to scream at the door. The need for blood was clawing at my insides. I *needed* to make someone pay for this. Needed to make the world stop caving in.

"Announce yourself," I growled at the door when no one spoke.

"I was sent to give blood." Vesper's muffled voice came from behind the closed door.

Relief shouldn't have exploded through me like it did.

"Come in," I said, straightening myself before sending a glare to Melia. "You're dismissed."

She paused before turning and heading to the door. Vesper gave her a glance and held the door open for her when she realized the handmaiden was leaving.

Her gaze followed her as she left, then she turned to me. Well, not me—the bloodied bird cage behind me. She silently closed the door and crossed the space...and went right past me.

"Don't you fucking—"

"That was some slap," she said. I turned to her. I hadn't heard her waiting behind the door. *I hadn't heard her at all.* Had I been so crazed by the bloodlust that I had been so unaware of my surroundings? I had always heard her. Always smelled her.

Reel it in, I hissed at myself, but it only made the monster inside angrier.

I watched in muted surprise as she slowly picked up each and every one of the feathers that had fallen to the ground before placing them back into the cage.

Stop it. I wanted to scream at her. *Stop fucking touching them!*

My entire body was shaking. I couldn't stop it. Anger was running through me so violently...but there was something else. Something else that had been there since the first night that I got on my knees and bared my neck to the prince.

It was becoming stronger. Taking over my body like a tidal wave, and it felt as heavy as lead. It was weighing me down, threatening to pull me into the floorboards and never let me out again.

Stop it. Stop it. Stop it. It was mine, you can't touch them!

But the words wouldn't come out through the knot in my throat. *Please don't.* I wanted to beg her to stop as she reached for the cover that had been thrown to the ground. I didn't want to look anymore. I didn't want to see anyone else destroy the one thing I owned. But with more gentleness than I had ever seen from her, she carefully covered the bird cage from view.

Please stop. Bloodred tears filled my eyes. *Please stop being kind.*

My fragile psyche couldn't handle it. I wanted her to lunge at me again. Take me out while I was vulnerable. Destroying the cage and all that was left in it would have been easier to stomach.

But instead, she had doused my anger with ice-cold water, leaving only that stored, heavy feeling that fought to be let out.

She lifted the cage with one hand and propped it against her shoulder, still not looking at me. She was searching the ground for any other feather that might have fallen.

"I'll take care of this and come back for your blood," she said, turning to me. Her face was unreadable and not at all like how it looked when she was trying to murder me.

"You weren't sent for blood." My voice was hoarse.

She paused as she passed me, her honey eyes meeting mine. *Fight me. Make this easier on me. Please.*

But she did none of that.

"Wait for me."

And with that, she left me alone in my cold room. The darkness lingering around my mind chose that moment to crowd in on me.

Wait for her?

I wanted to follow her. Wanted to tell her how pitiful it would be for *me* to wait for her.

But my feet couldn't move. I sat down right there on the floor and did exactly as she ordered.

I waited.

VESPER

The dumpster was on the floor just above the guards' quarters.

I didn't let the irony get past me that the family thought less of the guards than they did their own trash. Or that they kept most of it inside until it was ready to be taken out to the landfill once a week.

Another thing about their image.

They didn't want their trash to be seen by outsiders. They wanted everyone to see their picture-perfect palace and ignore the ugliness that lay rotting within.

Just like the princess. I paused after throwing the bird cage into the trash can along with the feathers. One of them got stuck to my uniform, and when I picked it up, the image of Aurelia's troubled expression flashed across my mind.

I had never seen her act like she did. Even when I was trying to kill her.

She was unrestrained. Panicking. Upset.

Something told me it wasn't just the bird that had made her like that, but maybe it was her breaking point.

Just another thing I shouldn't be doing.

I shouldn't have wandered up to her room to check on her. I

should have been plotting how to kill her. Maybe that had been the plan at first, but when I heard her voice through the door, how angry and pained it sounded...something switched in me.

As days—*no, hours*—passed at Princess Aurelia's side, the voice that reminded me to kill her became more like a whisper and the one that had me pitying her—it was like a siren.

"You did well." An all-too-familiar voice came from my right.

With a sigh, I turned to face Cedar. Her back was against the far wall, her eyes watching the door to her right. Her arms were crossed over her chest, but there was something about the tenseness of her face that told me she was less relaxed than she'd like to show.

"Meaning we kept her from dying?" I asked and held the feather carefully in my palm.

Cedar's eyes cut to mine, a small smirk playing at her lips. *I hate that smirk.*

"All you, friend," she said. "But it's not over."

"And you know that how?" I asked and walked toward her. When I reached her, I looked out the open door and down the hallway. Not a soul in sight.

"Can't tell you. But what I can tell you is that if you let this marriage happen, she's going to die," she said.

The seriousness of her threat caught me off guard, but there was another chill that ran through me when I thought about the possibility that the princess waiting up alone in her room would cease to exist.

"The prince doesn't treat her well, but he would be stupid to kill her," I muttered under my breath.

My heart sped up and panic had my chest tightening. Imagining the princess lying on the ground, cold, and covered in blood shouldn't have been as hard as it was.

Fuck. Damn it...What's wrong with me?

"The prince isn't capable of killing her," she said. "It's closer to her than that."

Slowly, I turned to face her. *Witches are dangerous.* I'd known that the entire time I worked with them...but never met one with as much power as she seemed to have.

"If you won't tell me how you know, then at least tell me what," I said.

Her eyes shot to the side, apprehension flashing across her features.

"He wasn't smart enough to come up with the idea to off her, but there are people beside her who were. People who hate her. And because of them, she will be blamed for something the prince will do. He will use her as a scapegoat."

Was that why he was meeting with her...stepsister? I wouldn't put it past them, but even *that* seemed cruel of them.

"You're a seer," I said. "That's how you know all this."

She rolled her eyes and let out a huff.

"Okay, I get it, you don't *want* to save the princess," she said, her tone annoyed. "But you will regret it if you don't."

"How do I even know you're telling the truth?" I asked, shifting closer to her. "What if this is you just trying to get me killed so you're the one who can off her yourself?"

She shook her head and gave me a sympathetic pat on the shoulder. Heat raced through me and up my neck. I hissed and sent her a glare.

Fuck her and her fucking magic. If I ever got back to my washed-up town, the first stop would be the bar to ask about why the hell Cedar's magic was as painful and potent as it was.

"Don't want the princess getting a look at that before it's time," she said before pausing, a contemplative look crossing her face. "She was never my job, Vesper."

Just as she was about to leave, I cleared my throat. She looked back at me with a questioning gaze.

I held up the lone feather for her.

"Given your *immense powers,* I think you can help me with this."

A true smile spread across her face at my sarcasm-laced words.

"Oooh, now you're just trying to butter me up," she teased with a light laugh. "But it'll work. I'm a sucker for compliments. Give me a little more, and I may just spill more about your girlfriend's future."

"So you *are* a seer," I said as I dropped the feather carefully into her hands.

"You and I both know that I don't need to be a seer to know the future."

Her knowing look caused a shiver to run through me.

Aurelia was still where I left her.

I had almost expected her to vanish. Maybe have another tantrum in the fountain.

I would have much preferred that instead of the way she was crouched on the floor. Her hair fell from all sides. The all-black dress she wore earlier that day blended in with the darkness of the room.

It reminded me too much of a child trying to hide from the monsters in the dark. It was pitiful and made me feel things I shouldn't.

I shouldn't have wanted to comfort the princess. I shouldn't have gone out of my way to throw away something that was causing her pain.

I want to save her.

I shouldn't have come to see her in the first place.

"How did you know?" she asked from her crouched position.

"Know what?" I asked and stalked closer, scared that one wrong move might flip another switch in her. She seemed very much like a wounded animal at that moment. Scared, unable to move, and just waiting for her perfect chance to attack.

"You weren't sent to give blood," she said. "I never asked for you."

She turned her head to the side, her bloodred eyes glowing in the darkness. Her face was stoic, but there was such a heaviness to the aura around her that no matter what mask she put on, the emotions she was feeling began to suffocate the room.

"Would you believe me if I told you I just had a feeling?" I asked. Her eyes narrowed.

I didn't really understand it either, nor did I believe it was fate drawing me up those stairs. I'd like to believe it was some pattern my conscious mind didn't fully recognize that had told my subconscious to get my ass upstairs before something bad happened.

But, in truth, I had no idea.

One moment I was sitting on my bed, decompressing after my shift, and the next I just felt the need to check up on the princess.

"If this is your way of telling me you're in love with me, I'm not interested."

Her bluntness caused a shocked laughter to spill from my lips.

"You're going through a hard time," I said, digging into my pocket for the magical item Cedar gave me. "The least you could do is tone down the attitude for, I dunno, a few minutes?"

I lifted it and showed it to her. The one bloodied feather clean and glowing slightly in the darkness. Cedar had fastened a vine-like silver chain with her magic and some spare scraps in the garbage room.

Not a good gift for a spoiled princess who was used to the biggest and shiniest jewels on this planet, but hopefully it would stop her from making that pained expression she was staring at me with.

I closed the few steps between us and placed it in her outstretched hand.

"I thought I smelled magic on you," she said, her eyes cutting to mine. "Are you harboring a witch in my palace?"

I let out a huff and shook my head.

"I would get rid of them if I knew how to," I admitted. "But they did say that you were in danger. That the prince and someone close to you were going to use you as a scapegoat. Is that true?"

It felt weird to tell her the truth. But it was also freeing in a way.

Her eyes searched my face. It felt different that time. Not in a criticizing type of way, but like she was desperately searching for an answer that I couldn't give her.

"I have it handled," she said and took a look at the feather in her hand. "Are you sure you still don't want in on the deal? This may be your last chance."

This may be my last chance. Maybe she had something planned? Had Cedar gotten it wrong?

I wouldn't be surprised if she did. Aurelia was cunning. I saw that much with what she had tried to do with the magical poison.

But would it work?

For some reason, I wanted it to.

"I don't want your father's head," I whispered. "He holds no value to me. But you could kill him if you wanted."

She let out a scoff. "Me? Kill Father?" She let out a bitter laugh. "What makes you say such a *stupid* thing?"

"I don't think it's stupid. I think you could, and I think your people would thank you." Another truth. One that was even more dangerous than the first.

Her reddened eyes met mine. I almost felt bad for the way hope lit them up. But it was diminished quickly.

"There is a reason why I worked to get on his good side all these years," she whispered. "After Mother died, I fought him—almost too much. And it cost me. You think the people are on my side? Maybe, but the people he employed certainly are not. They fear him enough to do whatever. Even torture their own princess."

I couldn't hear it. I didn't want to. I was afraid of what it would change in me.

"I can't help you with this, princess," I whispered.

She gave me a quick nod, all hope in her expression crumbled in seconds. Then, she turned her back to me.

"Leave, then. I have a lot to do."

I didn't want to, but my feet moved me to the door. I wanted to ask her to tell me what she knew. I wanted her to ask me to help. To ask me to save her.

Because, at this point, I'm not confident I could say no.

But there were no more words shared between us. Not as I opened and shut her bedroom door. And not as I walked down the dark hallway in silence, only for it to be broken by the sound of Aurelia's frustrated scream and the muted shattering of glass against the wall.

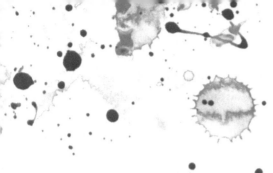

Aurelia

I was going to die.

It became clearer and clearer as the day of my wedding got closer.

I had no plan. At least, not one that would save me.

Vesper's words had been on a near-constant repeat in my head since she uttered them. *Why don't you kill him?*

Why didn't I kill him? It was a laughable notion to even entertain the thought of *me* killing someone like him.

She didn't understand what I went through after my mother's death. Didn't understand what he put me through to remind me that *he* was the one in charge.

My mother told me to stay fierce. That was exactly what I did, until it was beaten and starved out of me.

And most of all, I wanted to *live*. I didn't want to escape here as a corpse. I wanted to *rule*. I wanted to *thrive*. And nowhere in my mind was risking my life to murder my father a part of that plan.

So I needed something else. I needed to level the playing field.

My last-ditch effort had to have been the most humiliating yet, but I had to do *something*. Even if it meant relying on that spy.

"They are worse than my father will ever be," I said to the female vampire who had been a part of my family for the last decade. Eldra was her name, and she came with her husband in search of my mother. She was already dead by the time they arrived, but that didn't stop them from joining.

They worked in one of Father's many factories, hardly making ends meet.

Which brought us to our current problem.

"But *you* are there, princess," she answered with a kind smile. "We believe in *you*. Sure, maybe it will be hard in the beginning, but you will be there."

Bullshit. Maybe if there was even an ounce of truth in her words, there had to have been much more than that belief to have her do something so drastic.

"How much money did he offer you?" I asked, cutting to the chase.

She looked down at the floor, shame crossing her features.

"More than I had ever seen in my life, princess," she said. "My husband and I, we are tired. We would do anything for you, for your mother...but there are only so many more years we can handle this work."

I swallowed thickly, trying not to grind my teeth.

Hers was the tenth family I was talking to, and all of them offered something different.

Prince Icas had actually managed to do something right.

Not all the vampires he recruited to his family had been because of the witches, though many of the more powerful ones with money of their own were. The smaller ones were easy.

Money.

Bigger houses.

A chance at a family.

He was giving the people what they wanted. *A life.* Even if it was a lie, these vampires had been living in such horrid conditions under my father's reign that they couldn't help but believe him. Even if there was only a slim chance that what he said would actually come true, they would take it.

And I couldn't convince them otherwise.

Many had said the same thing. That their loyalty was to me. But when pushed, it became clear what their true desires were.

And it never had anything to do with me.

"I'm sorry, princess," she said when she noticed my silence. "Really, if there was any other—"

"I understand," I retorted with a forced smile. "Please don't apologize to me." *Even if it means my death.* "You're dismissed."

She hesitated, looking behind me at where Melia stood, before turning and leaving the back garden where I had all of them meet me.

There were only a few places in the palace where I could get away with these meetings. An overgrown garden, a dried-up fountain, or the edge of the property where the woods were so dense it looked like night even in the middle of the day.

The fountain held too many memories, and if I was caught around the edge of the property, the stepbitches and Prince Icas might try to tell Father it was because I was attempting to run away.

But I was running out of options.

"How many more?" I asked, not turning to Melia. I hated even looking at her, and my hands still itched to cut her throat. Fraternizing with the enemy wasn't on my bucket list. It was shameful at best, but again, I would do just about anything to get out of the palace alive.

"Fifty-three, princess," she replied.

I pursed my lips, unable to find the words.

I couldn't tell what was worse—the anger and helplessness the prince had invoked in me since the gala or how easy it was becoming to accept my death.

I didn't know how fast the prince's plan would work. Maybe his father would try to keep me safe from my father for some time. Maybe I would live there with them for months—years—before my father enacted his revenge for stealing from him.

Or, in order to save themselves from war, they might just give me up entirely once he found out.

"Get the guards to bring the car," I ordered her.

She shifted behind me, her pause calling my attention to her. She was looking at her hands as they wrung the cloth of her dress.

"They will kill you even sooner if you try to leave," she whispered.

I couldn't stop the smirk from pulling at my lips. *Is she done acting now?*

"I'm not leaving," I said. "I have a party tonight. One last one before I get married. Father and the others must know how important keeping these relationships is, no?"

She didn't fight me on it, even if it looked like she wanted to. Probably remembering what I was going to do to her the other night before Vesper walked in.

Her gift weighed heavily on my chest, hidden under my clothes.

I wasn't truly mad that there was a witch in my palace. It would have been stupid to think there weren't any. But Vesper knew them, and if she knew them...

I almost wish she'd just grow some balls and end me herself.

It would be much more entertaining than waiting for the others to do it. But every time she was near me, she kept giving me *that face.* The one that told me she didn't actually want to be there. That she longed to do something other than sink a knife into my chest.

And then she had to go and give me that fucking present.

It was probably the most thoughtful thing anyone has ever given me. Maybe even more so than the animal it came from.

It made me want to keep her. Made me wish that somehow I could stay in the palace with Vesper at my side, keeping her tied to me until the end of her short human life.

She was so...uncontrollable.

I thought I prided myself on being the uncontrollable one, playing my father while truly doing whatever I wanted.

But it was her. I might have been able to order her around on occasion, but there was no telling what she would do.

And I love it. I wanted to control that side of her.

My hand wrapped around the feather that heated softly against my skin.

One more try. One more try, and maybe I'll still have the chance to bind her to me forever.

I was surprised they even let me leave the compound. With the little mouse, especially.

I half expected them to stop me right before I got into the car, but I guess all of them knew just how important it was that I kept up appearances.

"Don't assume that I'll give you a repeat performance," Vesper said, crossing her arms over her chest and sending me a look.

She had been cautious since that night, never letting her words hold too much venom, her eyes always watching for my reaction.

How much does she know?

Apparently enough to ask me if I truly was going to die...but could she tell how close I was to utterly failing?

I had been able to pull myself out of almost every problem I'd had up until the moment the prince cornered me at the gala. But I was floundering and desperately trying to hold on to whatever sanity I had, even though it was hanging by a very thin, worn thread.

"Oh come on," I said, dropping my voice into a low purr. "Don't try and pretend like you aren't salivating at the idea of tasting my cunt again."

As if to prove my point, she swallowed thickly. The smallest coat of pink stained her cheeks.

Ah, how I wish to keep you for just a bit longer.

She had been such a refreshing break in the constant downpour that had been my life. With her, I didn't have to think about the prince or my duties to the palace.

I was just *existing*. And what a relief it was to just *be*.

"Is this a part of your plan?" she asked, doubt heavy in her voice.

"I didn't expect us to go to another one of these with your wedding so close."

"Don't remind me," I said with a scowl. "But yes. It's a part of my...plan."

More like a final effort. I wished I had any semblance of a plan.

"Please tell me it doesn't involve that *daddy* vampire." The word "daddy" was coated in disgust.

For the first time in days, I let out a real laugh. But instead of lifting the immeasurable weight off my chest, it just made it tighter. Like it was a reminder that this might be the last time I ever let out such a genuine laugh ever again.

The car came to a stop, and I gave her a halfhearted smile before stepping out.

No, it wasn't the daddy vampire. It was another vampire entirely. One more powerful than him, and one who could kill me in a second.

And she was waiting for me, right at the entrance.

It had taken more than a few bribes to get the human guards to send a message to her, but it worked.

Atlas Nox stood before me in all her glory. Long black hair was pinned at the sides and flowed down her back. Her usually hazel eyes had just a hint of red in them. And her full lips were pulled into a smirk.

She wore a black button-up that dipped low on her chest with matching black pants topped with a bloodred coat with black swirls meticulously sewn in. I think I even caught some small jewels shimmering in the dim light.

She didn't partake in families like most vampires of her status did. Instead, she decided to keep them as small clans, but had them dispersed around the country. Something reminiscent of the past. No one truly knew how many people pledged their allegiance to her or how big her army could get.

That was a part of her power.

I was lucky to even catch her in this part of the country.

Her face lit up as I came closer, and in an instant, her arms were around me, pulling me to her. I inhaled deeply, letting myself find even just the littlest bit of comfort in her embrace.

"Aurelia! How long has it been? You look stunning as usual."

"Atlas," I greeted and pulled away with a smile. "I would have gotten in contact sooner if I could have."

Her hands squeezed my shoulders.

"Yes, well, I know your father is—*oh*, who are you?" Her attention was immediately pulled to Vesper as she walked up behind us.

"A guard," she answered, though there was a tone to her voice that Atlas caught right away. In an instant, the happy-go-lucky version she had shown was gone, and in its place was a stare that made even my skin crawl.

"A plaything," I corrected her, and placed my hand on Atlas's hip. "Shall we?"

She gave Vesper a lingering glance before nodding and plastering another one of those brilliant smiles on her face.

"After you, my love."

VESPER

I hated that vampire.

Something was off about her, and I had an inkling of suspicion she was insane.

There was something about her aura that told me to stay away from her. She was dangerous. Maybe a little unhinged. Plus, she glared at me the entire time we were together.

If this was the princess's plan, then she must have really run out of options.

"I have no plans to start a war with your old man," she said, leaning back in the armchair. She had a glass of blood in her hand and picked it up in the most annoyingly elegant way.

The house wasn't as crowded that night, but Aurelia had still found us a more private room on the second floor. The music and laughter could be heard through the walls as they floated up the stairs, but not enough to impede their conversation.

"It's not war," Aurelia stated matter-of-factly, and took a sip of her blood as well. Well, not a sip...more like a gulp. *When was the last time she had blood?*

A better question was, *Why am I worried about it?* But since the incident with the bird, I couldn't *stop* worrying about her.

The last shred of self-control I had was waning pretty fast. I'd spent all night in bed just thinking of the various exits Aurelia *might* be taking. Anything I could do to help.

That was the dangerous thing—I couldn't stop myself from wanting to get involved. The only thing holding me back was her. If she even so much as *asked*, I would drop everything to help.

"Stealing his only blood daughter?" she asked with a raised brow. "Sounds like war to me."

"The correct term would be kidnapping, and it wouldn't be true because I would go willingly," she replied, crossing her legs and giving her a pointed look.

Atlas gave her an infuriating smirk in response.

"*Stealing*, my love," she corrected. "Anything his power touches is seen as his property."

The grinding of my teeth caught Atlas's attention, and a low growl rumbled in her chest.

"Should she even be listening to this?" she asked and placed her cup not so gently on the side table next to her. "How do you know she's not some spy for your father?"

Aurelia let out a huff of laughter.

"Because I tried to kill her," I answered for her.

This caused Atlas to pause. Then, slowly, she snuck back into her chair, a feral smile spreading across her face.

"Perfect!" She clapped her hands together so loudly it caused me to jump. "*She* can kidnap you then! No one would ever expect it!"

Aurelia's eyes darted to me, looking me up and down before shaking her head.

"I already tried to enlist her help," she said. "And she refused."

Atlas gave me a look that suddenly had me wanting to defend myself.

"You wanted me to kill a vampire king instead," I said under my breath. "That's not *helping*. That's a suicide mission."

Atlas clicked her tongue, "Yeah, see, that probably wouldn't work. If she couldn't finish it with you, I doubt she's very proficient at her job."

I'm going to kill her.

I reached for the sword on my back, ready to unsheathe it, when Aurelia cleared her throat.

"Enough picking on her," she said before looking straight at Atlas. "You may not want a war, but you have never given up a chance to get back at my father for what happened back then. What changed?"

I relaxed but kept my eyes on Atlas.

"She's talking about when he went around trying to steal my clans, and when they didn't join his family, he murdered them, if you were curious, hunter," Atlas said and lifted her glass in an almost-toast to me. "Something I bet you understand too well."

"I'm not a hunter," I growled low. *I hate that word.* And the connotations that went with it.

"Sorry, sorry," she said with a laugh. "What is it you call yourselves nowadays? Contractors? Semantics, really."

"*Atlas*," Aurelia warned.

She gave her a sheepish grin as an apology before her expression turned serious.

"There's been a rogue," she announced, her eyes locked on the leftover blood in her glass. "Well, multiple. We thought it was just one, but it turns out it's multiple."

"You don't deal with rogues," Aurelia pointed out.

"No," Atlas said through gritted teeth. "But after getting the attention of the human police, they started investigating the clans. Once the council heard, they began imposing restrictions on us."

I perked up at this.

"The rogue wouldn't happen to be down in Northern California, would it?" I asked.

Both of their heads turned in my direction.

"The first." Atlas placed her elbows on the couch and leaned forward. "Then up here. Then in Vancouver. Then all the way in Great Falls. In a matter of days, hundreds were killed. There's no way it's just one. Let me guess, your hunters have been notified?"

I sucked my teeth, unsure just how much I wanted to tell them. Aurelia was staring at me with an unreadable expression.

"The police haven't been able to keep it under control," I managed to say after a few moments of silence.

"What restrictions?" she asked, turning her attention back to Atlas.

"No more new clan members. They're watching us like hawks."

"I won't be a new clan member. I would just be—"

"They already killed ten of my people for going against it," she stated. For a second, it looked like there was real remorse on her face. "I really want to, but I can't. Not until this dies down, and when that happens—"

"It'll be too late," Aurelia whispered.

"Anything else," Atlas said, her eyebrows pulling together. For a moment, it looked like she truly cared about the princess. "Money. Safe passage. But you cannot stay with us. Not when we're already being attacked. I'm sorry, my love."

Aurelia gave her a forced smile before standing up.

"I appreciate the offer," she said. "Maybe one day I'll be able to take you up on it."

She cast me a glance and motioned for me to follow her out. *That's it? She's just going to leave?*

Panic started to rise in me. *Was this all that she had planned? And since it didn't work, now what?*

I didn't want to think of what this meant for the princess.

Atlas was up and following me as soon as I moved.

She was close. Close enough to alarm me...until her hand brushed across mine.

I shot her a look, but she motioned for me to remain quiet by putting a finger to her lips. I looked down at my hand to see a pitch-black medallion with a carving on it. Something that looked like a family crest.

I had seen it before, when my witch contact, Levana, was discussing magical relics with me. It was cool to the touch and smelled nothing like magic. If I hadn't known what it was, I might never have guessed a witch made it.

It was a communicator. Quickly, I stuffed it in my pocket and, without casting another glance at her, followed the princess out of the room.

"Think about my offer," she called after me. "I'll be here whenever you need me."

Aurelia let out a huff, not at all slowing her pace in front of me.

"That would do me no good," she muttered.

"What's the next plan?" I asked, speeding up to walk by her side.

"No plan, little mouse," she replied, sending me a bitter smile. "That was my last shot."

My hand shot out to grab her shoulder and turn her to look at me. *No.* There had to be something else.

The Princess Aurelia I had come to know during my short time here wouldn't just lie down and take it.

"Ask me to help you," I all but begged. "Anything."

I couldn't watch her do this to herself.

"Kill him," she said. "That's the only way. There are more of you, right? Use them. Whatever you need to do."

I gritted my teeth, trying desperately to stop myself from saying what I wanted.

The prophecy made you a target, princess. If it gets out that I abandoned my duty and am not actively trying to kill you, they will send someone else in a heartbeat.

While the prophecy dictated that I would be the one to end the Castle family, the secret organization that ruled us all would overlook it if it meant that they could still get the desired outcome.

Her death.

The prophecy was merely a tool to keep our families in line. To keep us feeling important. It became clear as soon as I stepped into the palace that this wasn't so much of a destiny as it was a spiked collar, with the organization holding the leash.

"Anything *else*," I whispered. "Please."

I would do it. Anything else. Anything that would guarantee our safety. *Her life.* The medallion in my pocket began to burn.

Atlas sensed it too, didn't she? Just how far gone I was for the princess?

I couldn't deny it anymore. Whatever delusion had kept me trying to kill her was gone.

I didn't want to. I never wanted to. There was no joy in making the princess suffer. No joy in watching her prepare for her death.

I could lie to myself before, say that *I* wanted to be the one who killed her.

But that's all it was. *A lie.*

The unvarnished truth was that I wished for nothing more in the world than for Princess Aurelia to live. And to live happily. *With me.*

She shook my hand off and cast her eyes down the hallway.

"I'll only be safe if he's gone," she said. "If you can't help me with that, you're useless."

And without another word, she left me there in the hall, feeling more lost than I ever felt in my life.

AURELIA

E arth-shattering things never came with a warning.

Just like on the eve of my mother's death, it was a calm, sunny day. It was misleading. Lulling you into a false sense of security, and then it would strike.

At least this time, I knew it was coming, no matter how hard I tried to deny it. No matter how hard I tried to avoid it. My destiny was about to hit me right in the face.

The one day every vampire princess was born to go through was coming faster than I could stop it. The same day they lived—and sometimes died—trying to obtain. For most, it was a sign of their power. The more powerful the family a princess married into, the more power she had.

But for me, it was a death sentence.

I was born for more. *So much more.* My potential was not that of a vampire princess who would just sit there looking pretty while her husband conquered the world.

I was the one who was supposed to rule. I knew I could do it. It was in my blood.

But after my mother died, there was no one to fight for my ascension to the family's throne. For my *rightful* place. And as much as I tried, there was no going against Father.

He was much more powerful and ruthless than I ever could be.

Marriage was my only way out. But in reality, I was just trading one cage for another.

The new one was seemingly even more horrendous than staying with my father and god-awful stepfamily.

*Father **stole** something from the Solei family.*

I had an inkling of what it was, but I couldn't bring myself to even consider the vile idea. But at the same time, it wasn't very surprising.

Vampires like them had no moral compass. They took what they wanted. Including other vampires. Anything to expand their range of power.

Krae wouldn't approve.

I couldn't help but wonder what our goddess was feeling watching this all unfold. My mother was so devoted to her, yet she stood by while she and her daughter suffered at the hands of a single man.

Sometimes I even wonder if she is real at all.

Even if she was, praying to her wouldn't do me any good. She had proven her uselessness to me enough.

Along with everyone else...even myself.

But wallowing in my own pity would do nothing for me, so I spent the last day of whatever freedom I had left in the back gardens that surrounded the property and reveled in the only place of my mother's that still stood standing.

I hoped—foolishly—that it would make me feel closer to her. Maybe give me the answers I was looking for. Some hint at how she survived all those years with my bastard of a father.

Of course, all I was met with was a reminder of how little one's life meant in the grand scheme of things.

My mother's favorite place was one filled with life. A place where flowers bloomed all year round. Where the essence of her soul could be felt by all those who entered. Walking into the garden felt like being pulled into my mother's warm embrace. A place that provided comfort.

But a place like that didn't exist after her death—at least not under Father's reign.

What was once a flourishing garden had turned into a long-dried-up fountain with overgrown weeds seeping through the cracks standing at the center of millions of roses my mother had planted. It hadn't been cared for in the years since she was gone, but for some reason, Father still kept it standing.

All the colorful beauty she spent years planting by herself, cutting open her hands, and spilling her blood into the soil was all demolished in the blink of an eye. My father attempted to destroy every bit that my mother left behind and replaced it with his own colorless void.

I liked to believe it was the people's decision to keep some part of my mother alive. That maybe he *had* tried to get the eyesore taken down, but no one would heed his requests out of respect for my mother.

Even after hours, I found myself still sitting on the edge of the fountain, looking down at the cracked blue tile she had specially created by one of the family's mosaic artists. Intricate blues, whites, and reds swirled around each other creating beautiful blossoms of color.

Even with all the grime and dirt that covered it over the years, it shone beautifully in the dimming sun. Not even the cracks could take away from its beauty.

I missed my mother in moments like that the most.

The moments when all the anger had finally subsided. When the reality of the situation had sunk in. And when I couldn't just talk my way out of it. *Hell,* I couldn't even *blackmail* my way out of it.

Money. Connections. They had no use. Not when the payoff was power.

Even beyond that...not when the real reason for the deal was something that was decided long before I was even born.

Those were the moments when my walls started to crumble. Every single brick that I carefully plastered together with all the rage that had been building inside my body was coming apart. I was no longer able to keep what lay behind locked away.

I am just waiting for my doom.

There was another complication, though. One that I prayed would just leave. I thought the assassin would just give up after a while, obviously not willing to help me in the way that mattered the most.

She should have left. After all, she had failed her job so spectacularly that it was comical.

Yet she was still here.

The sound of her footsteps crushing the roses beneath her feet caused an unexpected smile to spread across my lips. They weren't the light, careful footsteps of someone trained to kill. They were heavy-booted footfalls that cared nothing for the plants she was stepping on.

The plants my father adored so much.

"Destroying the wildlife, are we now?" I asked, turning to the intruder.

She stood tall in her all-black uniform, her hands in her pockets, and a contemplative look on her face. The dimming sun hit her face in a way that caused her various scars to shine in the light and her hair to glow.

She is too beautiful for this world.

It was hard not to get distracted by her. Especially when my brain was begging to forget about what was happening to me.

Her honey eyes passed over my face, actually looking at me.

It had been so long since someone had truly *seen* me the way she seemed to. I used to hate what the little mouse hid behind those eyes of hers. Dangerous thoughts, no doubt, but in that moment I would have paid anything to hear even just a snippet of what she was thinking.

Her gaze held mine for only a moment longer before she looked down, rubbing her booted foot on the ground harder.

Light wind wafted through the garden and caused her hair to get blown onto her face. The urge to run my hands through it—

maybe even grab a handful and force her to bare her neck to me—was strong.

"The temptation of damaging daddy's extravagant show of wealth was too great," she said, dragging her feet as she neared the fountain. Each flower that was destroyed under her booted foot felt like a little bit of a gift, each of them helping put a piece of myself back.

But she didn't sit. Instead, she lingered by my side. Her leg brushed across mine.

The action sent an odd jolt of electricity through me. It was such a simple move. Could even be called an accident.

But it felt much more meaningful than even the night we spent together, where her touch had been burned into my skin.

"Did I stay out here too long?" I asked, tilting my head, trying to recall just how long I had been sitting out there. I knew it had been hours, but how many?

Had Father or the prince finally decided to put an end to my freedom?

Her eyes met mine again before she looked at the fountain.

"It isn't *that* bad," she said, her eyes roaming over each crack in the tile. "Well, it's not great, but it shouldn't take long for someone to clean and repair it. I'm sure one of your staff could get it done in about a week."

What? Nothing about Father or the prince? Not even any questions about our meeting with Atlas?

She wants to talk about the fucking fountain?

I let out a scoff and looked away from it as a heaviness settled in my chest. I couldn't fight the vulnerable feeling. I should have handled it long ago, but for some reason...I never did.

Why didn't I?

No use now...

"Did you forget?" I asked with a bitter laugh. "I'm getting *married* tomorrow."

I don't know what I expected her to say, but her silence was like a stab in the chest. Somehow, I managed to still have the tiniest bit of hope that she had changed her mind about murdering my father.

But the silence weighed on.

Fuck, say something, why don't you?

The rage was returning, but instead of the tidal wave of power it once felt like, it was more like desperation clawing at my throat. It made me want to scream. It made me want to stomp my feet.

I wanted her to say something. *Anything.*

Say you changed your mind. Say you'll kill him for me. Tell me you'll—

"Should we have a bachelorette party?"

Her question made my head snap toward her so quickly my neck ached. Her gaze was back on me, unmoving. That stone-cold face of hers didn't even give one twitch to indicate if she was joking.

Because she isn't.

"Are you drunk or something?" I stood up and grabbed her face, forcing her to look at me. Her skin was hot and sent warm skitters down my arm. I wanted to bathe in it.

I searched her eyes, ignoring the way my body was betraying me, and took a deep inhale—only to burst out laughing.

A deep, unfiltered laugh forced itself out of my belly and echoed across the garden. It bounced against the palace walls and back at me.

The little mouse continues to surprise me.

"You *are*," I said with a mock gasp, finally realizing why her silence had seemed so odd. She was intoxicated.

It was so subtle, it was hard to pinpoint, but there was just the tiniest hint of sweet wine on her lips. I hadn't taken her for a wine drinker. If anything, I would have assumed she preferred something harder, but I guess there were still sides to her that I had no idea about.

She gave me a sly smirk, and a burst of excitement ran through me. *So we want to play now, don't we?*

Finally, she was giving me exactly what I wanted from her.

Maybe it was a pity move. Or maybe she too realized how little time we would have in each other's company before the end.

Either way, I wasn't going to complain.

"Like I said, bachelorette party. Want a taste?"

Fuck. If that invitation didn't cause heat to blossom in my belly, I didn't know what would.

"How am I to turn down such a considerate offer?"

My back hit the sharp bark with a thud, Vesper following my movement and sinking into the same tree with a sigh. The taste of her blood was still strong on the tip of my tongue. My entire body felt warm and bubbly.

I feel like I can breathe.

I finally felt how cool the night was. How the sun had fallen long before, and for once, the entire grounds were quiet.

Her blood had calmed my racing thoughts, and I was able to enjoy the peace that my mother's garden had once brought. I almost wished she hadn't given me her blood. Because then it wouldn't feel so much like a goodbye.

"You drank *way* more than you let on," I said with a giggle. Heat settled in my body, making it feel light as a feather.

When was the last time I let go like this?

It had to have been years before, when I still went to those blackmail parties for enjoyment. Where I would drink the alcohol-infused blood until I was a giggling mess. Where I would play with vampires and humans alike just because I could.

Where has that Aurelia gone?

Vesper side-eyed me and let out a light huff of a laugh of her own, but suddenly, I wasn't feeling so amused anymore.

"You ever just think that you're bad at holding your alcohol?"

I shook my head and leaned into her side. "I'll have you know I'm *great* at holding my alcohol."

A silence fell over us, sobering the mood.

I don't want to go, I wanted to say. *If this place was hell on earth, what kind of place will the new one be?*

And lastly... *Will you take me away from here?*

"Are you sure you won't take Atlas's offer?" she asked, her voice low.

"I can't," I whispered. *I can't survive out there on my own.*

A pitiful, painful realization. It would do me more harm than good if I tried to outrun Father and Prince Icas. I might get away for a few days, but they would find me. Not only that, but I had no clue how to live on my own in the outside world.

That's why I needed to rely on the people I met throughout my years in the palace.

"Why is your father giving you to them?" she asked, her hand brushing across my lap in search of mine.

I let her take it, if only for the comfort it brought in the moment.

"Apparently, my father owes the Solei family," I said. "Correction—he *stole* something. My guess is my mother, given how Icas's father wants me as a broodmare."

The flinch that traveled through Vesper was painful. Her hand gripped mine tightly, and her breathing hitched.

I knew the anger well, but instead of feeling the same, I felt... indifference. *Acceptance.* That was my future, after all.

"But if that wasn't enough," I said, letting myself lean into her even further, reveling in the warm body I felt against mine. "Prince Icas is offended. He hates how his father is using him, but he hates the way I've treated him even more. Someone he sees as weaker. Someone who belongs under his foot."

"A scapegoat," she added.

I nodded, my eyes traveling to the fountain just a few feet away. I didn't want to say it here. Not with the last remnant of Mother so close. It was insulting. But what did I have left?

"He's going to wage war," I whispered. "He's already recruiting those who pledged themselves to my family by using my name.

Using my fucking handmaiden—that snake—to stand in as me during these negotiations as a symbol of my allegiance. He has promised things he can't keep."

I let the words settle between us. Did she understand the severity? Had it finally dawned on her why I needed her to kill Father?

Prince Icas had already doomed me. There was no way out, and Father wouldn't cancel the engagement if I asked him to. Or *even believe me with those stepbitches by his side.*

They wanted me gone even more than Icas did. There was no telling what else they had planned.

"What is he promising?" she asked.

I clicked my tongue against the roof of my mouth. *Who cares if I reveal a little more?* It's not like I had much time left before Father found out.

"Anything from housing, money, less work, to...*dealing* with the witches."

I didn't know it was possible for Vesper to stiffen even further. Her heart raced at this.

I pushed myself up into a sitting position and turned to her, hoping to catch even a glimpse of understanding in her eyes.

"Do you see it now?" I questioned. Still searching her eyes for any hint that she was on my side. *I need you.* The words were on the tip of my tongue, but instead, what came out was something entirely different. "Do you see why you have to kill—"

"What would you do if you could leave here?" she asked. The suddenness of her question was like a slap in the face. Even after everything was revealed to her, she had no intention of helping.

She is a hunter through and through. She grimaced at that word when Atlas used it. Like it was something dirty and shameful...but that's all I could see in front of me.

A cold-blooded hunter who couldn't care for anything other than the job she failed to complete.

"I'm trying to tell you why—"

"*What* would you do?" she asked again through gritted teeth. My eyes fell to the hand farthest away from me. I hadn't seen it until that moment. How tightly she was balling it into a fist. The knuckles were completely white, the strength of her grip cutting off the blood flow.

"I want to paint," I whispered and leaned back against the tree. An unknown emotion caused my throat to strain. "Not just paint. Sculpt. Craft. Make anything that could..."

My voice tapered off in the end. *What difference does it make? What will saying any of this mean?* But a part of me was grateful for the redirect. Even if it meant letting go of the last bit of hope I had been holding on to.

Because then there would be nothing holding me back. Nothing I said would mean shit in the morning. There was something powerful pulling at my chest. Something begging me to just let the words out. To spill to the person who once dared to consider ending my life.

How pitiful is this? That the last person on earth I should feel safe with provided me the greatest comfort?

"Make someone *recognize* me. *See* me."

More silence. The sound of the wind traveled around us, weaving through the roses and sending some petals flying through the air.

"You're seen," she noted, her tone softer than before. "All day, every day, by the vampires in your family. They adore you."

I let out a sigh and sank back into the tree. The sharp bark digging into my body felt more like a hug than an attack. The alcohol-infused blood was running through my system, relaxing my muscles once again.

It paired well with the hopelessness.

"They adore my mother," I said. "*Not me.* I want them to love *me.* To move families for *me.* Not because of their loyalty to my mother, and certainly not because Icas has offered them money, or houses, or even decided to declare war on the fucking witches."

She sucked in a sharp breath.

"War with the witches?" she echoed, the same horror that I once felt shooting through my chest in her voice.

"That's what I meant when I said *dealing*. What did you think I meant?" I said, leaning back into her, letting my fingers brush across the stitches of her uniform.

"I don't know," she whispered after a moment. "Something—*anything*—but that. Vampires should know better. It won't be a war, it will be—"

"A massacre," I finished for her, a bitter smile spreading across my face. "I know. But he seems overly confident because he will use Father's and my name instead of his. He's stupid, but brave. There will be more than one casualty in my family, but his death won't be far behind."

There was nothing to say to that. *It was all out there.* And it was even more horrifying than either of us could imagine.

There was a reason that neither vampires nor humans would ever do something as stupid as fight with the witches. They were an anomaly and kept far too close to themselves for either side to ever gain an advantage over them.

"You'll remember me, won't you?" I said once the silence became too much. "As the one contract you wanted to kill but couldn't?"

There was another long silence as another breeze passed through the roses, carrying their scent to us. I hated how good they smelled. Hated that I would probably miss them.

It would have been perfect if she just kept playing along. I could forget about whatever moment we were having and go on to marry the prince because there would be nothing else holding me back. Fully content to forfeit my life.

But she decided to give me the worst wedding gift imaginable.

"I never wanted to kill you, Aurelia. *Never.*"

Hope. A vile, disgusting sickness that did nothing but ensure a person's tolerance for the worst. And after her words, the tiniest bit of it sparked in my chest.

VESPER

"On the floor," the king commanded. "Both of you."

He was quite comfortable in his large bed, pillows piled up on all sides. Two young humans were on either side of him, naked and leaning into him, while his vampire hand-maiden stood by the bed.

A sight I hadn't expected to see and made me work hard to control the disgust on my face.

His room was much different from the princess's and was the length of about three put together. Princess Aurelia's was that of a perfectly pampered princess. Consistently clean with pretty carpeting and white, fluffy bedding.

The king's was drowned in gold and black. The chandelier above us was dimmed, but even in the darkness, the gold shimmered. The walls and curtains were mainly black, except for the real gold accents. Large windows flanked us, connecting the two other rooms to his.

There were even more feeders just beyond them, but the most overwhelming thing was the number of guards. *Vampire guards.* All their bright-red eyes digging into mine.

The room itself looked like a dream, but the aura was sticky and it made me feel like something was crawling up my back. It didn't help that he was forcing us to wait in silence as he finished feeling up his maidens for the night.

Melia was the first to kneel on the ground and placed her head on it so fast, I was afraid she might knock herself out because of it.

Since the plan first popped into my head, I knew I was walking on thin ice. Knew that there was only one thing standing between me and certain death.

But even if I could pull it off like I imagined, there would be no guarantee I would leave with my life.

Or Aurelia's with hers.

There was no going back after this. I had gone completely rogue for the princess. And for what?

But I wanted nothing in return. *Truly.* The only thing that was pushing me to do something so reckless was the image of a hopeless and crying Aurelia. Seeing her like that would be forever burned into my mind, and just knowing the awful things the prince and his father planned...I found it hard to just watch as it happened.

I cast my gaze to the handmaiden beside me. She didn't dare look up, but I could still hear her pleas echoing in my mind as I dragged her down the hallway with my sword at her throat.

Please don't! They'll kill us both!

You don't know what those two are capable of!

It didn't hold the same guilt as when I put my weapon to Aurelia's throat. She was even pleading and crying, but none of it fazed me. I didn't care about her. Didn't care about her screams.

There was something much bigger at stake. Something I cared far more about. For the first time, I knew how to use the tools my father had beaten into me over the years.

The entire time I searched for the handmaiden, my mind was focused on one thing and one thing only—the hopelessness in Aurelia's eyes when I found her in the garden.

So maybe I haven't changed that radically after all. Maybe I just found my driving force.

I slowly lowered myself to the ground, my knees digging into the cold marble floor. The plush red carpet was a mere foot away, taunting me.

"You're lucky I'm not making you slit your own throat for coming to me with such an idiotic claim," he said with a scoff. "You do realize this will get you killed?"

Yeah, too fucking well, I thought bitterly. It was a half-baked plan.

In all honesty, I had never been good at the strategic part of my job. It's why I relied on the information provided to me. It's why I failed so catastrophically at killing Aurelia.

But even so, my mind was clear.

I couldn't kill the king, but I could do the next best thing.

"That's why I brought one of the traitors. I saw it with my own two eyes and was waiting until I could grab her for you, so there would be no doubt as to what I am saying," I told him, motioning to the shaking handmaiden. It was a lie, but I needed to use everything in my arsenal to get the king to believe me. Not only that, but I needed to play to his weakness. I needed to get him angry. Get him so angry he would think of nothing else other than getting back at those who wronged him. "Everything I said is true, all you need to do is ask her—"

"And why should I believe you?" the king asked, his voice bouncing off the walls.

My knees ached against the floor as I braced my body for violence. The beating of my heart the only thing keeping me steady.

Not for the first time since I entered the palace, fear had its ice-cold claws around my heart.

*This is a stupid, **stupid**, fucking decision.*

This could kill me. One slipup, and I would be dead at his feet before Aurelia even knew.

But if it works...she and I will be far away from each other, and she won't have to marry that demon.

There wasn't just one demon she had to save herself from. I had a duty. *The prophecy.* There was no telling what my father would do to me when I got back.

But it was better than having to kill her. It was heartbreaking to see her in that room as she fell to the floor in her darkened room, but it was the thing I needed.

I couldn't kill Aurelia, but I could kill for her.

"Because I may be risking my life," I said, keeping my eyes trained to the floor. "But you're risking your entire family. Everything you built. He was never here to abide by the terms you and his father set. The entire time, he was using it to scheme. If you let this continue, it will be the end of all your hard work."

I took the chance to look up at him as he pulled the females closer. They both let out giggles and rubbed up against him, their hands wandering his chest before going lower.

He let out a laugh. The warmness of it startled me.

"And you?" he asked. "What will you get out of this?"

Freedom was the wrong word. It felt cheap and coated my tongue with bitterness.

The truth was, I got nothing out of this. When I was sent back to my family, there was no telling what my punishment for breaking the prophecy would be.

But for Aurelia...I would risk it all.

I had watched her destroy herself over the time I had been her guard. I thought the magic poisoning was the worst that could happen, but no. It was the steady deterioration of the light in her eyes.

And she had fully given into her fate. *But not me.*

I hated the prophecies. Hated the witches who thought they could scam people with them. Worst of all, I despised the people who followed fate blindly. Not *once* trying to change it.

But I wouldn't hold it against the princess. She was cornered, never having seen a way out for the entirety of her existence.

I could forge this path for her, but I wouldn't be able to see her through it.

Maybe if I had just taken her up on murdering him, she would have it easier.

"I want to be discharged from Prince Icas's service," I said. "I want to be sent home. That is all."

He leaned forward, his eyes searching my face.

"You just brought to light one of the greatest betrayals this kingdom has ever seen...and you want to go home? No riches? A position in my ranks?"

Never. If I truly had my way, I would want nothing to do with the Castle family. But the damage had already been done since the first time my prophecy was uttered.

"It's as simple as that, sir," I replied, keeping my expression ice cold.

Believe me. Please. I didn't know who I was sending a prayer out to, but I hoped even just one god was listening.

A smirk spread across his face.

"And you, handmaiden?" he asked, his gaze falling on her. "What do you have to say about this? Have you been helping the prince steal people right from under my nose?"

I turned to Melia as well. Hesitantly, she lifted her gaze to him.

"Don't look at me," he spat, all warmth leaving his voice. "If it's true, you're a traitor. I don't want you to even look at me."

She quickly looked back down, her shaky breathing filling the room.

"Your Majesty, I would *n-never* attempt to harm the family—"

His fist slammed down on his side table, and the sound, along with a pained squeal from the woman at his side, echoed throughout the room.

"Don't try to placate me," he growled. I looked up just in time to catch him getting out of his bed and crossing the room to stand over Melia.

I thanked whatever god was listening that he was wearing loose pajama pants.

His hand shot down to her hair, and he yanked her face up.

Jesus. I didn't want to see him hurt her, but it was even harder to look away when I knew that she had played a part in Aurelia's possible demise.

I hated her almost as much as the prince.

"She may never have meant you harm," I said. "But she listened to the traitor. She did his dirty work. All under your nose. They tried to play you for a fool."

"No one plays me for a fool," he spat. The girls on the bed huddled together, obviously knowing far too well how easily the king could turn.

I was grateful he didn't direct his anger at me.

"At the gala as well," I continued. "He was going around, trying to get people on his side. To leave you. In broad daylight, where anyone could hear."

I wasn't sure it was true, but after Aurelia told me what the prince's plan was, her reaction at the gala made much more sense. So did his.

What hadn't made sense was why the prince was so close to her stepsister.

Until I remembered Cedar's words: *The prince isn't capable of killing the princess. It's closer than that.*

But even if my suspicions were correct, the king wouldn't believe his own wife and stepdaughter were in on it.

So the only choice was to pin it all on Prince Icas.

"Shut your mouth," he ordered me, then turned back to Melia. "Tell me the truth, and maybe I'll spare your life."

Melia's eyes filled with tears and sobs spilled from her lips.

"He's taken more than fifty of them already, my king," she said through quivering lips. "They're just waiting for the wedding to conclude before the mass exodus. What she said is true."

The king searched her face, that disgusting smirk showing up again. Like a light switch, his anger was gone, and in its place was a monster that liked to play with its food.

"And he asked you to help, and you used *my* name to do it?" he asked.

She shook her head.

"Aurelia's," she corrected. "And her mother's."

The smirk dropped, and all the playfulness in his eyes disappeared. One moment, Melia was being held in the air by her hair, and in the next, she had her neck snapped and was tossed to the floor like garbage.

The king looked over her with a boiling anger that made even my heart stop.

"Lock her up," he said to the guards stationed around the room. His reddened eyes dug into mine, the threat clear. "I have some things to verify before we let her run loose."

The human guard ran the electric shock stick against the bars of my damp cell with a menacing look on his face.

The damp smell of the cellar still itched my nose, no matter how many hours had passed. The coldness of the stone underneath me felt much harsher than whatever we had in the guards' quarters.

It was another floor down, with no sunlight, and the distinct scent of mildew filled the air.

The cell itself was about as large as the room Cedar and I shared, with a bed made of metal, no mattress, and a rusted toilet I didn't dare use.

I gave the guard a look as he waited for my reaction.

What did he expect? For me to jump? For me to cower?

He was a human, just like I was. If anything, I was above him because of my position at Aurelia's side. Maybe he knew that. Maybe that's why he had that smug fucking expression on his face as he looked down at me and flicked the button on the weapon once more.

Someone usually at the bottom of the barrel in this family suddenly found himself with a bit too much power.

The grinding of my teeth was beginning to cause my jaw to ache. My nails dug into my palms. All the annoyance from the meeting with the king and now being forced to suffer *this* was too much for me.

How many times has he passed by?

How many times has he said something offensive under his breath, knowing very well that I can hear him?

Unluckily for him, hours of sitting on the cold rock put me in a little bit of a mood, and that was my final straw. I stood up, rolling my shoulders and tilting my head from side to side. My tight muscles were yelling at me to get up and move around.

"Can I help you?" I asked him.

"Just checking on my favorite prisoner," he said with a taunting grin. "I heard the princess got tired of you and sent you down here. What happened?"

I strolled to the bars, holding his gaze. *He really thinks he's getting somewhere with this.*

There were a mere few feet between us. So close, I could smell the alcohol on his breath.

"Do you always drink on the job?" I asked, tilting my head. "I bet your head guard will have something to say about it when I tell him."

He shook his head and let out a laugh before leaning forward and dropping his voice to a whisper. "You're never getting out of here. You came here thinking you're hot shit, but look at you now. Do you even remember what you did to me?"

I raised my brow at him. "I don't even know you," I admitted.

His entire expression changed. The playful smirk dropped and was replaced with a sneer.

"The prince's palace," he said. "You and I were set to spar. You're the reason I was pushed to the lower ranks and am now stuck in this hellhole."

I racked my memory trying to remember his face, but the time at the prince's palace was such a blur. All I did there was attempt to move up as high as I could in the ranks before being given to the princess.

I huffed. "You must have sucked pretty hard to be *that* unmemorable."

He let out a growl and pushed his hand through the bars, the sharp sound of electricity drowning out everything else. I maneuvered to the side, the current zapping me on the bicep.

I let out a groan and took a step back. The human guard looked awfully fucking pleased with himself.

"But now *I'm* the one in charge—"

I lunged at the bars, my arm slipping past them and grabbing the collar of his shirt, and I used my body weight to slam him against the metal. He let out a pained moan as his face was forced against the dirty bars. There was nothing for him to grab on to, and his arms flailed.

I used my free hand to grab the offending stick and threw it far inside my cell.

"You have anything else to do other than annoy me?" I growled and twisted the collar of his shirt, cutting off his air supply. Then, I remembered an image of him under me as I flipped him in front of the head guards at the prince's palace. "I *do* remember you. You didn't even last a second. Even behind these bars, I can make you regret everything you just did and beg for your mother to come save you. Shall we find out just how much I can do with these bars between us?"

His mouth flopped open and closed like a washed-up fish. The fear was finally starting to show in his eyes, and he was realizing just how much he had fucked up.

It felt good.

I used to hate my job. Hated that I was good at it. Hated that I made people suffer. But people like him? I wanted to watch it all.

"Just kill him, why don't you?" a familiar, grating voice called from down the darkened hallway.

I could. It was very tempting. But the intruder reminded me just how short my leash was and just how easily the king could kill me if he so chose to.

My eyes drifted to the intruder.

With bright red hair casting an orange shine due to the oil lamps that lit the dungeon's hallways, she took up most of the hallway, and her presence was almost hypnotic with the way my eyes were all but forced to look at her.

Cedar. The fucking witch who proved to be a pain in the ass. There was something about her that alarmed me. She knew too much. Even before Aurelia told me about what the prince and her stepfamily were doing, she seemed to know it all.

But how?

She said she wasn't a seer...Had one sent her here? *Princess Aurelia was never my job.* So who was? Witches worked in covens. Had other people had the vision? And just how much had they seen?

All this time, I had been focusing on Aurelia...but maybe I should have been focusing on *her*.

She had her hands in her pockets and walked at an alarmingly calm pace, her eyes traveling around the dungeon, and that little smirk on her face told me just how much she was enjoying the show I was putting on.

I didn't let the guard go until he finally passed out from lack of oxygen. I didn't need his interference. Not when I had so much to question the witch about. His body fell to the ground in a heap.

"Keep showing up in places like this, and I *may* just think your mission here is me," I said, leaning against the bars. "You some kind of snake?"

The smile she gave me had a shiver run up my spine. I hated how much her green eyes seemed to see through me.

Maybe she does.

"Turning down my offer to save your skin?" she asked as she got to the bars, her hand slipping through them and brushing across my neck. "Or did you forget my magic is temporary?"

I jerked away from her. Panic and fear shooting through me.

"They'll smell you," I hissed.

She merely smiled at me. As if the knowledge of me working with a witch wouldn't be the death of me.

"Roll around on the ground a little, rub your own spit on it— whatever it is, I don't care, it's not my life."

I narrowed my eyes at her. *Obviously.*

"Why are you here, then?" I asked, eyeing her warily. The real question was—how did she know I was here? I never even went back to my room. I could have been anywhere. "Why does it matter to *you* if I'm killed?"

She shrugged. "I said I'd help you, so I'm here. Isn't that enough?"

I merely raised a brow at her. "Maybe a better question is how you found me. You choose one to answer."

She rolled her eyes. "Do you really think you have the power here? You're behind bars and waiting on the king's mercy, which we both know he's severely lacking."

I stayed silent, letting the pause fill the space between us. I wasn't joking, and she seemed to get that after a few long moments.

"You're my roommate," she said with a sigh. Her eyes cast back to the sleeping guard before looking back at me. The dim light illuminated her freckles, and for the second time, I realized there was a pattern to them. "If they find out about you, it will only bring trouble to me—trouble that I *can't* afford."

I looked at her for a hard moment. She didn't *seem* to be lying, but that sure as hell wasn't the entire truth.

As mysterious as she seemed to be, she didn't seem slimy. Not like the prince. And she was the one to warn me about the princess's life-threatening attack.

But was it life-threatening? A little voice said in the back of my mind. *What if she was making it all up just to keep you under control?*

She had seemingly been showing up out of nowhere, but always at the perfect time. The coincidences were piling up, and alarm bells were ringing at full volume in my head.

But I had trusted her once, and it wasn't like I was in any situation to refuse her help. She was right. The guard was, too. I was behind bars and at the mercy of a cruel king who could decide to kill me at a moment's notice.

I settled closer to her outstretched hand, letting her cold fingertips brush against my skin.

"*Perfect*," she all but purred, a feline smile spreading across her face.

This time, when her hand came into contact with my neck, it was like a sharp zap of energy. Even stronger than before, and the aftereffects left a tingle that ran from head to toe.

She did something different. Panic and anger rushed through me. Before I could stop myself, my hands were gripping the bars, and I was baring my teeth at her.

"What the fuck—"

Footsteps sounded from down the hall. Hard-booted feet. A sign of guards.

"Gotta go," she said with a wink and, right before my eyes, disappeared in a puff of black smoke.

This time, I truly did recoil. I had never seen a witch do something like that. *Never.* Nor had I ever realized they could manipulate their bodies like that.

But there was an even more pressing matter. The smell of magic wasn't just on me. It was filling the air all around me. Even my dull human senses could smell a hint of the burning, plant-like smell.

Shit. Shit. Shit.

I scrambled to hide farther back in my cell, picking up the electric weapon I had thrown there, and I found a good space to kneel down in.

All my muscles tensed, ready for a fight I couldn't win.

"What the hell is this?" A loud voice boomed as the group came across the unconscious guard. And then, to my utter relief, two *human* guards showed themselves right outside my cell. It was the way their skin gleamed in the dim light. The way their uniforms fit them.

Fuck Cedar and her mind games. She must have known that they were human, that would have been the only reason why she would have chanced doing what she did.

I waved the weapon at them.

"*Sorry,*" I said with a smile. "He just got a little annoying."

One of them let out a string of curses and put his hands on his hips. I almost expected him to start stomping his feet with how childish he was acting. *This is their head guard?*

"Move her! Obviously, she's gotten too comfortable for a prisoner."

"Waiting to be proven right actu—"

I was cut off by the now-conscious guard coughing fit. It only earned me another glare, but at least I would be leaving the magic-coated cell.

AURELIA

The bells were ringing.

Church bells from the next town over. The same ones they used for funerals. Normally, they were quiet on wedding days so as not to disturb the vampire palace so close to them. After all, the ringing was annoying after a while to our super hearing.

But that day, they went all out. Rung them all. Three, I counted. Every hour for almost a full thirty seconds.

They were celebrating with us.

The humans, who had once cowered in fear of us. Had shunned us. Had hunted us because of our monster status.

They were now celebrating *my* getting married to some ruthless vampire prince they probably didn't even recognize.

Maybe they were celebrating my departure, a bitter voice said in the back of my mind.

Maybe they were actually happy that I would be leaving. Or maybe they had heard rumors of the cruel fate that awaited me, and they were rejoicing that the spoiled vampire princess who caused so much fear was *finally* getting what she deserved.

I much preferred the latter. The hate was easier to digest.

I leaned my head against the cool window in my bedroom.

The smell of rose petals was strong on my skin and tickled my nose. For hours, I had handmaidens in my bathroom, scrubbing me from head to toe with scented lotions and soaps. They spent even longer on my hair, making sure it was silky smooth and carefully curled.

They didn't care how much I protested, citing that it had been an order from my father.

Of course. Even if he knew what awaited me, he still couldn't pass up the chance to make a statement. A pampered princess on her wedding day. Everything would need to be perfect. *I would need to be perfect.*

The longer I stayed against the window, the more it began to warm from the shining sun. For a moment, I let myself pretend it was the little mouse.

My delusion told me Vesper wouldn't have abandoned me.

Not after what she said.

I never wanted to kill you, Aurelia. Never.

But even then, wouldn't this be something she would want to see? Or maybe even a last chance to come put an end to my misery for good?

I had been so stuck in my own pity party that I didn't even think of the one final thing I could have asked her.

Ask me anything else.

She could kill me. I didn't want to die. Quite the opposite. With each passing second, I found the need to run away getting more and more overwhelming. The need to live was a hard thing to ignore.

But somehow, I knew that even if I asked, she still wouldn't do it. The little mouse had her fair share of chances, and each time it ended up with my fangs in her throat or her hands between my legs.

So where is she?

But the hours ticked by, each second getting me closer and closer to the time when I would be walking down the aisle, and she wasn't there.

I had nothing else to do but stay near that window and watch as the hundreds of staff prepared my wedding for me. It wouldn't be until sunset, but I could see them setting up right outside my window, and in my panic, I couldn't stop watching them.

Their hands were full. Some carrying expensive clothes, some carrying flowers. It was a bit comical watching how panicked they were when *I* was the one getting married. But my guess was that Father didn't want them preparing for the wedding until the actual wedding day.

Krae forbid that his throne room be occupied by something other than himself for even a day.

That was where the wedding would be held. It was a beautiful place for it, and I was grateful it was not in the cathedral where my mother passed instead.

The large crystal windows behind Father's throne would let the setting sun shine through and make for the perfect photo opportunity. But to get there, I had to walk down a bloodred carpet that spanned from the front of the palace to deep inside, with members of the family lining up along the way to see their late queen's daughter as she was handed off to another family.

I could imagine the headlines now.

Two of the most powerful vampire families finally united!

Princess Aurelia finally getting married off to the handsome Prince Icas!

They would never dare write anything bad about us—not with the amount of money my father gave them. But that didn't mean that we still didn't have to perfect our image.

The weight of it all was heavy on my shoulders. The longer I watched them, the harder it became to breathe. It became worse when I realized how low in the sky the sun had fallen.

I've been standing here staring at them for god knows how long and not even trying to get the fuck out of here?

The realization of just how much my own uselessness was about to fuck me over hit me like a truck.

There I was, waiting for someone who would never show. Someone whose entire job was to kill me. What did I fucking expect from her?

If she wouldn't come to me, I would fucking make her.

When I couldn't take it anymore, I stormed to the door, ready to demand that she come see me, but as soon as I opened it, I came face-to-face with not one but *two* guards.

Both of them turned to look at me with blank expressions. They weren't human. For the first time, Father decided to give me vampire guards instead of the normal human ones.

Shit. He knew I would get cold feet. Humans I could fight off easily, but vampires?

"Go get the silver-haired guard," I ordered them. "I'm thirsty."

The one on the right looked at the one on the left, but neither responded. *Fuck. Think of something, Aurelia!*

"Ignoring me?" I asked with a huff and placed my arms on their chests, ready to push them out of my way. I needed to get out of the room. "Useless—"

They both reached out, their hands capturing my wrists in a bruising grip. I looked up at them in shock. Not once had Father's guards dared to hurt me. Father was different, he could do whatever he wanted, but never anyone under him. It was an insult to his and my standing.

"Don't you fucking tou—"

"Your father's orders," the one on the left said, and with ease, they pushed me back into the room and slammed my door shut. The sound of it was such a shock that it was almost enough to silence me. *Almost.*

"We will let you out when it's time for the wedding," the other added, his voice muffled by the door.

I kicked the door, my foot causing the thick wood to dent. But it wasn't enough. Not to break it down or to give me a chance to escape.

"I haven't had anything to drink. You want me to starve?"

There was no answer. *Fine.*

I ran to my vanity, taking the whole fucking thing with me as I ran to the windows, letting out a guttural scream as I threw it at them.

The shattering of the glass was satisfying enough to cause me to let out a small victory noise.

I turned and ran to it, ready to jump out and secure my freedom, but just as my hands wrapped around the sharp edges, I paused.

Because below were three more guards, all looking up at me.

Vampires.

"Don't try it, princess," one of them called from below. "Go back to your room, and we'll come get you shortly."

One of them even had the audacity to chuckle under his breath.

The realization of just how stuck I was felt akin to ice-cold water being poured on me. *There is no escape.* Not then, not ever.

Growing up in the family, I always thought that I was used to the attention of thousands on me at any given moment.

Until my wedding.

It was nothing I had ever seen before. The grounds were *packed* with humans and vampires alike, all of them looking at me. The air was buzzing with excitement. Excited murmurs filled the crowd. I was more of a spectacle than anything else. A circus animal put in front of them to perform.

But all I could do was stand there at the end of the aisle, frozen, feeling their eyes wandering over my entire body. It felt dirty. It felt mortifying.

Father wouldn't degrade himself to walk with me, so I was accompanied by my guards, who stood close behind me at all times. No doubt for fear that I might run after my little *tantrum* in my room. They let me sit with the consequences of my own actions until they hauled me out of the room, kicking and screaming, to repair the window and get me dressed.

They weren't gentle then either, and there were even more of them at my side than ever before. Their presence behind me was stifling, maybe even more so than the guests.

At that moment, I realized just how boxed in I was. Guards at my back. Guests to my right and left. The prince, Father, and the stepbastards waiting for me at the end.

I could run, but then they would catch me. Maybe I could even dive into the crowd. But then what would the people think? What would Father do once the wedding was over and I had caused such a scene?

The setting sun had cooled the air, but the pressure of it all caused my skin to heat unbearably. My clothes were too tight. My hair too in my face. The tiara on my head too heavy.

But worst of all, Vesper was nowhere to be found. Her absence was glaringly obvious and more painful than I'd like to admit.

Music filtered down the aisle, signaling my time to start walking. It was dramatic. The strike of the organ keys mixed with the high-pitched sound of a string instrument sounded more like I was walking into war than into the arms of my prince.

The dress they had given me was made mostly of black lace that was intricately fitted to my body, underneath a light bloodred slip that showed through the fabric. A heavy ruby sat on my chest, with a few more pinned into my hair and about one on every finger.

My deep red shoes peeked out as I compelled my feet to move. *One after the other.*

That was all I could chant to myself. I tried not to look into the eyes of the people standing on either side of the aisle. Tried not to remember their names or what they thought of my mother. Tried not to think of what my father had given them.

It worked until I got to poor Henry.

He was forced to sit behind some human politician known for taking blood money donations, not even allowed in the front. *Corrupt* government officials were more important than our own *family.*

I wasn't surprised. Nothing about Father could surprise me... but I was *angry.*

Angry that our family had turned into this. Angry that there was nothing I could do about it. Angry that right beside him was a vampire the prince had somehow convinced to leave the family.

How did it come to this? How had the family become so twisted that the people who were loyal to me and my mother were forced to the back? Forced to stand next to people who would rather throw me under the bus for a measly house or some pocket change? Even when I begged them not to.

This wasn't the family I saw as a little girl. This wasn't what my mother had wanted.

My mother lived her life trying to do right by these people, and what did that get her in the end?

A disappointing daughter. A daughter who couldn't care less about the people who had tried to save her. Some even lost their lives by standing up to my father.

Why did it take me so long to realize this? Had I been so crazed with trying to fit into the mold of a vampire king's cruel daughter that I forgot everything else?

It didn't matter if they had originally joined for Mother—they stayed for *me.* Their loyalty was to *me.*

It didn't matter what Prince Icas offered them, at least not to the truly loyal ones. They would follow me. I just had to have the courage to act.

I gave up before I even tried.

The words were like a slap in the face and strong enough to cause me to stumble slightly. My mind spun. My chest ached. I wanted to cry. I wanted to scream.

If I had done anything even the slightest bit different, would this have changed?

Brushing it off with a smile, I righted myself before the stares could eat me alive. I had never felt so unnerved in my life. Never felt so weak.

Where the fuck is this coming from? I did the best that I could while trapped in my cage. Mother would have understood... wouldn't she? *Would the people?*

But after that one cruel sentence flitted through my mind...I couldn't help but notice all those who came out to see me.

Behind the rows of rich vampires and powerful humans, they were all there. I remembered them. Every single one. I could pick out the faces of those who kneeled down in front of my mother to greet me every time she and I walked through the palace grounds.

I remembered the ones who came to see me in the pouring rain after my mother died.

We weren't allowed a funeral, but they did their best to provide me with wreaths of petrified roses, a gesture to let me know Mother would stay just like that—frozen in their memories, never to be forgotten.

I looked at them all, using their faces as my guide down the aisle. Instead of racing to my husband, I was racing to their memories.

My stomach twisted itself into a knot. So tight, it threatened to bring up whatever leftover blood I had in my stomach. *Regret.* An aching, all-powerful feeling that caused a sense of shame to fall over me.

As soon as my feet hit the threshold of the throne room, all those familiar faces left. There was not one person in there who was a part of the family, save for Father's court members. The rest were from other families in the area, all of them packed into the throne room. Making a once vast space seem so crowded.

I recognized a few.

Elora and her rotten husband. She looked just as withered as the last time I saw her. But even then, she managed a smile for me.

Dalia and her husband were there, standing side by side, his father not far behind.

And then, right at the end, on his throne, sat my father. He wore his red ceremonial robe, which he usually reserved for initiating family members. It was the same dark red I was wearing, with intricate golden designs. My stepmother and her daughter were by him in all black.

They looked down at me with smug grins. Maybe to onlookers, their expressions would have looked supportive, but I knew better. I had seen that sly smirk one too many times to be fooled by it.

They were eating it up. Their attempt to get me out of their hair angered me, but it saddened me even more to realize just how complacent I had been.

Because of me, they were able to pull it off. Because of me, they would now be in charge of all the family members I left behind.

At last, my eyes found the man of the hour. Prince Icas stood at the bottom of the steps, waiting for me. His hair was slicked back, and he wore a white robe with dark red underneath. It was so showy, I was surprised my father even allowed it. He gave me a beaming smile that, I'm sure, melted at least *some* of the hearts in the room.

At least the ones who didn't know just how twisted he was behind that mask of his.

I don't want to do this.

Less than ten steps away from him, my stomach fell to my feet.

The dress felt too tight. Too itchy.

It was getting hard to breathe.

The room was spinning.

The voices were getting louder.

My hands were shaking. My legs felt like they might give out any second.

Can I still stop this? Can anyone?

Four steps. He reached out his hand for me.

I couldn't stop myself from recoiling. All the muscles in my body seized. The need to run was crushing me.

His eyes were on me, *waiting*. Then his smile dropped when he realized what was happening.

I can't do this. I'm sorry, Mother, I—

The sound of a sword being pulled was so fast and hidden underneath the intensity of the music that I almost missed it. *Almost.*

Until my eyes caught a movement behind the prince. A fast,

dark blob that materialized as it got closer. It was so fast that if I had so much as blinked, I would have missed it.

Silver hair that shone in the setting sun was the first thing I could make out. The second was the pale face filled with battle scars. Chains were fastened around her neck and wrists. A startling image that had pain expanding through me.

But it was followed by hope. *She came.*

My dead heart felt like it would explode out of my chest.

Then, when she got close enough, I could make out her honey-colored eyes narrowed in on her target. She wasn't fazed by the crowd or by the way my father was staring at her with a smile I hadn't seen in years.

Just like the first time I had seen her, her heart was calm. Beating steadily and evenly. A sound that comforted me as soon as it reached my ears. There was no fear in her scent. No panic in her expression. Totally and completely focused.

I knew she was hiding something back then, but I couldn't make it out at the time.

Not until I saw the monster hiding in her shadow.

Warm, thick blood splashed across my face as she shoved her sword through the prince's chest and twisted it before immediately pulling it back. The blood seeped into his white clothing, painting a beautifully gory image of his last moments.

Suddenly, the white made all the sense in the world.

The smile on the prince's face crumpled, but the light in his eyes was long gone before his body fell limply to the floor. It happened so fast. Much faster than every time she attempted to do the same to me.

He was gone. *Just like that.*

The music cut out. Screams filled the room. All the noise was drowned out by a rush in my ears.

Vesper stood there, her face covered in vampire blood, eyes trained on me. The relief that washed through me threatened to bring me to my knees. She looked even better covered in the blood of that bastard.

My shaky hand lifted to my face, trying to feel for any possible blood splatter. Instead, I came into contact with something worse.

My own smile.

And then Father climbed down the stairs, his hands up, trying to call for the crowd's attention. He was back in the spotlight after losing it for mere moments.

His mouth was moving, but I couldn't hear his words. I couldn't make sense of what was happening.

I'm free. **Free.**

But the relief didn't last long. Because Vesper looked up at him, waiting for his command even when her true commander lay dead at her feet. And then the little mouse *kneeled* at his feet.

VESPER

From *one cage to another.* I was just grateful my brother wasn't here to see it.

Ice-cold water was poured down on my weakened body, stinging any exposed skin. *Magical.* Of course they would resort to magic.

The craziest thing wasn't that the king wanted me to be the one to kill Prince Icas. Or that he had me do it at the bastard's very own wedding.

It was that he *let me go.*

A loose end that had the ability to make life hard for him. He wasn't a merciful king—killing someone in front of thousands and then declaring war between the families wasn't mercy. But I was *alive.* And home.

Well, in a basement. But home nonetheless.

That was the craziest thing. Not only had I lived to tell the tale of the king's wrath, but I was somehow right back home, like it never even happened at all. I expected to be tied to him for the rest of my life for what I figured out. Expected that he would need to keep a close eye on me.

It would have been better than the hell that awaited me at home.

"You were supposed to be the *savior*, Vesper. How could you fuck up so severely?"

I looked up at my father through blurred vision. Pain shot through my chest with each breath. My head was killing me. But none of it was as angering as his fucking face. He had that sad expression on his face, like he actually felt pain for "punishing" me.

The stark black tattoo on his neck was calling to me. In my delusional haze, I could have sworn the snake moved, opening its mouth and preparing to strike.

If only it could put me out of my fucking misery.

The basement was lit enough that he couldn't try to hide in the darkness. That he couldn't try to look the other way when he was torturing me. I was still stuck in my clothes from days before and chained to the cement walls that surrounded the room. I was forced into a kneeling position, the chains sufficiently tight to hold my arms and body up in case I was weak enough to faint during the assault.

The basement itself was soundproof. None of my screams would get out. No one would know what went on in the house. They would drive or walk by, thinking it was a picture-perfect suburban house. Though I learned long ago that the screams didn't make a difference.

Maybe at one point I had screamed for the attention of the people on the outside. Maybe on the off chance that someone would come save me. But no one heard. Not even if Mother had guests over like she sometimes did when I was down here getting my *punishment.*

That's when I learned just how unlikely it was that I would ever be saved. I accepted it after some time. Hoped my brother wouldn't have the same fate as me.

I didn't believe either of them ever truly felt bad for what they had done to me or my siblings. Father wasn't capable of a smidge of empathy, much like the vampire king. But, unlike him, he wasn't drunk on power. Not this time. He was *angry* and wanted to take it out on something. Mother was the scared one. Her expression told me as much when she saw me walk through the door.

They had truly expected me to die. Even if it wasn't a part of the seer's prophecy, they had hinted that what I was meant to do would change the fabric of all vampire families and the secret organization that ruled our family. It was only natural that the person who was to change the future so drastically would become a martyr.

But if I hadn't become one, what could they do? They couldn't force me into it any longer.

Maybe this is my father's way of trying to cover up what I've done, I thought bitterly. *By killing me himself.*

No one in our family or any of the other ones in the secret organization had ever gone against their prophecy. At least that we'd heard of. From the start, we were controlled by the seer's visions. Completing job after job. Starting families and then indoctrinating them into the same fucked-up family business.

"I tried," I forced out. My voice grated against my throat, scratchy from not having access to water for almost three days.

I had spent about a day in the Castle family dungeons, and Father locked me up as soon as I was dropped off in this city. Word had gotten out fast, but Father was faster. *He always was.* Somehow, someone had to have given him notice of what happened.

If someone like yourself made it in here, what makes you think there aren't more? Cedar's warning rang loud and clear in my head.

I had stopped the wedding, but what about after? I wouldn't be there to protect her.

Images of Aurelia's expression as I stabbed her almost husband were etched into my mind. She truly thought I had abandoned her. But then she *smiled.* A bone-chilling smile that made me realize just how bloodthirsty she really was.

I couldn't stop the laugh from spilling from my lips.

Seeing her covered in the blood of that asshole was probably the most beautiful sight I had ever seen in my life.

"You think this is fucking funny?" he snarled. "What happened to you? We've been preparing you for this for years. Don't you know what it means for this family?"

I struggled against my restraints.

"What I think is *funny* is how blind you are," I growled and attempted to lunge at him, knowing the restraints would hold me back.

The restraints on my neck and wrists dug into my already raw skin. The time in the second dungeon of the Castle palace, locked up for hours in such a similar way, had already done a number on my skin.

His hand tangled in my hair and jerked my head to the side.

"Not blind enough to ignore how you prepared for this," he said, his eyes coming to where magic concealed my tattoo. Cedar's magic hadn't worn off. "I know about your little outings to the witch's den."

"And you didn't say anything?" I asked. It was a surprise to me that he actually knew. Of course the family used magical items here and there, but the organization that ran us warned about working too closely with the witches.

No doubt for fear of what we would learn. Nothing bad had ever happened to me while working with the witches. Both Levana and Cedar had kept their word. Helped me when I needed it.

So what was it that they didn't want us to know?

Why was it that Father could get magic-infused items from them to torture his children with, yet we couldn't communicate with them on our own?

"I wanted to see just how far this rebellious *streak* of yours would go," he snarled and tossed my head to the side. Pain radiated from my temple.

"Or maybe they didn't allow you through their wards," I said with a bitter smile. "Maybe you knew I was meeting them, but you could never get close enough yourself. Must suck, doesn't it?"

He let out a growl and reached for a knife attached to his belt.

"Don't test me, *Vesper*."

"Do you know what this *prophecy* has done to me?" I spat out the word "prophecy" like it was a curse. "All the lives I've taken? All the families I've ruined? How do you even know that they were worth all this? Have you ever even talked to one of these people or—"

The next slap stung more than the others.

"It is not our job to care for these *monsters*," he retorted, his voice barely above a whisper. Almost as if he was ashamed we were even having this conversation.

I thought I had seen the end of my father's cruelty. Throughout the years of "training" and the punishments whenever I didn't act like the cold-blooded killer he wanted me to be.

The truth was, I was every bit the monster he made me. The problem was that he and I had different moral compasses.

Well, apparently, he didn't have one.

"We are the monsters," I said in a low voice. "No better than those *hunters*."

"We are nothing like them!" The booming of his voice had me flinching.

Yes, we are, and all the vampires saw right through it. They had a longer lifespan than we could ever hope for. They saw what the hunters had done—how they brought the world to the brink of chaos before disbanding.

Only us and all the other families involved in this organization couldn't see it. We were the ones who tried to deny the truth for what it was.

"You're not getting anything else out of me," I swore. "I did what I could. That's all you need to know. Hitting me won't change that the prophecy is no longer valid."

His eyes narrowed at me, his mouth set in a snarl.

My eyes shot to the basement door as it swung open with a creak. Mother's tired face peeked through, her wrinkles looking much clearer on her face than they had in years. The stress of my return was obvious on her face. But she wasn't alone.

She pushed into the room, a small body following behind her. Tate.

I thought seeing my brother again would give me some sort of joy, but all it did was give me a renewed sense of fear.

They wouldn't dare.

But one look at Father's face told me that he had even more sinister plans for him than I could even imagine.

I jerked against my chains with a growl.

They can't do this. Not after I had spent so much time trying to save him from exactly this fate. *He is too young.*

"He's supposed to be in sch—"

"This is more important," Father said, dismissing me and motioning for Tate to come forward. He stood frozen. His insecurity showed through his actions rather than on his face, like anyone else his age. He had already mastered the ice-cold expression Father had taught us.

Mother placed a hand on his back and gently pushed him forward. Her eyes glanced at me before her face steeled as well.

She is scared. That's why she was allowing this to happen. Scared of Father. Scared of what would happen to us.

She is a coward.

Tate tried not to look at me as he approached. The sound of his feet dragging across the cement floor cut through the small room.

"You can't take him out of school for stu—"

Another slap. Tate flinched and froze next to Father.

"Not another word," he warned, his gaze cold. "Now, Tate, this is an example for you. Vesper decided that she didn't want to fulfill her duties, and you know what we do to people like that?"

Tate mumbled under his breath.

"Louder."

"We punish them," he said just the tiniest bit louder.

My heart dropped into my stomach. Bitterness coated my tongue.

I hate them. I hate this fucking prophecy. I hate this fucking family.

"Right, now let's start."

AURELIA

How dare she try to get away from me that easily?

I don't know what annoyed me more.

The fact that she was the one to tell Father that Prince Icas had tried to steal family members, or that she negotiated her own release as a reward.

How did she find the courage to do it while I was sitting in my room like a coward?

The murder of Prince Icas opened so many doors for me. Unfortunately, the families would be going to war, but I would take that over having to be a fuck toy for him *and* his father. And it gave me the opportunity to rebuild what had been lost with Mother's death.

There were just a few things I needed to accomplish first before I decided to enact my plans.

"You always did have a thing for keeping pets," Father said as he looked over my proposed contract. "Clipping their wings so they would never leave you."

I gave him a sickly-sweet smile.

His office was as spotless as usual, but the stack of papers by his right hand and the slightly disheveled look of his robe told me that waging war had consequences.

Maybe even some that he hadn't fully thought through.

"Well, now that the prince is gone, I have to find my entertainment somewhere, don't I?"

His eyes looked over me before he let out a light laugh.

"I'm sure you do," he said. "Well, I don't much care what you plan to do with her. I kept my end of the deal, so there's no stopping *you*."

He handed me back the contract. Surprise tickled my senses. I expected him to be annoyed. Maybe even a bit suspicious. *It's the most relaxed I've ever seen him.*

"So you agree?"

"Sure," he answered with another laugh. "If you can find her, that is."

"Find her?" I echoed, panic sinking in. After all that happened, was there still a chance I wouldn't be able to find her?

Does Father know something I don't?

"We couldn't get an address from her," he answered with a shrug. "No one in the prince's ranks seemed to know much about her. And when we dropped her off, it was in a random city down south. She can be anywhere by now."

Anywhere? That wouldn't do.

"Which guards stayed behind?" I asked, leaning against his desk.

"Most of them. Go see for yourself in the basement, I'm sure they'd be thrilled to have a visit."

I tried not to show my distaste on my face, but Father saw through it.

"The chase should provide *some* entertainment, should it not?" he said, his tone almost...humorous.

"You seem very chipper for someone who had my husband stabbed in the chest and a war waged with a prominent vampire family," I volleyed back, unable to keep the words in any longer.

His smile only spread wider.

"War is what we vampires were made for," he replied, shifting in his seat to look out the window. It was a beautifully sunny day, much like the day of my wedding. "And this way, I get to keep what's mine. He'll lose anyway. He should surrender if he knows what's good for him."

I had to bite back the growl. *I'm not yours,* I wanted to hiss.

Atlas was right. Father never saw me as a daughter but as his property to use and sell as he pleased.

"Why did he want Mother so badly?" I asked.

Shadows flitted across his features before he managed to hide them.

"The same reason everyone wanted her," he said, his gaze coming back to meet mine. "The ancestral bloodline. It alone causes vampires to flock from all over to join our families."

"But Mother wasn't from a powerful family," I reasoned, tilting my head to the side. "If I recall correctly, she told me that her father didn't even have a large family. He was part of a clan."

He gave me a condescending smile.

"Don't worry about it. Shouldn't you be celebrating your newfound freedom? Maybe go find that guard of yours?"

I pursed my lips, not liking how easily he was dismissing me.

"Why did you let her live, Father?" I asked hesitantly.

"Would you rather I had killed her with that handmaiden of yours?"

I straightened at the tone of his voice.

"No, I was just—"

"Or maybe I should ask how your guard and your handmaiden knew about Prince Icas's plans yet somehow you didn't? Or if you did, why you chose not to tell your own father as soon as you found out?"

A chill ran up my spine. Of course Father wouldn't overlook it.

"I think that's enough questions for today," I said as I pushed myself off the desk. "Thank you for the approval, Father. I'll see you when I get back."

All humor was gone from his expression, and I barely made it out of the room with my head still on. But just as I was about to walk down the hallway to enact the first part of my plan, the stepspawn decided to show herself. She even had the audacity to pause and look nervous.

Fucking perfect. I couldn't hold back the laugh as I launched myself at her.

The spawn shuttered as I dragged the magic-coated knife across the bare skin of her neck. The magical drug that I coated the metal with dripped onto her neck, glittery pink blending in so perfectly with her skin.

I waited so long for this. So long to make her squirm. It wasn't hard to get the knife, but it had been much harder to keep it hidden while I ran around the palace, just waiting for my chance to enact my plan.

I had been hesitant before, maybe even a bit afraid. But not anymore. Not after I saw what awaited me.

Compared to the prince, she was nothing but an annoying gnat that I needed to squash, and my actions would serve as a reminder to her that she couldn't fuck with me anymore.

"I wanted to take my time with you," I murmured, looking her over as she tried to shy away from my touch. "But unfortunately, I have a little pet waiting for me."

I hadn't thought it through, but as soon as I saw the bitch alone, I knew I needed to get her secluded.

A random, unused bedroom would do. Although it was probably way too close to Father's office, with all the other things he was worried about, I doubt he would even care about what I did.

As long as she kept her screams down.

I used some spare fabric from my dress to tie her to the headboard of the bed while I sat on the plush mattress right beside her. I kept the room dark, but the light from the window was enough to see her squirm.

"What else does she have planned?" I asked as I dug the sharp end of the knife into her skin, just enough to break the surface. It should give her the faintest hint of the drug. I watched her eyes closely for a sign that it was working as intended.

"You're fucking crazy," she spat.

I gave her a pitying smile. She hadn't seen anything yet. I was showing restraint. The darkness that hid in the back of my mind wanted me to do so much more. I had years and years of built-up anger that I needed to get out.

The only issue was my poor little mouse. The one who thought she'd get away from me. But I couldn't let her go. Not just yet.

"I am," I agreed with a mock frown. "But saying that doesn't get us anywhere, does it?"

"Don't infect me with that shit—"

"This?" I asked and pushed the knife further into her skin. "Too much of this stuff is dangerous, you know. Especially for good little girls like you who have never dabbled in it. Want to guess how much it takes until it starts to hurt?"

"Once Mother finds out—" she cut off with a hiss as I pushed the knife in further. Dark blood flowed down her neck and stained the pretty blue of her dress.

"Or maybe you want to wear the black veins on your forehead permanently?" They were already forming. Slowly, faintly, but they were there.

If she knew anything about this drug, she would know that it would take a lot more and longer for that to happen, but what she didn't know only worked in my favor. I almost wished it was fully saturated with the drug so she could truly feel the pain she inflicted on me over the years.

Maybe I'll add it to the docket for the next time I want to play with her.

"She has nothing planned," she forced out through gritted teeth. "She has already done all she needs. You think you are off the hook just because Icas was killed? Father doesn't *trust* you. More than that, he sees just how many people are willing to leave for you. If you think you're safe—*you're wrong.*"

She let out a sinister laugh that only annoyed me more.

I dragged the knife down her neck. Her pained groans were like music to my ears.

"You're lucky he doesn't know about your involvement yet," I murmured. "How long do you think you can hide behind mommy's shadow? Or maybe I should let him know about your affair with Dalia's husband? I heard you and him had some alone time before my wedding."

Her face paled.

"What do you think?" I asked. "Something to level the playing field? Father would be furious if he heard you're spreading your legs and ruining vampire families."

"Dalia fucks his dad," she spat. "There is nothing keeping that family together. It's a joke."

I let out a laugh. "And you think your status is on par with Dalia's? Better yet, why would he choose you over her if this rumor spread?"

For the first time, it looked like I finally had the bitch where I wanted her. I had been sitting on that juicy piece of gossip for some time—it was just never the right time to use it. Nor did it hold as much weight as I was implying.

Playtime is over. As fun as messing with her was, I had someone much more important waiting for me.

"Try that shit again, and I'll skin you, understand?" I asked in a whisper and pushed the knife into the hard part of her chest. "This is a warning."

Before she had a chance to say anything else, I threw the knife across the room and pushed myself off the bed.

"Don't think you're getting off easy!" I told her as I left the room with a wicked laugh. The frustrated scream she let out only amused me more.

I'm coming for you, little mouse.

AURELIA

"What an *honor!*" A redheaded woman greeted me at the entrance to Vesper's old room. It was much smaller than I imagined, with only enough room for two twin beds, a small walkway between them, and a single end table for both.

It's not like I made day trips to the guard quarters, though, so I wasn't sure what to expect.

It certainly wasn't the smell of magic. It was barely there and artfully hidden by the smell of various herbs and the smell of roses from the front garden, but I could still sense it.

Perfect.

The woman was lying in her bed with one arm behind her head and gave me a lazy smile. She had an air about her that had my skin itching. She didn't even bother trying to get up to greet me.

I immediately disliked her.

"Where is she?" I demanded, putting my hands on my hips. She had the gall to look amused by my actions.

She sat up, holding her weight on her elbows. A feral-like smile spread across her face, and a light flashed across her eyes. She *was* enjoying the little one-sided game she was playing.

Is this how Vesper felt the entire time we were together?

I would have almost felt bad for the little mouse if I didn't know how much she secretly liked the games we played. I, on the other hand, didn't have time for whatever it was this woman was trying to do. I had to get Vesper back before I moved on.

There was something so infuriating about her little disappearing act that I needed to understand, or else I might truly go mad.

"She was discharged, princess, didn't you hea—"

"Enough with the bullshit, witch. I know you know more than you're letting on."

She let out a laugh and tilted her head to the side.

"Oh? How curious."

Curious. I wanted to snort at her attitude.

"Both you and Vesper sucked at hiding this little secret of yours," I said with a smile. "But I'm different. Tell me where she is, and I'll keep this secret for you."

She shook her head and stretched out on the bed, her movements languid and far too feral for my liking. She was unpredictable, even more so than her roommate.

Something zapped my spine. *A warning.* She was dangerous.

"How about we make a sweeter deal?" She waved her hand in the air. "How about...you owe me a *single* favor?"

This time, I truly did laugh aloud. *What the fuck is she on?*

"You don't just demand a *favor* from *me*," I said with a huff. "Did you forget who I am?"

"No," she replied, her smile dropping. "But I think you may have."

Her words were like a start to my heart.

"What do you mean—"

"Don't read too much into it, princess," she said, raising a brow. "You wanna go get your plaything back, or what?"

Each word had her winding me up more and more. It had the hair on the back of my neck standing up and my skin feeling hot. *What the fuck is her problem?* Besides Vesper, this was the first time anyone had ever treated me with such an attitude.

Though I much preferred her roommate's to hers.

"I don't blindly agree to things," I finally answered. There was no room for argument. I had no idea what she had up her sleeve, and I really didn't fucking trust her.

What if she wanted me to kill someone? Ruin my reputation? Even go against my father?

"No? Too bad." She turned around on the bed, giving me her back.

As annoying as the movement was, I was glad for it because at least then she couldn't see how comically wide my jaw had dropped.

I let out a growl and dug my nails into the meaty part of my palm.

I needed her. At least I thought I did. She seemed to know much more than she let on, and was probably the only person in this palace who could point me in the right direction.

Compromise. I can compromise.

After dealing with Prince Icas, my near-death, and my almost-unwanted breeding, compromising was nothing.

"As long as it doesn't hurt me or Vesper, put either of us in danger, or affect my status as princess," I said and took a deep breath, "I will agree to it."

She let out a laugh and turned back to me. *Fuck,* the satisfied look on her face when she knew she was getting her way was so annoying.

"You got it, princess," she said and bounced off the bed, her sudden movement causing me to jerk back.

"Where do you think you're going?" I asked as she sauntered right past me and left the room.

What the hell? Was I just bettered by a witch?

"You think I'd miss this?" she asked, looking over her shoulder with an amused grin. "I'll take you, but I'm tagging along."

It looked like any other human suburb.

The houses were well-kept. The grass was green. The neighbors were out and about, saying hello to whoever passed.

They seemed kind and not at all like the cold-hearted assassin who was sent to my palace. They seemed to be living happily in their own little human world, without any supernatural beings in sight.

It was so odd to be right in the middle of something seemingly so untouched by the rest of the creatures in the world.

If I were a normal vampire, it might have alarmed me. There weren't many places that were human only, and even if there were, they definitely weren't welcoming to our kind.

There was a shift in the air as soon as they caught sight of us. They would pause in their conversation, take in our state of dress, then abruptly try to get themselves back into the house as quickly as possible without making it look too obvious that they were running away from us.

It was amusing.

Was there something so scary about us that caused them to act that way?

"A word of advice, princess," the witch said, coming close to my side. Too close for comfort. "Don't get too close to any of the humans inside that house."

I wanted to push her off. Ignore her because of her attitude about the place. But there was something about the house in front of us that gave me a bad feeling. It looked just like the others, but there was an aura about it. It smelled too clean. I gave her a nod.

Where there was one assassin, there would be others. It was unlikely that Vesper was working alone, and the next logical guess was that this was some type of family business.

"Assuming they are more like Vesper than her neighbors seem to be," I murmured, my eyes shifting to hers for a moment. "Can I trust you?"

She let out a laugh and shook her head. "You're funny, princess. I see why Vesper likes you. Not at all. But a deal's a deal, no?"

A deal's a deal.

Brushing her off, I made my way to the door, overlooking the perfectly pristine front yard and carefully placed lawn decorations. It wasn't as grand as my father's palace, but I could recognize when someone was obsessed with their appearance in the same way.

They have something to hide.

The door opened before we even made it halfway.

A middle-aged human man opened the door to greet us. His hair was peppered gray, and his face was full of wrinkles, but his body seemed strong. He held himself up straight, his physique obviously well-trained. He looked like a normal human. Even dressed in casual human clothes that raised no alarm bells.

But it was his heart that had me pausing.

It was too steady. Just like Vesper's. *So it is a family thing.* And if I was guessing right, Vesper would have learned everything she knew from the man right in front of us.

And then there was something black peeking out of his collar and winding up his neck. Because of the high collar of his shirt, I couldn't make out much, but it looked to be an intricate tattoo.

A smirk pulled at my lips. *Was he the one who sent her to kill me?* If so, I couldn't help but imagine how surprised he was to see me show up at his door.

I reached into my coat pocket and handed the contract to Cedar.

"Is Vesper around?" I asked, giving him a sweet smile. "I have an offer for her."

He wasn't fooled by my tone.

"What *offer* are you talking about?" he asked, eyeing Cedar warily.

"A contract for her services," I explained. "If you let us talk to her, I'm sure she could fill you in—"

"I'm the head of the house," he said, his voice gruff. "All contracts go through me."

"Straight to the point," I said with a smirk. "I'm guessing I don't need to bother introducing myself."

I motioned for her to bring it to him. Maybe I couldn't trust her, but she had to be right about this family.

"No," he grunted with a frown. "I could smell your stink from down the road."

I couldn't help but laugh at how open his hatred for my kind was. I jerked my head toward him, signaling for Cedar to deliver the paper. He watched her approach, his body growing stiff.

"We really enjoyed Vesper's company, and I've come to offer her a position. Room and board included, plus pay for her services as my *personal* guard," I explained. "If I had known about her discharge, I would have intervened before she could leave, but I have been...preoccupied these last few days."

Dealing with the intricacies of Vesper forcing a sword through my husband-to-be's chest, to be exact. But judging by the look on his face, he might have been annoyed if I shared that fact.

He grabbed the folded paper from the witch, his eyes taking her in critically before unfolding it.

"I didn't know the Castle family hired witches now," he said under his breath.

"And contract killers now, too," I piped in, my smile widening as he met my gaze. "For a year, if she agrees."

The man looked up at me again, his gaze calculating. There was movement in the house. I could hear the shuffle and the extra heartbeat, but couldn't make out exactly who was in there. It was far too quiet.

Another trained one.

"If you know that, why would you let her back in?" he asked.

"I *really* enjoyed her company," I answered in a sickly-sweet tone again. "Don't worry, I don't plan on killing her."

Another stare, then a small huff. "Tate! Get your sister."

I heard the shuffling in the house. The footsteps were smaller, lighter. It was a child. It took only a few minutes for both Vesper and a miniature version of her to show themselves in the doorway.

Blood. Vesper's blood. I recognized it easily. My nostrils flared, and red started to cover my vision. I couldn't stop the growl coming from my chest. *Did he fucking do that to her?* I wanted to kill him. Force my arm through his rib cage and pull out his still-beating heart.

Fresh wounds wound up and down her arms. Her face was ashen. Her hair greasy and unwashed. Her eyes void of light. My chest ached for her. No matter how angry I was at her disappearance, there was nothing that could have prepared me for seeing her like *that.* She was even worse for wear than when I'd seen her plunging a sword into my ex-fiancé's chest.

Her brother was clenching her hand, looking traumatized.

If my family were any better than hers, I would consider taking him. If that was what Vesper looked like after only a few days, it made me worried for the boy. But it would seem both of us had some pretty fucked-up family dynamics.

I forced my feet to stay frozen in their spot. Tried to fight the violent thoughts of tearing the man's throat out. It was hard. Harder the longer I smelled her blood. Human wounds didn't heal like vampires', but hers seemed to be over the top. Deep gashes with no aftercare.

Vesper looked at us with tired eyes. My gaze lingered on a tattoo on her neck, presumably the same one her father was hiding. One I'd never seen before. A dark tattoo of a snake went up her neck and peeked out of her cut-off sleeve.

That had been hidden...but how?

Magic. It clicked why I had smelled magic on her the day she handed me the bird feather, the one that still hung underneath my clothing.

Something went off in the back of my mind. Something about humans with tattoos of the zodiac signs. *What was it?*

"Is this some kind of joke?" she asked. Her voice was scratchy, and it didn't even sound like it belonged to her.

"I came here with a serious offer," I said. *Stay planted. Do not fight them.* I chanted it over and over again in my head.

I thought I was the one stuck in a cage, hopeless with no way out...but had that been her this whole time? Had her not killing me somehow been the only act of defiance she could muster against these people?

"She's going," the man spoke for her. He didn't even look at her as he did it, his eyes still glued to mine. *The feeling's mutual.*

"No."

His head snapped around to her. Vesper forced Tate behind her and glared at her father. *She cares for someone.* It was...astonishing to see. The cold-hearted little mouse actually had a person she was willing to fight for. Even if the consequences had her looking so horrid.

"Send him to Gabriel, and I will go," she bargained. Gabriel? There was another?

"Ves, I don't wanna—"

"I'll check," she said, cutting off her little brother. "If he doesn't go, I'll be come right back. Is that what you want?"

I could hear the grinding of her father's teeth.

"Wellness checks, something I can easily facilitate," I said, pulling the attention back to me. "Do we have a deal?"

Vesper's gaze rested on Cedar. It would seem the witch annoyed her as much as she annoyed me.

"Interfering again?" Vesper asked, the venom strong in her words.

"Merely protecting the princess in your stead," Cedar said, though there was no smile in her tone. Ever since she had gotten close to the man in the doorway, she had turned serious.

"Let's get on with it," I told them, unwilling to let Vesper bleed out any longer. It was annoying that they were even letting her stand there when she looked so unsteady. "Before I accidentally sink my teeth into someone's neck."

But I wasn't looking at Vesper when I said it. I was looking at her father. The threat was clear. I was a very unhappy vampire.

VESPER

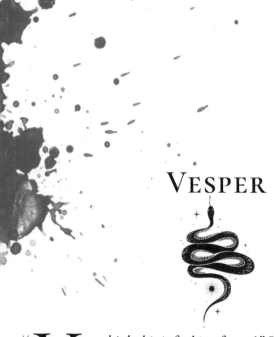

"You think this is fucking funny?" I asked as Aurelia led me down the hall.

My body ached. The wounds on my arms, face, and legs were slowly being healed by whatever magic Cedar had pumped into me on the car ride over, but it wasn't enough to make the pain go away.

It only added to

I was fuming. Her swooping in to rescue me was *not* part of the plan. The prince was gone. She shouldn't have interfered with whatever was going on in my life. Hell, she should have been rejoicing that I was gone.

So why the fuck am I back in this godforsaken place?

"I didn't think you disappearing on my wedding day only to find you had sworn your loyalty to my father very funny," she hissed, turning on her heels to face me. Her lips formed a pout, and her eyes were as sharp as ever.

Is she fucking kidding me? I was the whole reason she was able to get out of marrying him. To live. *Yet she was somehow still blaming me?*

I hadn't had a chance to take her in on the way back to the

palace. I was too busy trying to calm myself while simultaneously ignoring her and that damned witch who kept sticking her nose in places she shouldn't.

She looks good. Safe.

"Sworn loyalty?" I asked with a scoff. The anger was becoming unbearable. Boiling up inside me and heating my skin. "I was helping you! You know your crazy fucking father put me in the dungeon? You think I wanted to be down there?"

She let out an annoyed growl.

"You told a secret that wasn't yours to tell!" she blurted out, closing the space between us. She was so close, I could feel her front brushing across mine. The scent of her floral hair care wafted in my face.

The sun was shining in through the windows, sending colorful rainbows all over the intricate wallpaper, plush carpeted floors, and her face. It was beautiful. The way they splashed against her skin and lit up her blue eyes. The darkness of the dungeons made me forget just how mesmerizing she could be in the light.

"You should have stayed out of it."

She let out a huff of laughter.

"Sounds familiar, doesn't it?" she asked and cocked her head to the side, a sly smile forming on her face. "A little mouse not staying in her lane. *Interfering* when she shouldn't have. Maybe this is karma coming to bite you in the ass."

She was close enough to touch.

I hadn't realized just how much I needed to touch her until she invaded my space. It was like a parasite working its way into my brain and controlling my movements. I couldn't stop myself.

"What else would you have me do?" I asked, stepping closer. She moved to the side, trying to put some space between us, but I followed. A silly dance where we both knew the outcome we wanted but neither of us was ready to admit it. "Have you marry him? Have him use your name to start a war and get you killed?"

"You *killed* him and started the war anyway," she growled and tilted her head up to maintain eye contact with me.

"You don't seem all that upset about it, *princess*," I murmured, my voice dropping when I realized the wall was just behind her. She leaned against it, looking up at me with those angry eyes I adored so much. Her neck was outstretched, inviting me to wrap my hand around the delicate column.

I had thought about those eyes so much. Both while her father had me and while I was tied up in my house. As angry as I was, I was relieved more than anything that she was alive. The *exact* opposite of what my job entailed, but it was so much sweeter.

I leaned close, putting my hand on the wall beside her head. *So close.* Just one move, and our bodies would be pushed against each other.

"Well, are you?" I probed, needing her to answer. Needing her to admit that I actually did exactly what she wanted me to do. For her to realize that it was *me* who saved her. For her to confirm that throwing away any further contact with my family and the organization that controlled us wasn't all for nothing.

"He was mine to kill," she growled as her eyes searched my face, moving from my eyes down to my lips. "His blood should be on *my* hands. When people think of what happened at my wedding, they should be seeing me with my knife in his chest."

I couldn't help but smile at the image.

"But you choked. Froze right up until the very end," I murmured. Anger flashed across her face at the insult. "You did look quite breathtaking covered in his blood, though. I'd pay good money to see it again."

She tilted her head up even more, the anger starting to fade and something else taking its place.

This shouldn't happen. Not again.

But the electric tension that had been swirling around us was hard to ignore. Her breathing deepened, her chest rising and falling rapidly.

I gave into the urge to gently place my fingers around her neck before trailing them down to her chest. The gleam of the silver chain that was tucked into her clothing caused my heart to skip a beat. *She kept the present.* The softness of her skin was intoxicating. I let my fingers brush across the hem of her top before running them down the side of her breasts.

She ever so slightly arched into me.

"You should have told me what you were planning," she said breathlessly. I made it down to her waist, then to her mid-thigh, before bringing my hand up again.

Every other time before had been rushed, in the heat of the moment. Never once had I been able to indulge myself. To actually take in her little reactions to even the slightest brush of my fingers against her clothed body.

I wanted to study it. Commit it to memory so that I would never forget what happened between us.

"Is this my punishment?" I asked, letting my hand trail back up her leg. "You buying me as your pet? To have whenever you wish after I tried so hard to escape you?"

"Yes," she whispered, her breathing hard. My hand trailed to her waist before lightly teasing the underside of her breast. She didn't push me away or force me this time. She was letting me take my time with her. It felt more like a reward than a punishment. "I wanted to show you that there's no way to escape me. Even if you hadn't agreed to it, I would have made sure you were right back here kneeling at my feet, where you *belong.*"

Where I belong. The spoiled princess was making a comeback. Even after everything, Aurelia remained the same person she was before the wedding.

A selfish part of me was glad she hadn't changed. That she still wanted to play with me. To control me.

It was a part I was all too eager to play.

"Like this?" I asked, then slowly lowered myself to my knees, my face at her stomach. I let my lips brush across her clothed belly.

Her eyes hooded, and her mouth opened slightly, enough to give me a view of her fangs. It was so reminiscent of our first night together. I was kneeling between her legs the same way, and she was looking down at me like a queen perched on her throne.

"*Better*," she said with a light smirk.

But unlike then, I wasn't fighting the control she had over me. I took pleasure in it.

"And what if I try to escape these *horrid* conditions?" I teased her ankle with my fingers, slipping them under her skirt and slowly placing her leg over my shoulder. I kneaded the tense muscles. A move that had her relaxing against me.

"I'll find you," she vowed in a whisper. It wasn't an empty threat. Her gaze told me she would do exactly that. Over and over again until she grew bored of our cat-and-mouse game. "And then I'll bring you back here. Lock you up so you'd never have a chance to leave me ever again."

I pushed her skirt up, baring her underwear to me. Light pink with a lace frill. My mouth watered at the sight. I turned my head to the side, brushing a kiss against her thigh.

Her intake of breath had my own arousal growing. There was something so satisfying about turning the princess into a panting mess. About having her become something she wouldn't dare show anyone else.

"Be careful," I warned with a smile. "Or it might just sound like you missed me."

I leaned forward, placing a kiss over the growing wet spot in the thin fabric. She let out a high-pitched noise, her hips jerking against me, begging me to continue.

"And if I said I did?"

I hooked my fingers in the fabric and pushed it to the side.

"Go on," I breathed. "Tell me how much you missed me, and I'll reward you, princess."

I let my tongue brush across her folds, savoring the way she shuddered against me. *So easy.* The once ice-cold, cruel princess was falling apart with so little effort.

Having my face in her cunt in the middle of the hallway probably wasn't the best look after I killed her husband-to-be...but god, did it make me feel powerful.

She thought she was keeping *me* captive, but she was the one who came to find me. To drag me back just so she could feel my tongue against her. I was an obsession she couldn't get rid of, and she would do anything in her power to force me to her side.

She was the captive. She just hadn't realized it yet.

"I missed your mouth," she said, her hand threading through my hair and forcing my face into her cunt. My lips found her clit, sucking hard on it before making a trail to her entrance.

Fuck, I forgot how sinful she tastes.

"That's a good girl," she moaned. "Make my purchase worth it, hm?"

She asked for it. I fastened my lips to her clit again before pushing two fingers inside her.

If she wanted to be fucked, I had no choice but to oblige. Her moans were sweet as they filled the hallway. Her pussy clenched around my fingers as I pumped them in and out of her.

She arched into me, her hand keeping my head still so she could grind against my face. I could just make out her expression as I looked up at her. Her mouth was open, pleasure strewn across her face.

That's right, princess. Lose yourself in me.

"I'm so mad at you," she said through her moans. "I waited for you the entire day, and when you didn't show, I panicked. How dare you leave me right as I was about to get married off?"

I twisted my fingers inside her, pumping faster. Her wetness was dripping down her legs, making a mess of the carpet below, of my clothes.

I wanted more of it. I wanted everyone to know just how messy their perfect little princess got.

"And then when I saw you—*god*—I had never seen you like that before. So...unleashed."

She was going to come thinking about it. Her cunt started to flutter around me, and her movement became more erratic.

I pulled away from her, slowing down.

"Not so fast, princess," I said as I licked my lips. "You really think you deserve to come so easily after everything?"

She narrowed her eyes at me and tried to jerk her hips against me as the pace of my hand between her legs slowed, but I used my other hand to grip her hip.

"Don't play with me, *Vesper*." She said my name with so much venom, it made my stomach flip.

"Tell me you missed me, sweet princess," I whispered as I forced a third finger into her. She took it easily. Her whine was music to my ears.

"Touch yourself," she ordered. "Touch yourself, and I'll tell you how much I missed you."

Her expression told me she really didn't think I would do it.

I moved my hand away from her hip and held her gaze as I unbuttoned my pants.

"You act like this is such a degrading thing," I said with a shaky breath as I slipped my hand into my pants and circled my clit. It was already so painfully sensitive and engorged. "You act like me finding pleasure in yours isn't one of the most intoxicating things I ever felt."

She brought her own hand down to her clit, rubbing hard circles over it as she watched me fuck myself. Pleasure zapped up my spine, and heat exploded inside me.

"Taste me, little mouse," she said. "Use my cum to fuck yourself and tell me how it feels."

Fuck. I couldn't say no. I removed my hand from her cunt and forced it into my pants, mixing her wetness with my own as I pushed my fingers inside myself.

Her hands reached out and pulled my face back to her cunt.

"You're mine," she growled. "I did miss this. Missed *you*." Her movements became erratic again as she chased the orgasm she had lost. I matched her pace with my hand, fucking myself as if it were her.

She was intent on degrading me. On having me make myself come while she was the one riding my face.

It was that fiery spirit that had me clenching around my fingers.

The hand on my clit picked up speed, wetness spilling into my pants.

"You're so fucking messy," she said with a laugh. "I can't wait to see how else you'll embarrass yourself, little mouse. Now keep fucking yourself. Don't stop until you come."

I couldn't say anything if I wanted to. I was so bent on listening to her commands that all I could think of was obeying.

"Fuck, *fuck*." Her chants were the only indication she gave me before she exploded. Wetness coated my face as she rode out her orgasm. Her cries rang out, bouncing off the walls of the hallway.

I pulled away so I could catch the look on her face as she came down from her high, all while fucking myself.

"Are you going to come for me?" she asked in the sweetest tone, her nails dragging down my cheek.

I was. I couldn't hold back. I cursed under my breath as the first wave hit me. I couldn't keep my body up, so I fell into her as I shuttered through my orgasm. The heat was like a tidal wave exploding through my body and bringing me under as I tried to stay upright.

Only when it subsided was I able to look back up at her.

A satisfied smile spread across her face as I quickly buttoned my pants. Her eyes were clear, and the burdens that seemed to be permanently latched to her shoulders were gone.

She missed me.

How laughable was it that the only person who ever told me that was a spoiled vampire princess I was supposed to murder? Even more laughable was how it made my chest warm.

But it was short-lived, like most good things in the world. Her head snapped to the side, a growl rising from her chest.

I turned to see what alerted her, ready to jump into action until I saw *her*.

Goddamnit, could she ever leave me alone?

Cedar stood there at the end of the hallway, an annoyed look on her face.

I quickly fixed Aurelia's skirt so Cedar wouldn't see her exposed and sent her a glare. If there was anyone I needed to get rid of, it was her.

"You think I wanted to interrupt this?" she asked with a disgusted tone before pointing to her neck. "Unless you want the king to find out who you really are, you need a touch-up."

"Tell your friend to cover up her scent," Aurelia growled and pushed me out of the way before storming down the hallway.

VESPER

E ven if we had somehow found our way past the impossible walls in front of us, a happy ending still felt like a delusion. Like it couldn't exist.

Not for us.

I knew this wouldn't be problem-free. I knew that living in the palace with her was one of the least safe options for us. Especially while the king was preparing for war.

I knew Father was unhappy with the outcome of my job, and I also knew he would somehow come for me, so I was waiting for the universe to drop the other shoe.

"He's been taken to Gabriel," Cedar said as we walked down the hallway together. It had been my request that she be the one overseeing his transfer.

Not that I trusted her. If anything, she was the person I trusted the least in this world. But she knew far more about the situation than I wanted anyone else to know.

"Thank you," I said as, for the first time, real relief filled me.

I couldn't imagine what it would be like for Tate to be stuck at home with my parents. There was no telling what they would do now that I had failed them.

They hadn't been as hard on him as they'd been on me. The time I spent training at the boarding school getting my ass handed to me was time he spent going to a normal school, hanging out with kids his own age.

Of course, Father still trained him in his free time. Going over the importance of our role in society and why we did what we did.

But he never took the beatings that were meant to prepare us for even the toughest jobs.

Until the night I went back home. That was the first time they had him join in.

"They didn't let me near the drop-off," she said with a forced smile. "But I saw him meet with Gabriel. Or at least I think it was him. Same hair as you with the snake tattoo. Not many people out there look like that on purpose."

Her quip forced an unexpected burst of laughter to spill from my lips. I shook my head and sent her a grateful smile.

I wish I could have gone, but leaving the palace and the princess had its own set of risks.

"Thank you, *truly*. I've been worried about him. I can't tell you how much this means to me."

Her expression softened, and she slapped her hand against my bicep.

"I know," she said, then her eyes shifted to the hallway before coming back to me. "Things are looking good, Vesper. But keep your eyes peeled, okay?"

Her seriousness caused my heart to still.

I looked around the hallway. There were only a few maids at the end of it and they looked preoccupied with their duties.

I leaned close to her.

"It's not over, is it?" I whispered, my gaze shifting to hers. "Tell me what you know. *Please.*"

For the first time, a sort of regret crossed her face.

"I can't," she answered with a grimace. "Just know I'm on your side. Always, okay?"

"When have you ever been on my side?" I asked in a low hiss. "Tell me—am I or am I not your job?"

She let out a scoff and shook her head. "If you don't see everything I've done as being on your side, I don't know what to tell you." She looked down the hall, her eyes narrowing. "Good luck with everything."

A part of me wanted to call out to her as she turned and walked back down the way we came, but I stopped myself.

It wasn't my job to try and smooth this over. Yes, she had helped, but she wasn't being as truthful as she could be, and at that point, I couldn't afford to be in the dark much longer.

It isn't over. Her words told me that much, but her expression told me even more. *What does she know, and is that the cause of her pained expression?*

I shook my head. The princess was waiting for me. I didn't have much time to waste.

Our routine had been the same over the weeks following my "rescue" from my family's house.

I still stayed in the guard dorms. Mostly to save my own face. Most people knew the princess and I were together, but in a work sense. If I started staying in her room like she wanted me to, there would be no denying I was her plaything and not her guard.

The princess didn't care, even if the rumors surrounding the prince's demise went from him being a traitor to the princess having an affair.

I continued down the hallway, only to almost run right into one of the maids. I looked down to say something to her when she grabbed my wrists and pulled me into one of the dark, unused corridors.

Before I could even look at her face, my instincts kicked in, and in seconds, she was pushed up against the wall, my sword at her throat.

I was ready to slice it through her neck when her voice stopped me.

"Stop, Vesper! It's me!"

I paused, recognizing the voice. When I pulled back to take her in, my heart stopped in my chest.

I knew her. Not only did I know her, but our families were the same.

Long brown hair pulled up into a bun. Hazel eyes. Three—no, *four*—small moles on her face. She was in the standard maid uniform the palace supplied, but hers had a turtleneck instead of the standard crew neck.

Nadine.

I hadn't seen her in years. The last time had been at the boarding school my family sent me to. We were in a few classes together. At the time, the students tried to memorize every family symbol and child who was a part of the school. It was part of the information we were allowed to know about how the organization worked.

Our fathers knew each other. Just like us, they had gone to school together. But after we graduated, I never saw her again. That was the point. We were sent to different parts of the country, with each family settling in a specific place to carry out the orders given to us.

If she's here, this means...

My hand immediately went to her turtleneck to make sure the person in front of me really existed.

She shouldn't be here. No one should.

My breath caught when the pitch-black image of a dragon came into view. It was stark against her skin, the image startling me.

Fuck. Fuck. Fuck.

Had Cedar known? Was that why she gave me that look? I thought I had time. At least more than a few weeks before they would ship one of my own here.

I pinned her harder against the wall, my hand ready and my sword still on her neck.

Slice it. It will be easy. The issue would be getting rid of the body. Obviously, I couldn't just murder a maid in the middle of the palace and walk the halls with her bloody body over my shoulder.

"Did my father send you?" I whispered, my eyes narrowing at her.

My heart was erratic, beating loudly in my chest, and none of the techniques taught to me were any use in calming it down.

She caught me off guard.

Her eyes widened, and she brought her bottom lip between her teeth. A face of pure innocence. One that might have had another person putting away their weapon. But it only had me pushing it harder into her.

Maybe it would be worth getting caught. The princess could probably help me clean it up.

"I come with a message. But before I say it, please don't take this the wrong way. You have to understand that I never wanted—"

"Don't give me that bullshit. None of the act," I growled. "Did they or did they not send you here to make sure I completed my task?"

She grimaced. "Yes, but—"

I pushed her away in disgust. *A babysitter.* She would be the one to constantly feed information to my father and the organization, constantly watching and waiting until I completed my job.

We are not safe here. I need to kill her.

"Tell them I don't fucking need it," I growled and turned away, unable to keep my body from shaking with fury. "I have it under—"

"That's not all."

I turned back to look at her. The scared act she had been putting on was gone, and a full-on smile spread across her face. *This* was the type of person who went to the boarding school. She had a job to do, and not only would she get it done flawlessly, but she would also have fun doing it.

This is the type of person the school breeds.

Ruthless killers who took joy in the terror they were putting their victims through. She thought this was a game.

"You have a week," she said with a light laugh, "before I take matters into my own hands."

I'll kill her. Kill her and dump the body somewhere like they did the feeders. I will need to wait until night. Have Cedar guard the princess. No one will ever—

"Should I be worried that you're not paying attention to me?" Aurelia asked from her vanity, brushing her slightly damp hair from our time in the shower together.

She had told me about throwing her old one out the window. Looking at the room, one would never suspect she had ruined it. The window was back in place and allowed the sun to shine through. The vanity had been replaced with another one just like it. Not a thing was out of place.

Just like the king when it comes to covering up anything related to the failed wedding.

I wished their hiring was as good as their cleanup. Seriously, how many of us would be able to sneak in here before they noticed?

"Needy now, are we?" I asked, giving her my best attempt at a smile. She seemed to accept it.

She didn't need to panic, not over this. It was my mess, and I should be the one to clean it up. Maybe I could even get Cedar's help. If she wasn't too mad at me for my comment earlier, that was.

"Hey, our contract states that—"

"Have you ever thought of leaving?" I asked her.

She pursed her lips together and straightened. An oddly serious move from her.

"Many times," she admitted. "Growing up as a spoiled princess wasn't all it was cracked up to be."

There was a joke woven through her words, but there was something heavier behind them, too.

"I mean after the wedding," I said and shifted, my eyes searching the room. I don't know what I was looking for. *Something* to make sure there was no one listening in. The thought that Nadine could be anywhere, watching us, was getting to me.

The feeling of being watched, whether it was true or not, caused my skin to crawl. All I could think about was keeping the princess safe. Getting us out of here. *Anything.* They were too close for comfort.

Atlas crossed my mind. The magical artifact was hidden away in my room, so if worse came to worst—

"Are you asking me to run away with you?" she asked with a smile. When I met her gaze, she laughed and turned back to the mirror. "Father would be after us in an instant. Especially because he can't afford for his property to fall into the wrong hands. And don't get me started on that crazy father of yours. You still have a job to do, don't you remember?"

All too fucking well.

"Atlas, she has passage—"

"Is there something I should be concerned about, Vesper?" She was facing the mirror, but her eyes were on me.

I swallowed thickly. *Yes.* But I didn't want to burden her with it. I could handle it myself. I just needed time to *think.*

"Has your stepmother stopped bothering you?" I asked, unable to come up with anything else.

She held my gaze for a moment longer before looking back at herself. A smile played on her lips.

"I haven't had a chance to *visit* her yet," she said. "Though I will soon. It had to be perfect, you see—"

She was interrupted by a knock. Her eyes flitted to the door, and a smile spread across her face. "Oh, finally! Come in!"

And then, as if things couldn't get worse, Nadine's face peered into the room. My hand reached for the sword on my back. My body was tense.

"Sorry, miss, I just had to get oriented—"

"After Father killed the last one," Aurelia said, giving me a look. "I found myself in the market for another. She will be my new one, starting today. Came from Dalia's family with glowing reviews—"

I had to tune out her words, unable to keep my rage in check.

Nadine stood there, her hands folded against her stomach, looking like a picture-perfect handmaiden for a princess like Aurelia.

You have a week, her smile said. Her eyes were on me the entire time while Aurelia introduced her.

I debated killing her right then and there. We were alone in the room with only Aurelia. At least there would be no witnesses. But there was always a chance that she could sneak past me and hurt Aurelia before I had a chance to kill her.

They are better prepared than I thought. I could see the strategy. They were trying to fuck with my head. Get me scared, so I'd either hurry up or fuck up.

And it's working.

But if they thought I'd just let them interfere, they were fucking wrong.

"Get rid of her," I ordered Aurelia, not even sparing her a glance. "You don't need a handmaiden."

"And what, have *you* take over?" Aurelia asked with a scoff. The sound of her standing reached my ears, and her hand was on my shoulder in moments. "You can't expect a spoiled princess like me to live without a handmaiden, can you?"

She was saying it to annoy me. To continue our playful game.

But I wasn't playing anymore. Not when they were forcing my hand.

"Come help me with my hair. Father has guests today," she said and motioned for Nadine to follow her back to the vanity.

I stood by, watching helplessly. When the princess wasn't looking, Nadine sent me a wink. It took everything in me to stay planted.

I turned to watch them in the mirror as Aurelia explained how she wanted her hair. Nadine nodded along, her hands gently taking Aurelia's long locks in her hands before she began twisting them away from her face.

Those hands were too close to Aurelia's neck for me to relax. I had seen those same hands handle weapons, covered in the blood of our classmates. Her eyes met mine in the mirror, telling me she was remembering the same.

You have a week.

I'd be damned if I allowed her to be near Aurelia for even a second longer.

AURELIA

Stepmother had this habit.

Before important events, she would meet with a specific feeder.

One she would spend at least an hour with. She had a specific room, one on the other side of the house, far away from the king and her daughter.

She tried to keep it a secret, but the staff talked. Especially when they hated her as much as they did.

Apparently, I wasn't the only one whose life she tried to ruin. All it took was a little probing, and they spilled every single thing they knew about these meetings.

They thought it was an affair. Especially because of how giggly and satisfied she would be afterward.

An affair would be too simple, especially if I wanted to end her the way she tried to end me. But it was a start, and at first, all I truly needed was a warning.

So, I snuck into the room the staff pointed me to. It wasn't very remarkable. A large bed with a seating area off to the side. It was obvious what the room was supposed to be used for.

If what the staff said was correct, she would be entering the room a few minutes after me. The feeder would come later.

I made myself comfortable against the bedpost. Normally, I would sit on the bed, but it looked unused. Actually, the whole room seemed to be untouched. There was even a specific musky scent in the air that told me there hadn't been anyone in there for a long time.

Alarm bells rang in the back of my head. *This room didn't look used.*

All of it had been too easy. The staff too willing to share.

I had been cornered too many times in the last few months to fully believe that the person that was going to walk through those doors was my stepmother.

I had Vesper waiting for me downstairs where the guests would be. I needed to do this alone. But the way she reacted when we separated...

I don't think I'd seen Vesper act that way before. She had been... nervous. Maybe even a bit paranoid. Something happened. She hadn't wanted to tell me about it, even after I told her how unhappy it made me when she kept her plans secret.

Fine. If she wanted to keep it to herself, she could. I would find out myself, no matter how hard she tried to hide it.

The knob wiggled and had me reaching for the knife I kept hidden in my skirt. The same knife I used on the stepspawn, minus the magical drugs. Unfortunately, I used the last I had back then.

The door pushed open and instead of my stepmother, it was my newest handmaiden. She looked surprised to see me in here.

Of course it was too good to be true. I guess it's showtime.

It had almost been too easy to lure her out.

"Princess," she said in a hushed tone and slipped in, closing the door behind her. "You were supposed to be downstairs. The guests will be here any minut—"

"You work fast," I said with a smile, tilting my head and watching her.

"Excuse me?" she asked with a laugh. "Oh, you mean your hair? Well, Lady Dalia had pretty intricate—"

I cut her off with a laugh.

"You think I didn't ask my own friend about you?" I questioned, taking a step forward. My hand was tight around the dagger, ready to strike. "Not to mention how Vesper reacted to your presence. You truly think I'm some idiot who doesn't see when a snake has infiltrated her ranks?"

Her expression slowly morphed into a smile that confirmed all my suspicions.

I shouldn't have trusted Vesper as much as I did, but she hadn't failed me at that point. She truly seemed to be worried about me and took her job to protect me seriously.

Since she'd been back, we'd been nearly inseparable. But because of that, I hadn't been able to move freely. Or to pull the snake out of her nest.

This is for us. For Vesper and me.

"I'm not the snake," she said and reached behind her to pull out a small dagger of her own. I could smell the magic on it. "I'm *cleanup.*"

I pulled out my own weapon. When she got a look at it, she let out a huff of laughter.

Cleanup. No wonder Vesper was so worried. She was protecting her own failure. *It is kinda cute.* But I could take it from here.

I had been running around in a panic since the wedding, freezing like a deer in headlights and falling into a hopeless spiral.

I wouldn't be like that this time.

"Was that supposed to be for your stepmother?" she asked. "You're really something else, aren't you?"

I readied myself, recalling how Vesper attacked the night in my room. I was a vampire and had the upper hand, but they were trained in a way I never had been.

"It's for you," I said with a smile. "At least it is now. I just never expected you to move so fast."

She shifted slightly, placing her feet apart and crouching. She was readying to attack.

"I gave your plaything a week, but after seeing the way she tried to out me, I decided to take matters into my own hands," she admitted. "Pity—it was fun to see her squirm."

She launched herself at me. *I guess no more talking.*

She was fast. Faster than Vesper. But I could use that and her own strength against her.

As soon as she was less than a foot away from me, I jerked to the side. Her dagger embedded into the post behind me. She'd swung so hard, she couldn't pull it out right away. My free hand was on her wrist, my dagger hand pointing at her neck.

The smile on her face dropped when she realized what I was doing.

I opened my mouth wide and bit down right on the joint of her elbow. My fangs dug into her skin, slicing through it as easy as butter, until they hit bone. With one single bite, the bones cracked under my teeth.

Her pained scream split the air. I used her wrist to twist the broken arm behind her, while keeping my dagger at her throat. I got as close as possible to her face, a smile spreading across mine.

Her blood was sweet against my taste buds and sent a vibration through me. I was tempted to drain her just to watch her reaction.

It feels good. Her screams of anguish. Her pained expression. Knowing that I held her life in my hands.

It is addicting.

"How many others did you bring with you?" I asked. "And don't try to say you just paid off my staff to mislead me into coming in here. *How many?*"

She let out a laugh.

"Not as dumb as you've been made out to be, huh?"

"How many?" I asked again. "Maybe if you're honest, I'll let you off easy."

When she didn't answer, I put more pressure on her arm. Her lips formed into a snarl.

"I take that back. Letting go of your own killer is a dumb fucking idea."

I pushed the tip of the dagger into her throat. "I never said I'd let you go. But I could make your death less painful."

There was no way she was getting out of here alive, but I needed to get more information out of her. I had to know exactly how many people in this palace were out for my head.

But what I didn't expect was for her other hand to come out with another knife. I tried to jerk out of the way, but she pushed us both forward, causing us to fall on the bed.

I turned my head to the side as she brought the knife down to the mattress.

"I won't return the favor," she said with a sneer. "I don't take pride in cleaning up messes. Nor do I enjoy this little competition your fuck toy has created for us."

"Afraid someone else will get to me before you do?" I teased.

She gave me a smile. "Too late."

She pulled the knife back, but as she was about to bring it down on me, she was jerked away.

I scrambled up just in time to catch Vesper disarming her. The anger on her face was unlike anything I'd seen before. Pure, unrestrained anger. There was only one way to calm something like that.

I couldn't help but admire how beautiful she looked.

"I should have killed you sooner," Vesper growled. The girl jerked against her.

"Just get it over with," she huffed.

"Not until you tell me who else is here. Three? Five?"

She let out a laugh. "You really don't know, do you?"

I crossed the space between us and pointed the dagger at her stomach. Both their eyes flashed to me.

"What number are you?" I asked. This caused a playful look to pass over her face.

"Not dumb indeed," she breathed. "I'm number thirteen."

My gaze shot to Vesper. *Thirteen? The* look in her eyes told me she was just as surprised.

"Where are they?" Vesper asked and pushed her closer to my

knife. The tip dug into her skin, breaking it and letting her bright red blood spill out. She let out a groan.

"Acting innocent in front of your girlfriend?" she asked with a laugh. "Tell her how you killed them. Tell her how you mutilated their bodies and dropped them off outside the property. My job wasn't only to finish what you couldn't do, it was to end you. They're mad, Vesper, and they won't stop until you are both dead."

I knew Vesper hadn't done it. She was a killer like them, but there was no way she would have been able to kill all of them.

I pushed the knife into her stomach to the hilt.

"You talk too much," I growled. Pain flashed across her face as her mouth opened in a silent scream. Vesper covered both her mouth and nose, holding on tight until she slumped against us.

We stood there for a few moments in silence, both our minds reeling at not only what we had just done, but the threat that lay out there waiting for us.

It will never end.

"Who's killing them?" I asked in a whisper.

Her expression hardened. "Only one person could."

"It's time to tell the fucking truth," Vesper growled as she pushed Cedar against the wall.

The witch could have easily fought her off, but she let her hold the knife to her throat. She put her hands up, but unlike before, there was no smile on her face.

She was just as serious as we were.

The night air was cold, and I was forced to look over my shoulder at every rustle or sound for fear another one of Vesper's colleagues would sneak up on us.

Cedar hadn't been in her room when we first looked, but somehow we found her in the garden my mother once loved. The same one Vesper and I stayed in the night before my wedding.

I didn't like the coincidence.

"Please tell me you dumped her body somewhere, so I don't have to help you clean up," she said with a sigh.

"You knew, and you didn't warn us?" I asked, unable to keep the venom from my voice. Cedar looked at me with an annoyed expression.

"I warned Vesper!" she whined. "She was the one who decided to not listen."

The air felt cold against my skin. *Vesper knew they were coming? She didn't tell me. Again.*

My eyes shifted to the contract killer, but she seemed just as off guard as I was.

Who is telling the truth here?

"You said to watch out," Vesper growled. "You never said another one was coming. Or that she was the thirteenth."

Cedar's eyes shifted to the side. I moved so I was in direct sight.

"You've been killing them," I accused. "You knew they were coming, and you started killing them. Is that what you were sent here to do?"

Obviously, Vesper wasn't doing this. I didn't expect her to be *that* much of a liar. The urge to distrust her was strong, like with everyone else in my life...but she *saved* me. More than once. That had to mean something.

Cedar let out a huff.

"I don't kill hunters in my free time," she muttered under her breath.

Vesper didn't correct her this time.

"You're the only one who could."

Cedar gave her a look, a deep frown appearing on her face.

"I said I was on your side," she said, pushing Vesper off her. I smelled the magic before I saw Vesper being forced away from the witch by a gust of air. "Why do you think I was covering your tattoo for you? None of those other idiots even thought to do the same. They were dead on arrival."

Vesper froze. *Why? What is she getting at? I don't understand.*

Cedar seemed to get that I was confused.

"Your father knows," she told us. "At least about these guys. I mean, tattooing yourself with animals of the zodiac isn't really a subtle way to announce your affiliation."

That's what it was. It became clear then. I had heard about them in passing, but it had never been spelled out so clearly nor did I ever think I needed to worry about a silly human organization.

"But there were thirteen," I offered. "Shouldn't that mean they're running out of people to send? There are only supposed to be twelve animals."

Cedar snapped her fingers.

"*Yes*," she said with a smile. "There were thirteen. Tell us, Vesper. Why were there so many?"

The grinding of Vesper's teeth hit my senses.

"Each family gets assigned one," she explained, her head tilting just enough so I could see her face. "These families, as long as they don't piss off the organization, can stay in as long as they like. Others will get replaced when their usefulness wears off. There are some families out there who have been active for over seven generations. We aren't a small organization."

We aren't a small organization. That means they will come for me, and they won't stop. Hundreds of them. But why me? *What had I done?*

I had spent my entire life trying to save myself by melding into the role my father required of me. I hadn't gone out to start any wars, or killed any humans, and the blackmail parties held almost no importance.

"Why do they want me dead?" I asked, my voice dropping low.

Cedar looked at Vesper who let out a sigh. A discomfort spread across Vesper's features and had her body twitching. "I don't know *why*, just that it was prophesied."

I raised a brow at her.

"They get their jobs through seers," Cedar explained. Vesper shot her a look.

I still don't trust the witch, but maybe we need her. She knows too much.

"And you know that how?" I asked. Cedar took a step back and raised her hands again, a nervous laugh coming from her.

"Whoa, I'm here to help remember?"

"Honesty," Vesper growled, taking a step forward. "I need it if I'm going to keep her alive. I need to know how to stop them from coming."

"They won't stop," Cedar answered. "They never will. And in return, her father will continue killing them. Unless, of course, this war *you* started is enough to distract him. One already got in, so it wouldn't be a surprising conclusion."

"There has to be something you know that could help us," I pressed. Panic was rising in me now. If Father knew about these people, Vesper wouldn't be safe. If I stayed here, and knowing now one of them was already in, I wouldn't be safe either.

Cedar gave me a pity-filled look.

"Vesper knows how to end it," she whispered. My eyes shot to her.

"Then do it," I commanded. "This has to stop. My life—"

"She's lying," Vesper said quickly and took a step toward me.

Lying? The witch might have been cunning but there was nothing to indicate she had spoken a lie.

"You do know it," she said. "You just don't want to face it."

Vesper shot her a glare. Tension skyrocketed and Vesper looked like she was seriously considering ending the witch's life.

"Tell me what it is," I begged her. Her jaw clenched, her face conflicted.

"She has to complete the prophecy."

Vesper didn't look back at Cedar as she led me away. I was numb, unable to fight her pull. Unwilling to.

Does that mean I have to die?

VESPER

How many live executions have we been through in the past few weeks?

I had lost count. But at some point, after we murdered Aurelia's handmaiden, it was happening every single day.

It was because of the war. The king used it to exercise power and keep his family in check. After all, what was a war without some bloodshed?

But today was special.

The stage was set as it was every other day. It took over the side garden, with the fountain where Aurelia once had her tantrum hidden behind the large makeshift stage.

Normally, there would be three of the Solei family members or guards kneeling on the creaky wooden stage, but this time there were seven, all of their faces covered with bags. And a few of them were still struggling. Many of them had come to terms with the fact that they were going to die and didn't struggle by the time they were hoisted up in front of the crowd.

If they had gotten far enough to be tied up on the stage in front of the entire family, there was no going back. Nothing to save them. Rumor had it that the dungeon was filled with traitors. Many of the guards who had come with the family started to realize how fucked they were now that the two families were going to war and tried to run.

It never ended well.

Princess Aurelia was slightly in front of me, but close enough that her back brushed across my arm. Our attendance was mandatory. Almost as if it were a reminder that this was happening because of us. And, of course, we needed to show our support. We couldn't seem ungrateful in front of the king.

Especially Aurelia. She was still on thin ice with her father.

She looked up at the stage with a grim expression. The executions were wearing us all down. But not the king.

He stood tall with his shoulders back and a satisfied smile on his face. He would look over the crowd every so often as his most loyal guards were bringing up the eighth and final person.

Cedar was behind me, her presence suffocating. Since the night she spilled just how many people from the organization had been after us, I hadn't been able to relax.

Every night, I stayed with the princess. Every night, I looked outside of her windows, praying not to see another one of my people show up.

It should have been reassuring that I hadn't seen any of them yet. But instead, it made me all the more paranoid.

"Today we have a special show," the king said, stepping forward and pulling a golden sword from one of his guard's outstretched hands. He motioned for each guard to stand behind one of the victims-to-be. "Take off the bags!"

I hadn't been prepared for what was waiting for us under the head coverings...or *who*.

All of them—*all seven*—were people I knew. People I had gone to school with. Families I had gotten to know during my upbringing in the secret organization that ran my life.

I couldn't move. Couldn't breathe. It took great effort to remind my heart to keep beating. I took calming breaths through my teeth. *He found them. Found us.*

Just like Cedar had said...it had been him all along.

But what made him do this in front of everyone? Something big had happened. *Did one get too close?*

The thought alone of one of them getting close enough to warrant *this* caused the hair on the back of my neck to rise.

Two of them had rats on their necks. Three had horses. One dragon. And then there were two snakes.

Snakes. Meaning that at some point, far in the past...we had been tied by blood. Family. Like Tate. His young face and ghost of a smile flashed across my face.

Who are they? How far removed were we?

The families spanned generations. The more proficient the killers, the more they were rewarded, and the more likely they were to expand for the chance that their kids would someday carry on the family business.

I didn't want to look into their eyes, but forced myself to keep my gaze still on the stage.

No wonder Cedar had been so close to me. *She knew.* She was there to remind me how vital it was that I didn't react.

Last she told us, there had been thirteen... How many did this make? Had there been more?

I had been so diligent. Every night, I had been up, watching, waiting for them to show up. *And they were getting closer and closer...but how did I miss it?*

"These vile creatures have been sent to harm us," the king said. "And not in small numbers. I have been trying to keep this under the radar so there was no panic, but it looks like we are waging yet another war."

Aurelia's gaze shifted to mine. Even if it was just for a second, I could see the question on her face.

What are we going to do?

"We won't stop, not until she's dead!" one with the horse on her neck screamed. "You think this will scare us? There's nothing you can do to protect her!"

The king stalked across the stage and thrust his sword straight into her chest.

Her words rang through my head even as the blood gargled in her throat.

We won't stop. There's nothing you can do to protect her.

"This is number thirty-five," the king said, his voice lowering to a growl. "So take this as your warning—if you're out there watching, you can try, but it will all end the same."

Thirty-five. And I missed every single one of them.

How close had they gotten? How many times had I been sleeping next to the princess, completely unaware, while they were just a few steps away?

He pulled his sword out of her chest, her body jerking against it as the light dimmed from her eyes. He motioned for the other guards to finish the job. There was no hesitation in their movements as they sliced their throats.

One of the ones with the snake on their neck looked at me, a flash of recognition going through their eyes just before the end.

They won't stop until she's dead. And if I made it, how many others were already in the ranks, lying low?

I looked around the crowd, trying to catch even a single person's gaze, but none of them dared to pull their eyes from the blood bath.

Does that make them more suspicious? What if they were just putting on a show? Acting as if they were truly a part of the family, only to try and stab the princess in the heart.

All of them looked suspicious to me. The voices in the back of my mind kept criticizing them, pulling apart their appearances and trying to remember if I'd ever seen them in the palace before this.

I am missing something. It's been happening right under my nose, and they were going to try to kill her. Princess Aurelia can't die. Not after everything I've done to help her. She can't. I won't let it. Not over my dead bod—

"Reel it in," Cedar whispered, her body much closer than I remembered. Her words were enough to stop me from spiraling and shock me back into my body.

Vesper knows how to end it. She had warned me. She had *warned* me, and I hadn't listened. It was my fault. They were dying needlessly because of me. The princess was in danger because of me.

I needed to end it.

They were already cleaning up the bodies. People around us were yelling, chanting, calling for more revenge.

The king had them right where he wanted them. My gaze traveled to him, but his eyes were already on me. He saw right through me. I could feel it. *He knows.*

We were surrounded. It didn't matter if it was her father or the organization.

There is only one way out.

Aurelia's hand found mine and squeezed. Cedar was by my side, her arm brushing across mine.

The witch knew... But did the princess? Did she know what I was about to do?

As I looked into her eyes, I knew she didn't. I knew that she still had hope.

Hope that I would have to crush.

I was spiraling. Panicking. I had never felt so uncontrolled in my life.

I had always had a plan. Had been following a specific path my entire life and never veered off of it.

Until I met Aurelia.

Until I decided that I needed to save her. And there was no looking back after that.

My father sent me here thinking that maybe I would change my mind. That maybe his beatings would have reminded me of what was important.

But they had only reinforced the same idea.

The organization is cruel, violent, and will stop at nothing to see the end of their prophecy.

The universe had been telling me this. Yelling it at me the entire time. Through Cedar. Through Princess Aurelia's father. Through my own fucking experiences.

I had to end it. And I was the only one who could.

Cedar's words from that night played over and over in my head. *She has to complete the prophecy. She has to complete the prophecy. She has to complete the prophecy.*

She pitied me, I could see it in her face. But that didn't make the realization of what I had to do any less painful.

I have to do it. I have to kill Aurelia.

There were generations and generations of trained killers coming for her. Not only had one gotten past the king, but she had almost gotten past me as well. Who was to say there wouldn't be more?

And the one on the stand all but cried out a call for action for anyone who was still hiding.

They would be furious after watching their comrades die. They would want revenge. But how many more would we face? How many more did the king have locked in his prisons?

And all the time I had been in the palace, they had been coming for her. *And I didn't know.*

The king slowly and quietly plucked them out and destroyed them before I was even made aware of it. It didn't make me fear for my own safety. At that point, I couldn't care less about what happened to me. If I even so much as left the palace, I was dead.

Probably if I stay too. Someone had to have spilled something to him for me to get *that* look while he was killing them. Was it a warning? A promise?

I could fight him and the organization off, but not for long. Not alone.

But Aurelia wouldn't be able to hold her own. One maybe. But two? Three? An army?

We weren't safe in the palace. Aurelia wasn't safe.

And there would be no end to this—not until the prophecy came true.

I hated how right Cedar was. Whatever seer knowledge she had was inevitable. There was no changing a prophecy. We could try to run from it. I could try to reject it. Hell, the organization could even try to change it by sending other families in my place.

But we wouldn't see an end...not until I was the one to end the Castle line for good. Or at least that's what the world needed to think.

"We're leaving," Aurelia said as soon as we got to her room. She ran around faster than my eyes could make out. All I could see was the luggage she threw on the bed and the pieces of clothing she shoved inside it. "I'll contact Atlas. She will help us in the meantime. The witch is coming too. I don't give a fuck if she tries to fight this."

"Aurelia..."

"We pack tonight, leave tomorrow night," she went on. "Father has another engagement tomorrow. I need to attend that, so they don't notice I'm gone right away. But after that, I don't have another for three more days. During that time, we should be able to get—"

"*Aurelia...*"

"We'll use herbs to cover our scent," she said, her wild eyes flashing to mine. "There's a stream off to the back of the property. We will go there, cover our scent, then be on our way. No one will—"

I cut her off by holding onto her arms. I hated how panicked she was. Hated how I was the one who made her like this.

I should have realized what it meant to come back here. Should have realized that even stepping foot into the palace was a mistake.

But I couldn't help but be grateful for it. I didn't want her to deal with this alone. Not when she didn't have to.

But that didn't make what we needed to do any less painful. I would hate myself for it. She would hate me. There was no way to even guarantee that it would work...but I was running out of options.

"I'm glad I came to the palace," I said, letting my hand brush across her cheek. "I'm sorry for everything. I know you've been put in a difficult spot because of me."

She gave me a pinched look. "My life has always been hard, Vesper. At least when you came, I had something to look forward to. I don't care if we have to be on the run for the rest of our lives. I don't care if we're constantly looking over our shoulder. We will make it work, I know it."

She has too much faith in me.

We couldn't run. Not just yet. There were probably more people just like me in the palace, waiting for their chance to get at the princess. Who's to say they wouldn't burst in any moment?

Even then, when would this stop? We could run, but how far could we get before we were ambushed?

We needed a better way out. We needed to finish the prophecy.

"Do you trust me?" I asked, searching her face. "I have a plan."

I didn't want to do this. I wanted us to live a life together, even if it meant having to bend to her father's will. To hide my tattoo forever. I'd even carve it out of me if I needed to. At least then we would be surrounded by guards. She would be comfortable in the place she had always known.

Don't make me do this, I prayed.

But I didn't know who I was pleading to anymore. Was it a god? The universe?

Myself?

There was no person or being out there who could help me. I would have to do this part on my own.

Up until then, I had been training my whole life for the moment when I could see the prophecy through. I had gone through grueling training and abuse to make me into the cold-blooded killer they desired.

But they never prepared me for the heartbreak it would cause.

I could feel it. My heart being ripped in two as I made my decision.

I grabbed the hilt of my sword with a shaking hand. But unlike when Nadine cornered me, my heart was calm. There was no panic in my body. Nothing pushing me to rush this. Just a serene heart and an unwavering decision to do whatever I needed to keep us safe.

She gave me a sad smile.

"Do I have any other choice?" she asked. I hated seeing her like that. I wanted her fiery spirit. I wanted her to yell, kick, and scream.

I didn't want this to be easy.

"Believe me when I say I never wanted this," I said, my thumb rubbing against her cheek. I committed her face to memory. "I fell for you. I wasn't supposed to, but I did."

"Just tell me what we need to do," she whispered. Her pleading had my chest twisting in pain. "Please, Vesper."

Fuck. I couldn't take it. My heart felt like it was being ripped out of my chest. My throat began to close, and my eyes began to sting.

There would be no way out. Not for me, and not for her. We either lived fighting for our lives or died together.

I have to complete the prophecy. And this way, maybe both of us can be free.

"Forgive me."

I leaned down, my lips brushing hers, so she didn't see the weapon at her side before the blade pierced her chest. I pulled away, forcing myself to take in everything she was feeling. Hurt, Anguish. Betrayal. All of it clear on her face.

I deserve to see it. Deserve to feel this way.

There was nothing I could do except hold her as her blood seeped out of her wound and onto my sword. It was deep and straight through. She wouldn't last long with a wound like that untreated, even as a vampire.

She opened her mouth to speak, but no sound came out. The wound was too deep. Blood pooled in the back of her throat and started leaking out of the sides of her mouth.

Her eyes fluttered closed. How awful was it that the last thing she saw was her own lover murdering her? That even on the brink of death, she would be reminded of just how wrong she had been to trust me.

"I'm sorry," I whispered, and leaned down to kiss her.
Please forgive me.

AURELIA AND VESPERS STORY ISN'T OVER YET!

Head over to my newsletter for a special sneak preview of book two or preorder the next installment here.

WANT EXCLUSIVE NSFW ART?

For NSFW EC art (and other series) join my Patreon!
I also update my novellas on there every other week and they are the FIRST to get
  ARCS of all my newest releases!
Check it out here or go to https://www.patreon.com/ellemaebooks

ACKNOWLEDGMENTS

Thank you to everyone who has supported my vampire journey so far!

My first ever book started with vampires and I am so happy to continue with them.

From my teenage years and well into my adulthood, vampires have always held a special place in my heart. Whether it be TV shows, manga, books, I always love a good vampire story and am ecstatic that my readers feel the same!

Stay tuned for more lesbian vampires~

IF YOU LIKED THIS, PLEASE REVIEW!

Reviews really help indie authors get their books out there so, please make sure to share your thoughts!

About the Author

Elle is a native Californian who has lived in Los Angeles for most of her life. From the very start, she has been in love with all things fantasy and reading. As soon as Elle found out that writing books could be a career, she picked up a pen and paper. While the first ones were about scorned love and missed opportunities of lunchtime love, she has grown to love the fantasy genre and looks forward to making a difference in the world with her stories.

Loved this book? Please leave a review!

For more behind the scene content, check out my Patreon or sign up to my newsletter!

https://elegant-mountain-68199.myflodesk.com/y8a9duflae

 x.com/mae_books

 instagram.com/edenrosebooks

goodreads.com/ellemae

Made in United States
Troutdale, OR
06/22/2024

20739575R00176